HEART
OF
VALOR

ALAN MORRIS

GUARDIANS OF THE NORTH

HEART
OF
VALOR

BETHANY HOUSE PUBLISHERS
MINNEAPOLIS, MINNESOTA 55438

Published by Bethany House Publishers
A Ministry of Bethany Fellowship, Inc.
11300 Hampshire Avenue South
Minneapolis, Minnesota 55438

Printed in the United States of America.

Library of Gongress Cataloging-in-Publication Data

Morris, Alan B., 1959–
    Heart of valor / by Alan Morris.
      p. cm. — (Guardians of the north ; 2)
    ISBN 1-55661-693-7
     1. Title. II. Series: Morris, Alan B., 1959–   Guardians of the
north ; 2.
PS3563.087395H4   1996
813'.54—dc20   96-45771
                                        CIP

Part Four: Till Judgment Break

CONTENTS

To my mother

Strength and honor are her clothing.
She openeth her mouth in wisdom,
and in her tongue is the law of kindness.
A woman that feareth the Lord, she shall be praised.
I arise up, and call you blessed.

The Proverbs of Solomon

ALAN MORRIS is a full-time writer who has also coauthored a series of books with his father, best-selling author Gilbert Morris. Learning the craft of writing from his father, this is Alan's first solo series. He makes his home in the Rocky Mountains of Colorado.

PART ONE

SOUR SWEET MUSIC

*How sour sweet music is,
when time is broke, and no
proportion kept!
So is it in the music of men's
lives.*

William Shakespeare
Richard II

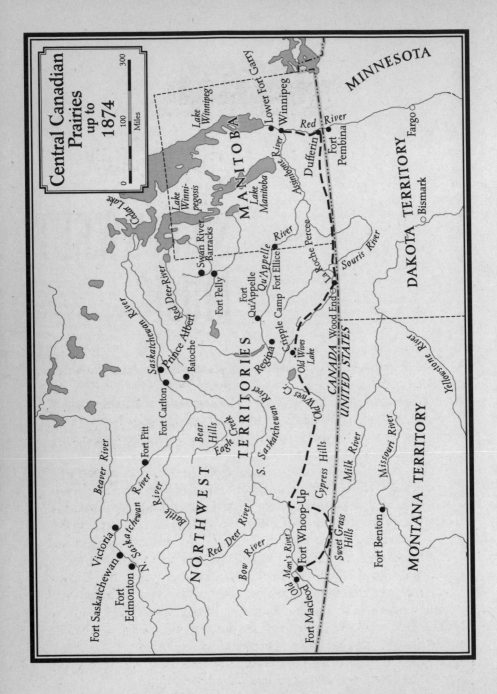

Central Canadian Prairies up to 1874

0 100 300 Miles

MINNESOTA

DAKOTA TERRITORY

Fargo

Bismark

MONTANA TERRITORY

NORTHWEST TERRITORIES

MANITOBA

Lake Winnipeg

Lake Winni-pegosis

Lake Manitoba

Cedar Lake

Swan River Barracks

Fort Pelly

Fort Qu'Appelle

Qu'Appelle River

Lower Fort Garry

Winnipeg

Red River

Dufferin

Fort Pembina

Assiniboine River

La Roche Percee

Souris River

Wood End

CANADA

UNITED STATES

Yellowstone River

Prince Albert

Batoche

Fort Carlton

Saskatchewan River

Red Deer River

Cripple Camp

Fort Ellice

Regina

Old Wives Lake

Old Wives C.

Cypress Hills

Fort Pitt

Fort Saskatchewan

Fort Edmonton

N. Saskatchewan River

Victoria

Beaver River

Battle River

Bear Hills

Eagle Creek

S. Saskatchewan River

Red Deer River

Bow River

Fort Whoop-Up

Old Man's River

Fort Macleod

Sweet Grass Hills

Milk River

Missouri River

Fort Benton

CHAPTER ONE

Hissing Snow

The ill-kempt man who opened the cabin door balanced a bald-headed baby on one arm and a shotgun in the other.

With sickening clarity, Del Dekko stared into the huge black hole at the end of the barrel he found pointed directly between his bulging brown eyes. He moaned inwardly and somehow stifled the urgent desire to duck out of the way.

Dekko had deliberately positioned himself between Sub-Inspectors Hunter Stone and Jaye Eliot Vickersham as they'd walked to the door through the deep snow, hoping to avoid this very thing. During that walk, he'd cackled himself into a rare good mood, picturing the three of them in his mind: two tall, handsome, scarlet-jacketed Mounties on either side of a short grizzled scout who hadn't had a bath in a week. From another viewpoint, Dekko had imagined that they looked like some sort of sandwich that had gone wrong in the making. Two rich, fragrant slices of bread on either side of a less-than-savory interior. Say, a fish head sandwich. The thought struck Dekko as extremely funny.

The shotgun aimed in his direction blew away his brief good mood as surely as if its owner had pulled the trigger.

"Good morning, sir," Vickersham greeted heartily from Dekko's right, as though the settler had just invited them in for tea. Standing an even six feet tall, Vickersham was thin but wiry. Beneath short brown hair, his face was narrow and open, with thin lips and an angular jaw. His unfailing politeness and ever pleasant expression made him seem more handsome than he was.

To Dekko's relief, the shotgun moved to a spot between him and Vickersham. But just as his humor had been short-lived, so was his ease. The barrel began moving in a disturbing side-to-side motion from Vickersham to Stone, which meant Dekko was never really out of the line of fire. He watched it, half hypnotized.

"What do you want?" the settler asked in a surprisingly high voice. Behind him rose the chaotic din of many children at play. The aroma of roasted chicken sporadically touched the air, while the warmth from the cabin fought with the cold outside.

"North-West Mounted Police, sir," Hunter Stone spoke up for the first time. His deep baritone contrasted sharply with the settler's whine. Well over six feet with a well-proportioned frame, Stone had sandy-blond hair and ice-gray eyes. His face was more square than oval, with a strong cleft chin and determined jaw, leaving him with the presence of being both handsome and authoritative.

From the corner of Stone's eye, he saw Dekko's head moving from side to side, following the shotgun's path, and Stone hoped he didn't make a sudden move. Stone sensed that Del was ready to bolt. "We're here to—"

"How do I know you're Mounties?"

Stone and Vickersham glanced at each other in puzzlement.

"Well," Vickersham said, "we're wearing the uniform. . . ." He trailed off, as if that explained everything.

"Don't mean anything. *Anyone* can wear a uniform."

A brief, shocked pause ensued.

"Why, that's *preposterous!*" Vickersham argued in his clipped British accent. Indignation soaking his tone, he sniffed, "*No man* may wear the scarlet unless he's a member of the Mounted!"

"Step back," the settler ordered.

Stone said, "Sir, if you'll just let us—"

"I said, step back!" The shotgun's aim came to rest on Stone's chest.

Dekko was the first to retreat. He began stepping backward all the way to where they'd tied the horses.

Stone and Vickersham each moved back three paces until they were out from under the narrow porch roof and standing in the bright sunshine. Neither of them turned to watch Dekko make his clumsy exit.

The settler moved outside and closed the door. Once the latch caught, the door was opened again by a girl of about fifteen. "Pa?"

"Get back inside and bolt the door! Now!"

The girl's moon face disappeared instantly. The settler whirled back to face Stone and Vickersham. His watery eyes followed Dekko, and waving the shotgun in that direction, he asked, "Where's he going?"

"He's sort of skittish around guns," Stone informed him mildly. "Especially when they're pointed at him. Would you mind. . . ?"

The settler grinned for the first time, revealing greenish teeth. "I'd heard you Mounties weren't afraid of nothing."

"Actually, I was thinking about the baby. I don't think it's a good idea to combine guns and infants, do you?" Stone's gray, almost colorless eyes moved to the baby, who looked to be about a year old. The child was staring back at Stone's chest in fascination. Stone suddenly realized that the brilliant sunlight reflecting off of his scarlet coat and the snow behind him was just too rich a sight for a baby to ignore.

The settler looked at the child, and for a moment all three men were staring at him. The baby didn't notice his sudden popularity. A tiny finger was jammed solidly in his mouth, and a pendulum of drool swung from his chin. The man lowered the gun until it was pointed at the ground and then brought his attention back to the Mounties. "All right. But tell that fella behind you to stop. He's making me nervous."

Vickersham turned and called, "Del! Hold right there."

Dekko stopped instantly with one foot raised and cocked behind him.

Vickersham watched him for a moment, then said, "You can put your foot down, Del. Just don't go any farther. There's a good chap."

Dekko put his foot down.

The settler considered him briefly, then observed slightly in wonder, "He looks like a scarecrow out there."

Stone glanced back at Dekko. Fifty feet away in a world of pure white, Del stood absolutely still, dressed in his worn, knee-length brown boots, gray pants with a hole in the thigh, and dirty bearskin coat. He did, indeed, look like a scarecrow, but somehow infinitely more pitiful. In the midst of a barren landscape, Dekko's lack of farm crops to guard left him appearing as an *unemployed* scarecrow. Stone shook his head at the sight and turned back to the settler. "We only wanted a bit of your time, sir. We've been assigned to take a census in the area, and we need to ask you a few questions."

"A census, huh? What'd you boys do to deserve that?"

"I beg your pardon, Mr. . . . ?" Vickersham asked.

"Sikes. Jim Sikes."

Vickersham, who'd been holding a leather-bound notebook the whole time, tucked it under his arm and removed the spotless white glove on his left hand. Opening the book and taking pen in hand, he began writing and asked, "What do you mean 'deserve,' Mr. Sikes?"

"Well, think about it. You're out in the middle of nowhere in the blue-lipped cold asking people questions! I mean, if this is choice work, what do they do to you boys for *punishment*?" Sikes let loose a barking laugh that grated on the Mounties' ears.

Stone chose to ignore him. "How long have you been out here, Mr. Sikes?"

Waving the shotgun at the stark, skeletal outline of an unfinished addition beside the house, Sikes answered, "About a year. As you can see, I've got bigger dreams than this one-room cabin."

"And how many in your house?" Vickersham asked, writing in his notebook.

His forehead wrinkling in a scowl, Sikes' suddenly pleasant demeanor vanished. "How many? Uh . . . how many . . . let's see. There's Adam, Abigail, Aaron, Amy . . . uh . . . no, wait a minute. There's Adam, Aaron, Abigail, *Afton*, then Amy and . . . no, no, no, that's not right, either."

Stone looked at Vickersham, who had stopped writing until Sikes made up his mind.

Sikes counted to himself while gazing at the cloudless blue sky, his fingers working as he mentally counted children.

To Stone's amazement, Sikes went through all the fingers holding the shotgun, then all the fingers holding the baby, then started all over again.

"Seventeen," Sikes declared confidently. "No, wait"—he looked at the baby in his arm—"eighteen, counting Artemus here." He tickled the child's chin. "Almost forgot you, Artemus. Can you believe that?"

Stone didn't know which was worse: the number of humans living in the tiny cabin or the baby's name. He heard Del crunching through the snow behind him.

"You named that child Artemus?" Del asked incredulously.

Sikes' eyes narrowed. "You got a problem with that, mister?"

"No, but the kid sure will."

"Del," Stone said, "shut up."

"But he named the kid Artemus, Hunter! Ain't there a law against that somewheres?" The shotgun came halfway up, and Del's eyes went to it like a snake's to a mouse.

"Mister, I don't remember asking you—"

"Mr. Sikes," Vickersham broke in smoothly, "it's a wonderful name. Does it run in the family?"

"Why, yes, it was my wife's father's middle name."

"Poor feller," Del mumbled behind a grimy hand.

Stone, standing with his hands behind his back, brought his elbow around in a stiff arc to connect with Del's shoulder. Dekko stumbled forward a half step, nearly fell face first in the snow, and gave Stone a pained look. Stone ignored him.

"I'm sure it made her father very proud, Mr. Sikes," Vickersham continued. Raising his notebook, he licked the tip of his pencil and said, "Sikes. Eighteen. Thank you for your time, sir. We'll be going now."

Del leaned forward and waved at the baby. "Bye, Artemus. Good luck. You're gonna need it."

Artemus watched the wiggling fingers and yawned hugely.

Stone and Vickersham each took an arm and together half carried Del toward the horses.

"Kid's gonna get more beatings in his life than a three-legged mule," Del muttered. "I'm comin', I'm comin'!"

The glittering snow lay before them like a solid field of frozen cotton. They visited four more cabins; one contained a lone man, while the others were crammed full of settlers and their many children.

"What is it with these settlers having so many kids?" Del asked as they left the fourth home.

"Perhaps procreation is a prerequisite for that profession," Vickersham reasoned, with a secret wink at Stone.

Del was so stunned by the statement, he couldn't think of a thing to say.

Stone added, "Well, that career does call for countless co-workers."

Del watched him warily with one suspicious brown eye, while the other stared somewhere to Stone's left. Looking at Del was very confusing for people not accustomed to it. Stone had discovered that when he'd first met him. After the initial shock that day, he'd focused on the eye looking back at him, but when he'd faced Del again, it was the other eye that was centered on him. Now, after knowing Del for a year and a half, Stone was convinced that he purposely switched eyes to confuse people and make them uncomfortable.

"Someday," Del promised dangerously, "you fellas are gonna have me on one too many times. Then I'll turn on ya. Kinda like a dog that's part wolf. You ain't neeeever quite sure if he's gonna wake up one day and feel wolfy."

"Wolfy?" Vickersham asked incredulously.

"*I* sure don't want a wolfy dog," Stone said. When he smiled at Del, he noticed that he'd changed eyes on him again. "Would you stop that?"

"Stop what?"

"You know."

"I don't know what you're talkin' about." Del glanced at Vickersham, then back to Stone . . . with the *other* eye.

"That!" Stone pointed triumphantly, his finger inches from Del's eyes. "That's what I'm talking about!"

Del stared at him, acting bewildered.

Vickersham wiped his mouth with his gloved hand, hiding a smile.

"Vic, help me here."

"With what, Hunter?" he asked innocently.

"Come on, Vic, you know."

Del said in exasperation, "*I* know, *he* knows. . . . What is it we're supposed to know?" Shaking his head, he added sadly, "I swear, Hunter, if this was summertime, I'd say you'd been out in the sun too long."

Stone found himself frustrated because he'd really wanted an answer once and for all concerning Del's eyes. Instead, he started laughing, and when he saw Del glaring at him strangely, still keeping up his act, Stone laughed even harder. Vickersham joined him, and soon, despite himself, even Del began to smile.

When their laughter subsided, Vickersham said, "I never really noticed before how much you *don't* laugh until you do, Hunter. You should try it more often."

"Yeah, you're just too serious, Hunter," Del added. "Sometimes being around you is as depressing as a graveyard on a wet Sunday."

Stone kept his smile but said nothing. Deep down, he knew they were right. Since his wife, Betsy, had been murdered by a renegade Crow named Red Wolf nearly two years before, he'd lost part of himself. His anger, mourning, and subsequent isolation had pushed him to the very edge of insanity. He could still remember the first time he'd laughed six months after Betsy's death—a genuine belly laugh, not a chuckle. *Six months!* he thought even now, with a shake of his head.

The reason he'd laughed was because of something that Reena O'Donnell, his missionary friend, had said or done. He couldn't remember exactly what. He *did* recall that the weather had been cold, and when the corners of his mouth had turned up, the crazy thought had flashed through his mind that the lower half of his face might shatter and crumble away due to the cold and the movement of unused muscles around his mouth.

While married to Betsy, he had laughed every day. Since she'd been gone, amusement had been hard to come by.

"How many more houses in the area, Del?" Vic asked.

"One, and then we can veer back to the fort. I don't know whether you two brains have figured it out or not, but we've been making a wide semicircle all day."

"We're not blind, Del. I just didn't know how many more cabins there were before we reached Fort Macleod."

Del sat up straighter in his saddle and sniffed loftily. Whenever he found himself with more knowledge than his two friends, he played it to the hilt. "Well, now you know. You brave and gallant Mounties would be lost without us scouts."

"So true."

"That's all you got to say, Vic? 'So true'? I was ready to hear a speech about how smart you are in your fancy outfits. Speakin' o' which, I sure am glad I don't have to wear them red targets on *my* back. Injuns could draw a bead on you two quicker than a blind buffalo calf in a six-by-six corral."

"The vast majority of the Indians respect the scarlet," Vickersham contended stubbornly, sitting up straighter in his saddle. His long, fine nose and sharp chin jutted into the air with pride. Unconsciously, he ran his gauntleted hand down the sleeve of his jacket, smoothing wrinkles that didn't exist.

"It ain't the vast majority I'm talkin' about. It's them what get whiskeyed up and start thinkin' they're bulletproof. What if one of 'em up and decide they want one of them jackets to prove their manhood, or impress a woman, or just to be downright ornery? Never mind if there's blood on it when they get it. Blood wouldn't show. Neither would a few arrow holes."

"What was that you were saying about a graveyard on a wet Sunday, Del?" Stone asked.

"Huh?"

"He means," Vickersham explained, "that you are having and expressing very dreary thoughts, Del."

"Just the way things are," Del maintained, beginning to sulk. "The Mounties have arrested a couple of whiskey traders in the Territory, and most of you think it'll be smooth sailing from here on out. I'm here to tell you that there's plenty more left, and they ain't gonna just faint dead away and beg for mercy when they see those pretty red coats." He concluded his speech by leaning over and spitting a mud-colored stream of tobacco juice between the horses.

"We know that, Del," Stone agreed patiently, automatically steering his horse, Buck, away from the well-aimed sputum.

"*You* do, Hunter. But then, you've always had your cap set straight. You're suspicious of *everybody*."

"Well, I wouldn't say that."

"I would, and I just did. Now these fellas like Vic, they think everyone's gonna treat 'em like the king they is and bow down."

"I'm an English lord, Del. Not a king."

"Whatever. Point is, there's some nasty men out there."

As if punctuating Del's ominous remark, the sun dipped behind a few clouds hovering over the distant Rocky Mountains on the west horizon. Stone welcomed the relief from the blinding reflection it had caused on the snow. He was suddenly aware of a ringing headache.

Vickersham wasn't willing to let Del's slight go without an explanation. "It *does* make a difference, Del. As I've told you before, I'm a lord, but it basically comes down to being a courtesy title. My older brother inherits everything."

"Yeah, yeah, yeah. And you got tired of layin' around in merry old England with nothing to do. So you come to Canada to find adventure. I've heard that story thousands of times. Why don't you make up a new history, just for variety's sake?"

Stone and Vickersham were accustomed to Del expressing his mind when the mood took him. Stone usually found it amusing and somewhat comforting, much like the comfort drawn from the fact that the sun would rise the next morning. Del could be counted on to reveal his doubts and opinions no matter how outlandish. However, the truth of the matter was that he had sometimes proved uncanny in his reflections and predictions. What bothered Stone the most on this day was that he'd been thinking along the same lines as Del, which was disturbing enough in itself. The Mounties had had an almost miraculous five months of nonviolence while establishing themselves in the wild and unruly Territories. Could it last? Or had it merely been a matter of the worst ruffians being the most skillful at eluding them? Despite hoping for the former, Stone believed in the latter and felt a twinge of guilt for feeling that way. Maybe Del was right. Maybe he *was* too suspicious of human nature.

"Reena seems to be having a difficult time, eh?" Vickersham commented.

"She's a tough girl," Stone said.

"Tough as they come," Del announced proudly, as if he had something to do with Reena's hardiness of mind and body.

"It's that Dew Eagle," Vic continued. "He's a bad one, I'm afraid."

Stone patted Buck's neck and rubbed vigorously. The high-stepping through the snow had been difficult and tiring for the horses, but Buck showed no signs of fatigue. Stone was grateful for the hardy buckskin he'd raised from a colt. "The Blackfeet are more set in their traditions than the Assiniboine that she lived with before. They're also more suspicious of whites. Especially Dew Eagle."

"Dew Eagle's problem has more to do with whiskey than it does with anything else," Del said. "He'd kill his own mother for it, and once he gets on a tear there's no stopping him."

"Not yet, anyway," Stone said quietly.

"Is Reena getting discouraged, Hunter?" Vickersham asked.

"Humph," Del snorted. "That'll happen when crows turn white."

Stone smiled. "If she is, she's not letting on. You know Reena."

"Yes, I do," Vic said dreamily. "We should stop by and see her since the Blackfoot camp is on our way."

Stone glanced at Vickersham sharply but said nothing. Vic was his best friend, but Stone couldn't help feeling a twinge of jealousy whenever Vic spoke of his obvious fondness for Reena.

Vickersham noticed Stone's look out of the corner of his eye. "A gentleman can't help but be attracted to such a beautiful, upstanding woman, Hunter."

"I know, Vic. It's all right."

Del peered at Stone carefully and spoke his mind. "Just because she nursed you back to life after Red Wolf nearly sent you to the Great Beyond ain't no reason to think you own her."

"Nobody owns Reena, Del."

"All right, then," Del sniffed.

"Look, we *all* care about her. There's nothing wrong with that."

"I said all right, didn't I? You're the one that's so sensitive about her. Why don't you just marry her?"

Stone felt himself losing his temper with Del. "I don't *want* to marry her. She's just a friend—a good friend."

"Humph. You're just saying that 'cause she won't *have* you." Del sensed that he'd pushed too far and smiled. "'Course, she won't have *any* of us."

"She's more concerned about her mission work right now,"

Vickersham said. "Just another reason to admire her, if you ask me."

Stone sat up straighter and pointed ahead. "Del, that wouldn't be where the next home is located, would it?"

A dark trail of smoke snaked into the sky in the distance. They hadn't noticed it against the mountains and clouds on the horizon until now.

Del squinted. "Yep, that's about it. Some feller by the name of Jester lives there, I think."

Stone and Vickersham suddenly spurred their horses into awkward runs through the deep snow.

"What are you doing?" Del cried. "You're gonna tire them horses out before you get there!"

"Come on!" Vickersham yelled over his shoulder. "Someone could need help!"

Del shook his head and called back futilely, "*You're* the one gonna need help if that horse breaks down!" As expected, neither Mountie slowed down, and with a sigh Del urged his own mount forward. "All three of us gonna be on foot and freezin' to death 'fore nightfall. Mark my words," he finished to no one in particular.

Stone and Vickersham kept pace with each other for over a mile, then Buck began to outdistance Nelson, Vic's horse. Buck needed no further urging from Stone; as always, he sensed his owner's desire for speed. Stone kept his eyes on the smoke in the distance, and soon a burning cabin materialized. He had a gut-wrenching flashback to two years previously, when he'd played out the same scenario. Only that time, it had been his own home on fire. Without knowing it, he reached back and slapped Buck's laboring hindquarters with the reins, caught up in the memory of terror and fatal urgency. That day, in addition to losing his farm, his stock, his whole *life*, he'd unknowingly kissed Betsy for the last time. Red Wolf had kidnapped her and eventually killed her.

He'd pursued Red Wolf relentlessly, finally catching him in the Cypress Hills. The resulting battle had left Stone close to death, and Red Wolf wounded, but able to escape. Reena O'Donnell had found Stone, taken him back to the Assiniboine camp, and cared for him while he hovered between life and death. After a harrowing night when his blinding, burning thirst for revenge had almost cost an Indian boy his life, Stone had finally come to his senses and joined the Mounties. It had been the smartest thing he'd ever done in his life.

After a few moments of thoughtless fury, Stone's vision cleared and he stopped Buck a safe distance away from the blazing cabin and jumped down. As he raced toward the blaze, shielding his eyes and face from the heat, he passed the flat remains of a small barn that he hadn't noticed before. Above the roar of the inferno, he faintly heard the snow sizzling and hissing around the base of the destroyed structure.

A bloody arm wrapped in a smoking, fire-dotted sleeve appeared in the doorway under the burning porch, the hand clenching pitifully. Stone rushed forward, feeling heat so intense he imagined his skin was peeling away from his bones. He heard a shout behind him and knew that Vickersham had arrived. What he'd shouted, Stone didn't know.

Reaching the now-burning arm, he slapped out the flames with his gloved hands in order to get a grip. He pulled on it, felt momentary resistance, and then he dragged the smoking body from the doorway. Cinders from the burning porch fell all around him, hitting his neck with searing pain. The porch would go at any second. He doubled his strength and heaved the body free from the porch.

Vickersham suddenly appeared at his side and helped him drag the figure a safe distance away through the snow. The ragged clothing, on what they now saw was a man, smoked and popped in flames. They turned the man face upward.

His hair, eyebrows, and eyelashes were completely gone, and he trembled and shook violently. He screamed in agony as Stone and Vickersham heaped snow over his exposed, blackened skin. "Is anyone else inside?" Stone shouted, but the man was beyond hearing.

With a creaking groan, the cabin collapsed behind them in a roar of hungry fire and snapping joints, sending a shower of countless embers into the sky. Stone and Vickersham leaned forward as the man began moaning, shaking his head from side to side, and talking unintelligibly. "I hope to heaven no one *was* in there," Vic said.

"Ssss—ssss—" the man they thought to be Jester stuttered.

"Yes?" Stone asked, grasping Jester's flailing hand. Jester squeezed his hand, then let go and went to Stone's thigh. Stone grimaced in pain at the strength of Jester's grip and asked again, "Yes? What did you say?"

Jester's body was racked with excruciating spasms as he tried to speak again. "Ssss—ssswweee—sweet! Sweet!"

Stone and Vickersham looked at each other over the grisly, writhing man.

"Sweet! Sweet!" Jester gasped.

"What's sweet?" Vickersham shouted. "Is your sweet wife inside? Your sweet daughter? What?"

Jester's eyes began to glaze, and Stone felt a loosening of the dying man's grip on his thigh.

"Oh, mercy!" Del cried as he appeared beside them. "Oh no! Was anyone else in there?"

"What are you saying, mister?" Stone asked as he leaned down. His nose was almost touching Jester's, and he nearly choked from the smell of smoke and burned flesh.

"Sweet!" Jester gasped, barely audible, and then his head fell to the side into the snow as his eyes lost all life.

CHAPTER TWO

Dew Eagle

Early the next morning, twenty miles away, Reena O'Donnell sat cross-legged very close to the fire in her tepee with a buffalo robe snugged around her shoulders. She couldn't seem to get warm enough, and the scratchiness in her throat promised a cold or something worse.

To an unseen bystander, Reena could well have been mistaken for a native Blackfoot woman except for two distinctions: the sky-blue eyes that glowed to turquoise from the firelight, and the Holy Bible opened in her hands. Her thick raven hair spilled over her shoulders and onto her fringed buckskin dress. She was totally at ease in her sitting position as she stared not at the Bible but into the crackling fire.

Dark circles were etched under her eyes like ink stains. The normal healthy glow on her young face had been replaced with a pallor the shade of chalk. The Bible weighed heavy in her slim hands. She'd spent another restless, fever-ridden night and knew she should try to get more sleep, but her body was sore from lying down for so long.

The previous five months had been difficult for Reena. After growing up in Chicago and feeling the Lord call her to missionary work, she'd come to Canada and established a mission and a relationship with the Assiniboine Indians in the Cypress Hills. Many of the Assiniboines had turned to Christ, and Reena had eventually felt the need to move on to another tribe, the Blackfoot. But leaving the Assiniboine Indians had wrenched her heart, for they had become like family to her, especially Lone Elk, the chief, and his wife, Gray Dawn.

But leave she did, for a distrustful, unruly tribe of Blackfoot. Mistakenly, she'd assumed that her transition into the new tribe would be as comfortable as it had been with the Assiniboine. Not so. She'd been regarded with suspicion and open hostility from the majority, while the minority gave her a lukewarm reception, at best. Only recently had she been allowed to move her tepee into the village from her isolated spot fifty yards away.

"Reena?"

With a start, Reena realized that she'd been half asleep when the call came from outside the flap of her tepee. Getting to her feet slowly, she said, "Yes?" and through the flap came Raindrop, her sole friend in the tribe.

"Are you awake?" Raindrop asked in Blackfoot.

"Yes, *piik.*" Reena pulled the buffalo robe tighter around her as a blast of cold morning air followed Raindrop inside. The Blackfoot language had proven to be a serious challenge, just as the Assiniboine had. Eight to ten hours every day for four months, Reena had practiced, learned, and translated the Indian language with the help of Raindrop and two of her friends. Since the Blackfeet descended from Algonquian stock and the Assiniboine from Siouan—two completely different nations—Reena had had to start all over again. She thanked God every day that she apparently had a special talent with languages. By no means was it easy for her, but she sensed that she was a fast learner.

Raindrop immediately removed her own fur robe, revealing a red buckskin dress decorated with colorful beads. Her face was homely and round but strangely attractive in its open honesty.

"You look like you were asleep," Raindrop stated, eyeing Reena closely. "I can come back later."

"No, no, I wasn't sleeping." Reena waved her to the fire, and they sat cross-legged, facing each other.

Leaning forward, Raindrop scrutinized Reena carefully before shaking her head. "You look terrible, Reena."

"Thank you. Did you just come here to cheer me up?"

Raindrop's seriousness didn't fade a bit. "No, I did not."

"That's a joke, Raindrop." Reena used the English word "joke," for there was no translation in Blackfoot. "You remember what a joke is?"

A smile split Raindrop's face. "Yes." Then she gave an all too poor imitation of a laugh. "I remember 'joke.' " Raindrop's duty done, the laugh was cut off abruptly. Her face turned grave as she stared into the fire.

"What is it, Raindrop?" Reena knew before the girl answered what the problem would be.

"It is—"

"What did he do now?"

"It is what he did *not* do. He did not come home last night."

Reena sighed heavily. Raindrop's husband, Plenty Trees, was less than attentive to his wife; the only thing he really cared about was whiskey.

"He took Blue Mountain's baby blanket, Reena. The one I made before he was born." Raindrop's expression turned to pure hatred for a moment, then was replaced with a look of resigned defeat. "I know he has sold it for whiskey. I know it."

"Maybe he took it for warmth," Reena said, then dropped her eyes from Raindrop's gaze. The excuse sounded foolish even to Reena.

"What if he is caught? I know he steals horses. They will hang him, and then what will Blue Mountain and I do?"

Reena was hearing a familiar story. Many of the braves followed Dew Eagle, a member of the secret and dreaded Horn Society. Dew Eagle supposedly had mystical powers. It was whispered that he consorted with magical animals and spirits. Reena had tried to convince those who would listen that if these spirits weren't of the one God, they were false and evil. This outlook was met with surprise and skepticism, and the people continued to fear Dew Eagle.

Along with the mystique surrounding the Blackfoot Horn Society, Dew Eagle was a strong, charismatic young man who naturally drew men to him. Despite a face that was less than handsome and unfortunately acne-scarred, he also enjoyed the attentions of many women. On the few times Reena had talked with him face-to-face—or rather, listened to him speak *at* her—she'd seen flashes of what attracted them: it was his eyes. Dew Eagle had smoldering black eyes that burned with intensity—an intensity that stoked human emotions, such as love, hate, joy, and passion for a cause. Reena had the unsettling idea that he could turn on the depth of his gaze by mere force of will to get what he wanted.

Reena knew that Dew Eagle could be a powerful and positive chief for the Blackfoot, yet he chose to intimidate and control by fear. Powder Moon, the true chief, was old and barely able to rise to his feet, much less lead the tribe. He had no son and had appointed no successor. Dew Eagle wasn't even waiting for a chief to be chosen, and if one was, Reena couldn't think of a man in the tribe who would stand up to Dew Eagle. The leadership was his by default, but he would never be completely accepted until Powder Moon abdicated or died.

Reena could have accepted Dew Eagle had he merely been a bad seed that was intent on domination. She could have witnessed to him and *made* him give her an audience to hear of her mission. But Dew Eagle was caught up in the evil that was tearing the Blackfoot nation apart all over the Territory: whiskey. He became as a man possessed when he was drunk. There was no reasoning with him, nor pleading, nor making him feel guilty for his violent acts when he was under the influence. To make it worse, he could drink for *days* before he'd had enough.

Raindrop shifted her bulk, and the movement brought Reena back to the matter at hand. She asked her friend a question that unfortunately she probably also knew the answer to. "Is Plenty Trees off with Dew Eagle?"

"Yes. Dew Eagle came for him in the afternoon."

"Did Dew Eagle *make* him go?" Reena knew this wasn't unheard of.

"No. I wish I could say that he did. But no, he didn't."

"How many were with him?"

"I don't know."

Reena knew there was nothing they could do. Raindrop couldn't tell Plenty Trees what and what not to do. "We have to keep praying for him, Raindrop."

"It does not work!"

"We have to give God time."

"How much more?"

"We don't know. We don't always know the will of God, and I promise you He has a reason for waiting to deliver your husband."

Raindrop stood abruptly, swatting the floor dirt from her clothes. "I *have* prayed! I asked you for help before, and you said pray! You always say pray! I think Plenty Trees will learn to behave if I swat him with a stick."

"Raindrop, wait!" Reena got to her feet, nearly stumbling with the wave of weakness that swept over her. She put her hand on the Indian girl's arm, towering over the girl at her own five-foot-eight height. Raindrop shook her off and threw on her robe with a whirl. Following the girl outside, Reena heard her gasp.

Dew Eagle was standing directly outside the tepee, surrounded by Plenty Trees and five other braves.

Reena could tell immediately that they were drunk. One of them swayed precariously on his feet, ready to tumble at any time. Another wore only a vest for protection from the cold and held a bottle containing black liquid that sloshed about as he performed a small dance. But the most frightening sight was Dew Eagle's black eyes. He ignored Raindrop and stared at Reena with a predatory gaze. Reena wondered if he'd been listening at the tepee flap to their conversation.

"Plenty Trees, where have you been?" Raindrop asked, attempting to sound stern through her fear and dread. "And where is Blue Mountain's blanket?"

"Don't question me, woman."

Raindrop blanched. "You can't speak to me that way!"

"I will speak any way I want," Plenty Trees slurred.

"You only treat me that way when *he's* around," Raindrop asserted, jerking her chin in Dew Eagle's direction.

Plenty Trees glanced at the other men, as if to draw sympathy and support. The unsteady one simply remained unsteady; another was contemplating his dirty fingernails; the other three just seemed confused. Dew Eagle kept his eyes on Reena—all over Reena.

"I want an answer, Plenty Trees, to both questions!"

Dew Eagle spoke for the first time. "Tell your woman to shut her mouth." His voice was a deep baritone that left uncomfortable rumblings in the chilly air.

"You can't talk to me like that!" Raindrop cried.

The black eyes lit on her, and she visibly cringed. "I was not talking to you."

"What do you want, Dew Eagle?" Reena asked. She quickly

grew tired of his drunken, cruel games, and he knew it.

"Ah, One God Woman speaks."

The name wasn't an insult on any other lips but Dew Eagle's. The Blackfeet had given her that name soon after her arrival, and it had stuck. Reena didn't mind it; in fact, she was proud of it, both in its context and the feeling of belonging it allowed her by having her own Indian name. But when Dew Eagle spoke the words, they were heavy with contempt and arrogance.

Dew Eagle took a clumsy step toward Reena, who firmly stood her ground. "You do not look too well, One God Woman. It seems our winter does not agree with you."

"I'm fine."

With another step, a leer began to form on Dew Eagle's face. "Perhaps you are too cold at night. Perhaps you need someone to keep you warm."

"My home is very warm at all times, though *you'll* never find that out."

"I *have* been in your home."

"When?"

"At night, while you are sleeping."

A chill swept through Reena, but not from the cold. "You're lying."

"Am I?"

He took another step, and now he was standing right in front of her. His powerful arms hung loosely at his sides, but Reena suddenly imagined them reaching for her, hands like claws, to squeeze the life out of her. The intense eyes were bloodshot but focused. Reena wanted very badly to step back, but she forced herself to remain where she stood.

"One night I was an ant crawling through your tepee on my way to the moon. Another time, I passed through as a wolf searching for a rabbit."

The dawning sun peeped over the horizon behind Reena, shining directly into Dew Eagle's face. He squinted painfully but kept his eyes on her.

"The next time I was a shadow cast by your sleeping body on the other side of the dying fire. I could smell your dreams and see your sweet breath on the air."

Grateful that he'd made a silly mistake, Reena smiled. "You

mean see my dreams and smell my breath, don't you?"

"I meant exactly what I said. Your dreams smell good—strong and rich with desires, yet innocent of how to handle them."

Reena felt her face flush. "I think you have quite an imagination, Dew Eagle. You know as well as I do that you've never been in my tepee while I was there. And you can't change your physical form and become an animal anytime you want to."

"Who is the Hunter?" he asked with a knowing grin.

Reena's eyes widened before she had a chance to recover. "Who?" *How in the world did he know about Hunter?* she wondered in shock.

"Your pretty face betrays you. You know who I speak of. What does he hunt?"

Reena tried desperately to remember if she'd ever mentioned Hunter to him before, or anyone associated with him. She hadn't even told Raindrop anything about him. Hunter had visited her a few times, but he'd never talked with any Blackfeet but Powder Moon. *Had the old chief told Dew Eagle about Hunter?*

Dew Eagle watched her mind working, and his grin grew into a laugh, revealing strong white teeth. The men behind him laughed too, though they had no idea what was so funny. "The Hunter is important to you. You dream of him sometimes. But he is also out of reach, like a firm, sweet apple on the high branch of a tree too skinny to climb." Incredibly, Dew Eagle took another step toward Reena until their faces were almost touching. They were exactly the same height, and she could smell stale whiskey on him.

"I don't know what you're talking about," Reena said firmly, though she felt anything but firm inside. How did he know this? *How does he know that I care for Hunter but have to keep him at arm's length because he's not a Christian? How does he know that I dream of him?* The stench of rank whiskey was strong, and she felt a wave of nausea and weakness pass over her. She couldn't stand close to him much longer, but she didn't want to appear as if she were giving in to his bullying.

Dew Eagle continued, "I am a hunter also. Do you dream of me, too?"

Reena felt a powerful surge of dizziness overcome her, causing her to break eye contact and sway precariously. Without realizing it, she'd had her knees locked, and the blood supply to her brain had dwindled. She was also dimly aware that she hadn't eaten in over twenty hours. Just as she felt herself falling, hands grasped her arms and gently helped her down into a sitting position.

"Leave her alone!" Raindrop said fiercely from behind Reena, closing her arms protectively around Reena.

Dew Eagle's eyes narrowed to slits. "I grow tired of your woman's mouth, Plenty Trees. Maybe she should fill it with something else. Bring me the whiskey."

Plenty Trees looked from Raindrop to Dew Eagle uncertainly.

"Don't do it, Plenty Trees," Raindrop said, looking up defiantly at Dew Eagle from her knees.

Reena found her equilibrium, though she was having trouble following the conversation, and glanced up at him, too. He appeared impossibly tall from her position. She saw that his deerskin leggings were stained from grease where he'd wiped his hands.

Dew Eagle turned slowly. "I said, bring me the whiskey, Plenty Trees."

Under the full force of Dew Eagle's glare, Plenty Trees took the bottle from the coatless Indian and walked slowly to stand beside Dew Eagle, who snatched the whiskey out of his hand with a withering look.

With exaggerated movements and knowing he had everyone's full attention, Dew Eagle raised the bottle to his mouth and removed the cork with his teeth.

"What are you going to do?" Plenty Trees asked in a shaky voice.

Dew Eagle didn't answer. Slowly he stretched out his arm until the bottle was over the women's heads. Reena and Raindrop watched, openmouthed and disbelieving. The bottle began to tilt.

"No!" Raindrop breathed.

"Oh, Lord," Reena whispered, closing her eyes and bowing her head.

Dew Eagle, smiling now, watched as the dark liquid edged to the mouth of the bottle.

"Dew Eagle," Plenty Trees managed in a choked voice. He glanced around quickly for support from the other braves, but they were staring at the bottle, too. "Wait, Dew Eagle, I don't think—"

Out came the whiskey and splashed over Raindrop's head as she ducked. Reena heard the splashing, then felt some of it in her hair.

The stink was astounding. Then the stream was on top of *her* head, and her stomach heaved.

Plenty Trees watched in shock for an instant, then reached up to take the bottle away.

A huge explosion rent the air, and the bottle suddenly shattered into a thousand shards.

"Back away from those women, *now!*"

Dew Eagle and Plenty Trees, covered with the whiskey themselves, looked up to see a red-coated Mountie aiming a pistol at them from thirty feet away. Both had taken a step back from the startling disintegration of the bottle, and Dew Eagle felt sharp stinging on his skin. As soon as his mind registered the cuts on his body, they began to burn painfully from the alcohol in the whiskey that had sprayed all over him.

"I said back away! And you other men don't move an inch!"

Reena looked up through wet strands of hair. "Hunter!" she cried, overjoyed, then realized her mistake and turned to Dew Eagle. His face cut in three places, he looked at her sharply with dawning understanding.

Stone waved the gun at the five bystanders and ordered in a low, dangerous voice, "Get out of here. Now." The braves ran off without a look at Dew Eagle. Stone dismounted, pointing the pistol at the remaining two men.

Reena and Raindrop distastefully smoothed their wet hair back from their faces and rose to their feet. Reena stumbled to Stone, while Raindrop fixed her husband with a gaze of such intensity that he lowered his head.

"So . . . you are the Hunter," Dew Eagle said in Blackfoot. He smiled through the blood on his face.

"Shut up." Stone squeezed Reena in the crook of his arm. "Are you all right?"

Not trusting herself to say anything for fear of bursting into tears, Reena nodded. She leaned into his arms for shelter, realizing she was getting the whiskey on him but not caring. Her wet hair was suddenly freezing, and she shivered uncontrollably.

"Put that down," Stone ordered, waving the gun at the bottle neck with razor edges that was still intact in Dew Eagle's hand. Dew Eagle glanced at the glass in surprise, then dropped it in the snow, still grinning.

Stone whispered to Reena, "Does she speak English?"

"A little, but not much."

"Tell her to go to my saddlebags and take out the rope, would you?"

Reena told Raindrop without turning around or breaking their embrace. She didn't want to take a chance on seeing Dew Eagle's face right now; she just wanted to be held. The stench of whiskey was again threatening to make her sick.

Raindrop retrieved the rope and stood next to them.

"Ask her if she knows how to tie knots," Stone said.

"She knows," Reena replied, her voice muffled against his jacket. In Blackfoot, Reena told Raindrop, "Tie their hands behind them," then looked up at Stone. "Both of them?"

"Both of them."

Reena nodded at Raindrop.

"Lie down on your faces," Stone instructed the men, making clear what he wanted by waving the gun. Raindrop pointed to the ground and said something harshly.

Both men looked down at the snow.

"Now!" Stone snapped.

They got down—Dew Eagle slowly and defiantly. Raindrop began tying him first, none too gently.

"What are you going to do?" Reena asked.

"Tell them they're under arrest for—"

"Dew Eagle understands English. He just doesn't want to admit it or use it."

"Good. Why don't you go inside? I'll take care of them."

"Will you come see me before you go?"

"Yes. My visit sure did get cut off before it began."

"I'm sorry."

"Reena, you look sick."

"The smell . . . it's . . ."

"Go inside."

Gratefully, Reena went to her tepee, anxious to wash the whiskey from her hair.

Stone glanced around and for the first time noticed the crowd that had gathered. Most of the people were sleepy-eyed as they stared at the men on the ground. Stone holstered his pistol, patted the air in front of him with his hands, and said, "Go back to your tepees. These men are under arrest and must go with me to Fort Macleod. Do you understand?" They stared at him blankly.

Raindrop finished tying Plenty Trees, harshly whispered something to the back of his head that Stone didn't understand, and rose. In rapid Blackfoot she told the crowd something, and they began to file away with uncertain looks at Stone. Raindrop glanced at him.

"Thank you," Stone said, smiling.

Raindrop nodded, then made her way to Reena's tepee, passing Plenty Trees with more severe words that obviously stung him.

Stone knelt beside Dew Eagle. "What was that little scene supposed to accomplish besides getting you thrown in jail?"

Dew Eagle strained to keep his face out of the snow, the muscles in his neck standing out like cords of rope. He muttered something through clenched teeth.

"What was that?"

Dew Eagle repeated himself, louder this time.

"I'm sorry, I haven't had time to learn the Blackfoot language yet."

"I said, can we get up now?"

"Oh, you speak English! That'll move things along nicely. Of course you can get up." Stone helped them both to their feet; then, less than gently, he slapped the snow from the front of their clothes. When he stood before them, he was a full head and shoulders taller. "My name is Sub-Inspector Stone with the North-West Mounted Police. You're under arrest for the illegal possession of whiskey and assault against women."

"We don't follow your laws!" Dew Eagle spat.

Stone stepped close to him and looked down into his ebony eyes. "As of today, you do."

CHAPTER THREE

Border Line

After burying Jester, Stone and Vickersham decided that Stone should go back to Fort Macleod by way of the Blackfoot camp, while Vickersham and Dekko followed the tracks in the snow leading away from the burned-out cabin. After Stone's departure, Vic and Del discussed whether to begin tracking immediately or to wait until daylight.

"Mighty tough to track through snow at night," Del cautioned.

"But it might snow again tonight and cover up the tracks."

"Sky was clear as a winder pane all day today."

"You and I both know something could blow in from the mountains overnight."

Del shrugged. "Your call."

Vickersham considered the rapidly darkening sky. The North Star was already visible, and the only clouds to be seen were over the Rockies where the sun had set.

"I kinda like it right here," Del commented, then waved to the still-burning cabin. "Got a fire already started for camp."

"That's morbid, Del."

"It's the *truth*!"

Vic took one more look at the sky. "All right. We stay here tonight, then get an early start in the morning."

They pitched tent by the burned-out cabin, and both men slept well by the coals. Vickersham tried not to feel guilty about taking warmth and comfort from another man's tragedy, but he ended up worrying for only a few minutes before he fell asleep.

Once during the night, Vickersham heard the tinkle of breaking glass over Del's loud snoring. In a flash he was out of his blanket and armed. Outside, he carefully scanned the area and waited for five minutes, shivering in only shirt sleeves. He saw no movement and heard no more noise, so he went back to bed.

The next morning, Vickersham was relieved to find that no snow had fallen while they slept. Remembering the noise in the night, he walked around the homestead searching for footprints, but found none except their own. Passing by the barn site, he stepped inside the ash-strewn perimeter and walked about until his boot crunched down on a pile of broken glass. He hadn't seen it because the glass was burned black. After sifting through the ruins, he estimated that at least thirty bottles had been stored there. Vickersham didn't think they had contained water.

"Del, have a look at this," he called.

Dekko sauntered over, squatted down, and peered at the uncovered glass in the pile. Then he stood and walked a wide circle around it. "Whiskey."

"Do you think so?"

"Yep. A buncha these bottles exploded. What does that tell ya?"

"It tells me, my dear Del, that our dead friend Jester had more whiskey here than he could drink in six months. Also—"

"I've told you to stop callin' me 'dear.' "

"Also," Vickersham continued, as if Dekko hadn't interrupted, "the fire didn't originate in this shed, because it's too far from the cabin, and the cabin burned down. Someone, whether it be Jester or persons as yet unknown, deliberately set fire to these buildings. I would say, with no particular proof except his death, that this disaster was contrary to Jester's wishes. Therefore, another party must be involved."

"Figgered that out all by yourself, eh? That Jester didn't burn down his own home and himself in the process? You English earls are quick as whips."

"English *lord*, Del."

"Whatever."

"And we mustn't eliminate *any* possibility until we have solid proof. Maybe Jester had a reason for burning his property, and villainous persons came along and threw the poor chap inside the very inferno he'd created.''

Del hawked and spat, then gave Vickersham a wry look. "Villainous persons? I swear, Vic. My granddaddy used to say something that fits you perfect: 'Some people are educated beyond their intelligence.' ''

"I do agree with your learned grandfather in his observances of the human tendencies, but I daresay I take offense when the remark is directed to me," Vickersham sniffed.

"Kinda thought you would."

They packed up their tent, hastily made and consumed coffee, bacon, and biscuits, and started tracking. The hoofprints indicated four horses and a few cattle, and they had no trouble following them since they had left the only disturbance in the snow except for an occasional small animal print.

The men traveled in comfortable silence, with Vickersham recalling how he and Del happened to meet three years before. Vickersham had arrived by train in Dufferin from Toronto, intent on seeing the great North-West Territory. Having no idea where to proceed to find a scout, he'd gone to the local jail and asked the town constable.

"Yeah, I've got you a scout."

"Where would I locate him?"

The constable jerked his thumb behind him toward the cells. "In there."

Del had been arrested for card cheating, and after he'd jumped at the chance to get out of jail, Vic had talked the constable into releasing Del into his custody if he promised to keep Del away from Dufferin. Vic had promised. Remembering Del in the cell, pitiful in his dejected state and eager as a puppy to please a total stranger, Vickersham laughed out loud.

"What's so funny?" Del asked suspiciously.

"I was just thinking, Del."

"Oh, boy."

"What would you have done if you'd traveled with me awhile and couldn't stand me? Would you have stood by your contract with me?"

"I *did* travel with you awhile, and I *couldn't* stand you. And what's this about a contract?"

"Well, we didn't have a signed contract as such, but we had a gentlemen's agreement, I thought."

"Nobody ever accused me of being a gentleman. And I never signed nothin'."

Vickersham cast a speculative eye on him. "Come now, Del. It's just you and me out here. You like me, and you know it."

"Who told you that?" When Vic only stared, Del grunted and grudgingly said, "Yeah, I guess I like ya, but ya know why?"

"Other than my rapier wit and solid moral constitution? No, I suppose I don't."

"'Cause you remind me of how I don't wanna be!" Del cackled. When he saw Vic turn to face straight ahead and his half-smile fade, Del realized that his companion was serious, even though he'd been joking. "What's the matter?"

"Nothing."

"You're lying."

Vickersham looked at him quickly. "I *never* lie."

"Well, *something's* bothering you."

Vickersham shook his head. "Just forget it."

"Come on, Vic. What is it?"

Vickersham shifted the reins to his other hand. He spotted a ground squirrel staring at them from beside a pine tree. Its black, expressionless eyes followed them with muted interest, the small forearms cocked in a praying gesture. It had only eyes and a chirping squeak with which to communicate. So isolated, it seemed.

"Vic?"

He looked at Del. "You and Hunter are my only friends, Del. No man can call another 'friend' unless they've shared their lives . . . an *important* part of their lives. I thought I had many friends in England, but they were only acquaintances who admired me for my title and my connections. There was nothing deep down. Do you understand?"

Del couldn't meet his eyes. "I think so."

"What do we do, Del? What's out there for us? Do you remember what Hunter did when he found out that the murdering Indian had kidnapped Reena?"

"Sure I do. I was there."

"Hunter's a good man, a brave, noble man who abhors injustice, protects the innocent, and knows what's right and wrong, despite the law. The law is there for a purpose, I know, but it's not human and can only see so far. Hunter saw beyond the law of man at that time. He'd been through so much just to *find* a place with the Mounties. A place where honor and justice existed without question—his home, so to speak—and he abandoned that home for what he knew was right."

"I never saw a man so tore up when he disobeyed Macleod like that and deserted. But what are you getting at, Vic?"

"I'm wondering what's out there for us after this life, even if we do right by the law and follow a noble sense of right and wrong. Do you believe in hell, Del?"

"I . . . uh . . . well . . . what's the matter with you today?"

"Just thinking, Del. Just thinking."

"Well, stop thinkin'. You scare me sometimes with the things you come up with."

"Why should you be scared if you don't believe in hell?" Vic turned to look at the squirrel again, but he was gone. Then he whispered, "There's the rub."

———

They traveled all morning and into early afternoon before stopping for a lunch of jerky and beans. The tracks hadn't wavered from their southerly direction.

Del brought up the subject that both men were carefully avoiding yet painfully aware of. "Been a while since we crossed the St. Mary's River."

"Yes, I know."

"Be at the U.S. border soon."

"Mmm."

After a pause, Del blurted, "Cain't cross it to track fugitives."

"I *know*, Del."

Del nodded and stared toward the flat, unbroken horizon to the south. His nose was red with cold above his bushy beard. "You wanna keep goin'?"

"Of course."

"Thought you'd say that," Del sighed.

Vickersham stood and threw out the remains of his coffee. His chocolate-brown eyes followed Del's gaze to the south. "Those men may have no idea where the border is. For all we know they could stop on this side of it for a rest. Then we'd have them."

"Mighty long odds if you ask me."

Vickersham didn't answer him but continued to stare south thoughtfully.

"'Course . . . nobody *asked* me," Del mumbled as he put out the fire. "Nobody *ever* asks—"

"Someone's coming, Del."

"What?" Del asked, spinning around to see. "Who'd be out here in the middle of nowheres besides us fools?"

Vickersham's shoulders visibly relaxed. "It's Mr. Potts."

Del squinted but could only see a dot in the distance. "How do you know that?"

"Mr. Potts leans slightly to the left while riding. He took an arrow to the right . . . um . . . buttock in a war raid when he lived with the Blackfeet. Remember?"

"How could I remember? I weren't even there."

"I mean remember when he *told* us about it!"

"Oh yeah." Del hadn't taken his eyes from the rider and finally shook his head in exasperation. "I swear, Vic, you got the eyesight of an eagle. I just see a little speck."

"Comes from clean living, my good man," Vickersham grinned.

Del grimaced and decided to ignore the remark. "What do you think Jerry's doing out here?"

"Let's mount up and go find out. Maybe he's spotted the men we've been tracking."

"I say we wait right here for *him*. He's comin' right at us."

"Improper manners," Vickersham said as he swung onto his horse. "No need to make the man nervous while he wonders who we are."

"Vic!" Del cried in disbelief. "There *ain't* no manners out here! When you gonna learn that? 'Sides, Jerry Potts never had a nervous minute in his life! He's probably already spotted that red coat of yours."

"Come along, Del, there's a good chap," Vickersham said calmly, spurring the horse without waiting for his friend.

"I'd like to chap the top o' your head sometime," Del grumbled darkly, reaching for his horse's reins. The bay nipped at his outstretched hand, and Del swiped at his nose. "I don't need none o' *your* behavior today! Got enough on my hands dealin' with Mr. Snob.''

Jerry Potts had the saddest face Vickersham had ever seen. Heavy lids hovered over dark eyes that seemed dull with disinterest but somehow managed to take in every detail of his surroundings. Above Potts' downturned mouth was a wide, droopy mustache that received a daily trimming. Small, round-shouldered, bow-legged, and pigeon-toed, Potts looked anything but the uncanny scout he'd proved to be.

"Mr. Potts, how are you this fine day?" Vickersham asked as they came together.

"Sub-Inspector," Potts greeted with a nasal twang, in typically Potts-like few words. One of Assistant Commissioner Macleod's favorite stories was of the time he'd initially hired Potts to lead the Police to Fort Whoop-up following the long and treacherous march west in 1874. Bone weary, hungry, and irritable, Macleod had asked Potts, "What's beyond that next hill?" Potts had replied, " 'Nother hill.''

The son of a Scotsman, and his mother a Piegan Indian, Jerry was extremely versatile. He could blend in with either white man or Indian as the occasion demanded; strangely enough, his command of respect from both races was total. At seventeen, Potts had tracked down his father's killer, an Indian, into the man's own camp and killed him. The killer's fellow tribesmen acknowledged Potts' courage and let him go. His knowledge of the Territories' terrain was absolute, and he'd proven himself invaluable to the Police for his interpretive skills with the Plains Indians.

Del rode up beside Vickersham and asked, "What are you doin' out here, Jerry?"

Potts ignored him and leaned over to pat Del's horse, which made no attempt to bite. "Hello, Charlie.''

"How come you always say hello to my horse before me?"

"Like 'im better.''

"Humph. Well, his name ain't Charlie, Jerry. How many times do I have to tell you that?''

Potts tilted his head, questioning.

"Churly.''

"Hello, Churly.'' Potts patted the horse's nose and again looked at Del with another unspoken question.

Del rolled his eyes. "Jerry, you ain't got the memory God gave a stump! We named him Churly 'cause of the word . . . uh . . . the word . . . What was that word again, Vic?"

"What were you saying to Mr. Potts about memory, Del?"

"Never mind the smart aleck comments. What was the word?"

"Churlish, Del." Vickersham looked at Potts and began to explain: "When Del purchased the horse in—"

"*I'll* tell the story. He's *my* horse," Del interrupted. "After I got him, Churly was actin' up somethin' awful—bitin' me, tryin' to stomp me, and Vic said"—Del puffed himself up and gave a remarkable imitation of Vickersham's voice and accent. " 'I say, that bay is awfully churlish, what?' So I named him Churly."

"After you asked me what the word meant," Vickersham added.

"Do you *always* have to say that when I tell the story?"

Potts favored Vic with the same questioning look he'd given Del.

Vickersham said, "It means bad tempered . . . ill behaved . . . slightly akin to Del here."

"Ohhh, so you wanna get personal, huh?" Del managed to growl through tight lips.

Vic turned to Potts and asked, "What *are* you doing out here, if you don't mind my asking?"

"Telegrams," Potts replied, patting his saddlebags.

No telegraph line existed between the government in Ottawa and Fort Macleod. The closest line reached Fort Benton in Montana Territory, and to Macleod's chagrin, he was forced to send a man to pick up the latest dispatches every week. Assistant Commissioner James Farquharson Macleod was not known for his patience; he was known for his courage, foresight, and ability to get things done. The trip to Fort Benton irked him like no other inconvenience.

"Any news?" Del asked innocently.

Potts gave him a sour look.

"Well, excuse me fer askin'!"

"It's none of our affair, Del, you know that," Vickersham told him.

"Ain't you fellas ever heard of gossip?"

Potts asked Vickersham, "What's your story?"

Vickersham explained the incident at Jester's cabin and the subsequent following of the tracks. "Have you seen anything, Mr. Potts?"

"Jerry. Saw some tracks, but—"

"You didn't know whose they were. I'm going to follow them as far as I can," Vickersham declared.

Potts shook his head, then jerked it back the way he'd come. "Border right there."

Vickersham felt like cursing but held his temper. He took a deep breath and glanced at Del. "All these miles for nothing, my friend."

Potts waited patiently, though obviously ready to ride on.

"I suppose we'll head back to Fort Macleod with you. There's nothing else to do."

The three men turned north, and Potts favored Del with his longest speech yet. "How's about lettin' me ride Charlie?"

"*Churly!* And no, you cain't!"

———

Stone placed a hand on Reena's brow and grimaced when he felt the heat. Looking up at Raindrop, who stood nearby in Reena's tepee, he spread his hands, placed them against his chest, and rubbed his forehead and throat—Indian sign language for "sick." At least Stone thought it was.

Raindrop's eyes widened, and she disappeared. Stone sincerely hoped he hadn't told her that Reena was dead.

"I'm not sick," Reena said weakly.

Stone tucked the elk-skin blanket tighter around her until only her head was showing.

"Stop it. I'm not sick."

"Will these people take care of you?"

"Of course they will!"

Nodding slowly in contemplation, Stone watched the two lines form between her eyebrows as they always did when she was being mulish.

"I mean, they'd take care of me *if* I was sick."

"Why are you so stubborn?"

"Hunter Stone! Who are *you* to call *me* stubborn?"

"I'm not when it comes to being sick. I'll whine and be pitiful with the best of them."

Reena glanced at the poles in the ceiling. "Lord, forgive him for that."

"What?"

"Lying."

"I wasn't lying!"

"Who do you think you're talking to, Hunter? I'm the one who nursed you for two months after Red Wolf almost killed you! Every time I turned around you were trying to get up and saddle Buck to go hunt down that Crow." Her eyes narrowed. "Don't you re-member the time you got up—about a week after you were nearly dead!—and burst the stitches that Gray Dawn had so carefully sewn?"

"Well, I—"

"It wasn't any fun having her sew them up again, was it?" Reena smiled sweetly, though she felt terrible. She loved their good-na-tured banter, and now she had him.

"It wasn't so bad," Stone argued, but he couldn't meet her eyes.

"Now who's being stubborn?" Reena brought her arm out from under the blanket and placed her hand on his. "How have you been? It seems like it's been a long time."

"It has—almost three weeks."

"Busy?"

Stone nodded and began kneading the palm of her hand with his thumbs.

"Oh, that feels wonderful," Reena murmured. "You can stay here and do that for hours."

"I wish I could, but there's that little matter of Dew Eagle."

"Do you really have to arrest him?"

"Of course I do! Why?"

"When he gets back here, he's going to be even more bitter and spiteful than he already is. I'm not looking forward to that. How long will he be in jail?"

"Is he drunk?"

"Couldn't you smell the whiskey on his breath? Yes, he's drunk."

"Then I can get him on possession of whiskey and drunkenness. Did he steal the liquor?"

"I don't know, he'd just come back—wait!" Reena's face fell as she remembered. "No, he probably didn't steal it. Plenty Trees, the other man, sold his baby's blanket that Raindrop had made."

Stone's face darkened. "I'll ask around when I get back to the fort. Maybe someone's heard of whiskey being stolen and I can pin the charge onto Dew Eagle."

"Hunter, you can't do that!"

"I know, but I wish I could. So what do we have here? Possession, drunk and disorderly, and assault. I'll try to up the charge of assault to indecent assault, and our friend Dew Eagle may be looking at a fine of one hundred dollars or more."

"Who will be the judge?"

"Commissioner Macleod. If he doesn't have time, it'll be Inspector Walsh. In either case, Dew Eagle will get the maximum penalty because neither man is lenient."

As the Commanding Officer of the Mounted Police and a magistrate, Macleod's authority in the remote frontier was almost absolute. To anyone who entertained thoughts of defying that authority, Macleod left no doubt that justice would be swiftly enforced with heavy penalties. He was fair, however, and the justice always fit the crimes. Macleod made it a point never to abuse the extraordinary powers he possessed.

Reena said, "But Dew Eagle doesn't *have* that kind of money."

"Then he'll get prison and hard labor."

"I don't know, Hunter," Reena said doubtfully, shaking her head, "he'll be so mean when he gets back."

Stone stopped massaging her hand and let it rest between his. "These men have to be punished for their crimes. That's why we're here. Besides, I've seen the sort of labor these men have to do, and it would be enough to break the meanness in *me*."

"You don't have any meanness," she said softly.

"You keep telling me that. Maybe one day I'll believe you." Stone smiled, then asked, "Is there anything you need? Something Vic or I could bring to you? Do the Blackfeet have the medicine you'll need, or—"

"I'll be fine, Hunter. Raindrop will take care of me."

"You're sure?"

"Yes. Now go! Dew Eagle and Plenty Trees are probably freezing."

"I really need to get to the fort to see if Vic and Del are back."

He explained how they'd come upon the burned-out cabin and the dying Jester, and that Vic and Del had gone after the men who had set the fire. "I'll come back as soon as I can."

"Don't worry about me. Just take care of yourself."

Stone paused and said, "It would be different if you were still with Lone Elk. I wouldn't have to worry about you."

Reena nodded. "I miss the Assiniboines so much."

"They were good people. *Are* good people."

"The Blackfeet are so different . . . so distant to me."

Stone nodded and said nothing.

"It seems I'll never get close to them."

"If I know you, I'd say it's just a matter of time and patience. I don't see how anyone could *not* trust you."

Reena met his eyes, and Stone saw a gratefulness in her face that gave him a rush of satisfaction. He still found it hard to believe that they'd known each other for only a year and a half. They'd been through more in that short time than most friends and acquaintances experience in a lifetime: pain, fear, emotional turmoil, victory, defeat, joy, and near death. Reena was his best friend, and he cared about her more than anyone in the world.

Even as he thought of his affection for her, a dark current of remorse and even guilt coursed through him at the memory of Betsy. She had died a horrible, lonely death, and she'd been blameless. Stone couldn't shake the feeling that she'd somehow paid the price for his sin of taking her to the Territories. His desire had been for peace and solitude on the wide open prairie, away from cities and people. The punishment for his dream had been a dreadful brush with an untamed native of the plains who'd taken everything from him in the matter of a few days.

In seeking peace, he'd found war. While fulfilling a dream, he'd lived a nightmare.

Reena was staring at him strangely. "What are you thinking?"

"Nothing, really," Stone shrugged.

Glancing heavenward again, Reena teased, "That's two lies. You've got a lot of praying to do tonight."

CHAPTER FOUR

Macleod: The Man and the Fort

Fort Macleod was situated on a level strip of land within one of the curves of the Old Man's River. Macleod and Jerry Potts had chosen the site for its plentiful supply of water and wood and as a good prospect for a natural hay crop. The high banks of the river shielded the fort from the north wind. From a strategical point of view, it commanded the route frequented by the whiskey traders from the United States. Many a man had registered complete shock, when innocently passing by the river he found scarlet-coated troops waiting to relieve him of his trade. He often watched stupefied as his moneymaking whiskey was poured onto the ground in front of his eyes.

Constructed of twelve-foot cottonwoods set in three-foot ditches to create nine-foot walls, Fort Macleod quickly shaped into a shelter for the winter of 1874. The square measured two hundred feet across and enclosed a hospital, stables, living quarters, jails, stores, a kitchen, and a blacksmith shop. It had been constructed in that order, since the newly arrived and exhausted Mounted Police gave priority to sick men and to horses.

Stone arrived with Dew Eagle and Plenty Trees on the same night they left the Blackfoot village. The three men had remained totally silent during the ride. Stone, a quiet man anyway, knew of nothing to communicate to the Indians. As far as he was concerned, they were aware of their troubled situation, and he sure didn't want

47

to make small talk with abusers of women.

Plenty Trees stared straight ahead at the back of his horse's head the whole time, a look of extreme dejection clouding his young face. One time Dew Eagle said something to him, but Plenty Trees ignored him.

Dew Eagle, however, kept his back straight and, wearing a confident smile, arrogantly glanced at Stone from time to time. Stone considered wiping the grin from his face by telling him the penalty that likely awaited him but decided against it. He would find out soon enough. Stone merely grinned back at Dew Eagle a few times, then ignored him.

After identifying himself at the gate, Stone led his prisoners into the fort. The night was the warmest they'd had in weeks, and Stone knew that a Chinook wind had arrived. The Chinooks blew in suddenly from over the Rockies with little warning and elevated the temperatures by thirty or forty degrees. The warm weather sometimes lasted up to a week. The Mounties had come to love the winds and had begun celebrating them by cooking a barbecue on the grounds of the fort. Supper was over by the time Stone arrived with his prisoners, but a large portion of the garrison seemed to be lounging and visiting about the compound. Some bowled with a ball and crudely carved pins, while others smoked cigars and pipes while they talked. The delicious aroma of barbecue still hung in the air as the men boisterously worked out their cabin fever.

"Hunter! Over here!"

Stone turned to find Vickersham, Del, and Jerry Potts standing with four constables by the cook fire.

"*More* prisoners?" Del asked incredulously, his strange eyes glinting red from the fire. "Blazes, son, don't you ever take a day off from arrestin' folks? Hey, Vic. Stone went to visit a pretty lady and ends up bringing back these two ugly fellas!"

"That's Hunter," Vickersham shrugged.

"Hello, sir!" called a huge, baby-faced constable. He'd been throwing a ball with another Mountie when he'd spotted Stone and rushed over.

"Becker."

"Oh, boy," Del grumbled loud enough for everyone, including Becker, to hear. "There's the bear cub."

Becker overlooked Del's comment. "Where you been, sir?"

Stone sighed and favored Vic with a secret smile before answering. "I've been on census duty, then visited Miss O'Donnell. Would you like my full report before I give it to Colonel Macleod?"

"No!" Becker replied, his eyes wide. "The colonel should get it first."

The men exploded in laughter. Becker, at nineteen, was the newest recruit in C Company, and his naiveté and enthusiasm were already legendary. Bright, inquisitive blue eyes complemented his handsome face, along with a determined square chin. An unfortunate white scar ran down the side of his face from just below the eye to the jawline, as if some cruel fate had determined that the handsome face was just too attractive. He stood six feet four inches and was one of the few men who could look Stone in the eye flat-footed. Del nicknamed Becker "bear cub" because his physique was extraordinarily well muscled. The haft of a knife sprouting from his belt was the only nonregulation item on his person. Stone knew it wasn't the only knife he carried, just the only one visible.

"Can I go with you on patrol next time?" Becker asked Stone.

"I don't assign the men, Becker. You know that."

"What did these unfortunate fellows do, Hunter?" Vickersham asked, nodding toward Dew Eagle and Plenty Trees.

Stone's face darkened as he turned to the Blackfeet. "The one with the red headband is Dew Eagle. He was getting ready to pour a bottle of whiskey over Reena and an Indian woman named Raindrop. The other one, Plenty Trees, Raindrop's husband, stood gallantly by and watched. Both of them were intoxicated."

The good-natured smiles vanished from every face within hearing distance. Stone glanced around and saw eyes usually reserved for mischief and merriment turn almost vicious in their disapproval.

"I think they're sober now," Hunter added.

Dew Eagle met every gaze with his usual defiance, while Plenty Trees didn't look up from his lap.

"Maybe they *aren't* sober yet," announced Sergeant Preston Stride, who'd suddenly appeared beside Buck. "Maybe they need a little help."

"Hear, hear," Sub-Constable Ken Garner added.

Stone looked down approvingly at Stride. The sergeant had been in the British regular army and was without question the best in Fort Macleod at his craft of training and disciplining men. Stone and Vickersham had both recommended Stride for promotion, but he'd begged them to withdraw their requests. He was happy right where he was among his "lambs," as he called them when none of the lambs were around. From the lambs' point of view, Stride was father, mother, teacher, boss, and, most of all, leader. They would follow Stride if he walked off the edge of a cliff.

"We could tie their feet to their stirrups and drag them around in the snow for a bit," Stride continued in his proper English accent. "That'd do it."

"None of that talk, Sergeant," Vic admonished gently.

"Yes, sir."

Stone said, "Becker, you and Hallman get these men off their horses. Be careful. Their hands are tied behind them."

"With pleasure, sir."

Becker and Hallman passed by Stone as he dismounted and said to Vickersham, "Vic, Reena's—"

A thud and a grunt sounded behind Stone. When he turned he saw Dew Eagle lying on his belly in the snow, his face covered with patches of the white stuff. Becker stood over him, his face full of innocence.

"Becker—" Stone growled.

"He fell off his horse, sir," Becker claimed, a sudden look of innocence lighting his face.

Snickers came from behind Stone, but before he could turn around, a voice thundered, "Pick that man up!"

Every man in the area except for the two Indians and Becker snapped to attention. There was no mistaking that bark. Becker hurriedly helped Dew Eagle to his feet, then assumed attention.

Assistant Commissioner James Macleod strode into the group that had somehow expanded to about thirty men. "What's the story here, Sub-Inspector Stone?" Six feet, with a straight European nose, bushy beard, and dark piercing eyes, Macleod's presence was electric to all around him.

"My fault, sir," Stone began. "I wasn't watching when—"

"Begging the colonel's pardon, sir," Vic interrupted, "Sub-Inspector Stone had his back turned to the . . . incident—"

"I'll see both of you in my quarters pronto!" Macleod roared. Then he stepped right up to Stone's ear and said, "Grab a bite to eat first, Stone. But don't let anyone see you dawdling—can't have that, eh?"

Stone didn't move from his stiff posture but was greatly relieved. He hadn't eaten all day and had been looking forward to some barbecue. Macleod, on top of every situation as usual, probably knew Stone had just arrived and was hungry.

Macleod turned on a heel and strode toward his quarters. After he'd gone, the men sighed as one.

Becker walked up to Stone and Vickersham with one hand on Dew Eagle's arm. "I'm sorry, sir. I didn't mean to get you both in hot water, I was just—"

"Just trying to help him off his horse, I know," Stone nodded, then considered the Blackfoot. "Do you have anything to say before you're locked up?"

Dew Eagle, his face wet and glistening from the melted snow, said darkly, "I had heard the white men in red coats were fair in their treatment. The ones who told me that were wrong." His black eyes went to Becker.

Stone stepped closer and looked down at him with contempt. "I had heard the Blackfoot treated women with respect. Those people were wrong, too."

Dew Eagle didn't flinch from Stone's hot glare, and Vickersham smoothly stepped between them. "I think you'll find—Dew Eagle, is it?—that on the whole the Mounted are an honorable unit." This time, it was Vickersham's turn to glare at Becker. "Some young, wild recruits must learn that we do treat our prisoners fairly."

Becker hung his head and said, "Yes, sir."

Vic whispered to Dew Eagle so that only the four of them could hear, "But I must say that young Becker's action, though it will not go unpunished, is nothing compared to what *you* will suffer for what you've done."

Stone watched his friend's face turn icy and marveled again at how the change made him look dangerous. Vickersham's usual calm and pleasant demeanor could disappear in an instant when he was riled.

"Now," Vic continued, stepping back from Dew Eagle, "for your punishment, Constable Becker."

"Yes, sir."

"Do you have pen and paper?"

51

"Umm . . . I have a *pencil* and paper, sir," Becker said in confusion.

"That will do. I want you to write twenty times for Sub-Inspector Stone and me—not one time less, mind you—'I will not push abusers of women off their horses again.' Do you understand?"

"I *pulled* him off, sir."

"Very well. 'I will not *pull* abusers of women off their horses again.' Is that understood?"

"Yes, sir."

"Are you certain?"

"Quite certain, sir."

"How many times?"

"Twenty, sir."

"Outstanding. We'll want that by. . . ?" Vickersham turned to Stone questioningly.

"Next week ought to do."

"Next week, Constable."

"Yes, sir . . . um . . . sirs."

Stone didn't take his eyes from Dew Eagle during the exchange and saw the man's face flush in rage.

Vic leaned close to Dew Eagle again. "You're lucky I wear this uniform. Do *you* understand?"

Not waiting for a reply, Vickersham turned and said, "Constable, you and Hallman take these prisoners to the jail at once. And take care they don't trip over anything, will you?"

———

On the wall of Macleod's private office hung a sketch by Richard Barrington Nevitt, Assistant Surgeon. Nevitt had captured a portrait of the fort from a distance with the Union Jack flying triumphantly in the center. A mounted deer head with a six-point rack stared glassily from beside it. On one side of the oak desk against a wall was a hand-carved ivory chess set, a game Macleod loved with a passion. A partially filled bookcase stood on the opposite side. Despite the dirt floor, which every building contained, the room seemed spotless.

Macleod, seated at the desk, handed a note to an aide. "Give this to Sergeant Stride." The aide nodded to the two sub-inspectors and left. Macleod didn't rise when Stone and Vickersham entered but returned their salutes and motioned them toward two straight-backed chairs beside the bookcase. "At ease, gentlemen. I didn't call you here to discuss the incident in the yard, but obviously I have questions." His eyebrows raised inquisitively as he opened a box sitting on the desk and removed a cigar.

Lying was not an option for either Stone or Vickersham, especially to the most respected man in the force. Vic said, "Totally my fault, sir. I should have acted the moment it happened."

"The moment *what* happened?" Macleod offered the box of cigars, which both men declined.

"Constable Becker was helping the Indian off his horse, and . . . well, you know Becker. He's a bit enthusiastic about things and took offense at the crime of the Indian in question."

"In all honesty, sir," Stone added, "every one of us did."

"What was the offense?"

Stone told him.

Macleod nodded slowly and leaned back in his chair. Appearing to take his time, he struck a match on the heel of his boot and lit the cigar. Four perfect smoke rings emerged from his mouth as he shook out the match. Stone was aware of a clock ticking somewhere, but he hadn't spotted it yet.

"What are your charges, Stone?"

"Possession, drunk and disorderly, assault, Colonel."

After a pause and another puff, Macleod asked, "And how is Miss O'Donnell?"

"It didn't help that she's sick, sir. A respiratory thing, I think. But she's a remarkably strong young woman and seems to have taken it in stride. More controlled than I would have been under the circumstances."

"That's not saying much, Stone. You're barely under control at the best of times."

Stone wasn't sure if the hint of a smile played around Macleod's lips. "I'm not sure how to take that, sir."

"Look at your production and promotions, Sub-Inspector. I believe that speaks for my point of view."

"Thank you, sir."

"Don't pat yourself on the back too much. I believe you know my stance on the incident with that Red Wolf character. Your behavior, though courageous, was reckless and thoughtless."

"I never pat myself on the back, sir," Stone said grimly.

"I know," Macleod murmured. Then, strangely, "Believe me, I know." Hatless, Macleod's balding pate shone in the lamplight. He considered Stone through squinted eyes as he puffed. "You remind me of myself when I was your age, Stone."

"I take that as high praise, Colonel."

"Not so fast, Sub-Inspector. You lack a certain quality that keeps you from being the complete soldier."

"What's that, sir?" Stone was completely intrigued, as he knew Macleod wanted him to be. Macleod's presence was so awe-inspiring that men, even his enemies, hung on his every word.

Macleod turned his penetrating gaze to Vickersham. "Do you know what it is, Vickersham?"

Vic, too, had been engrossed with Macleod's hypnotic mien. His eyes widened for a moment before he said softly, "I think so, sir."

"Then why don't you tell him?"

"Me, sir? But what if I'm wrong?"

"Then that would mean Stone has *two* areas for improvement."

Stone shifted uneasily in his chair. *What is this?* he asked himself. Stone had always been uncomfortable talking about himself and suddenly found that he was extremely disturbed when being examined by others right to his face. He turned to Vic, one of his best friends, who pinched a pleat in his trousers before meeting Stone's eyes.

"I don't think it's any real secret, Hunter. You have an awful temper, you know." Vickersham tried to smile but failed.

Stone relaxed in relief. *Is that all? I was afraid he would say I was cruel or lazy or incompetent!*

"An *uncontrolled* temper," Macleod clarified, breaking into Stone's self-congratulations. "I don't worry about you when you're with Vickersham, since he seems to be the only one who can get through that stubborn head of yours." Macleod smiled slightly at this. "But how in the world you kept yourself from beating the stuffing out of that Indian today, I'll never know. Even I might have had a hard time with restraint in that situation. But it's unacceptable behavior in the Mounted, and one day your anger will get you into trouble. I speak from experience, not in judgment."

Both Stone and Vickersham waited and hoped for an explanation from Macleod, but they were disappointed. Macleod stared for a moment at the glowing tip of the cigar before commenting. "Up the charge to indecent assault. I don't see why that wouldn't hold water."

"I'll be glad to, sir," Stone said carefully. He was trying to hide his satisfaction while he thought of Dew Eagle's face as he stood in Macleod's courtroom and heard his sentence. *If Macleod says it'll hold water, it'll hold water. After all, he's the judge.*

A sharp rapping on the door produced Sergeant Stride and Becker. "Constable Dirk Becker, sir, as ordered."

"Thank you, Sergeant. Will you come in, too?"

"Sir!" Stride marched forward and braced to attention, his eyes straight ahead. Becker tried to emulate Stride's crispness, but his eyes seemed ready to bug out of his head. Stone doubted he'd ever been in the colonel's office, much less in a private audience with him.

"At ease, men, I'll be with you in a moment." Macleod turned back to Stone and Vickersham. "Due to the seriousness of the event at Jester's farm today, I'd like to hear your version of the story. Not that I don't trust Sub-Inspector Vickersham or Dekko, but I'd also like Sergeant Stride to hear it."

Stone told of Jester's slow, painful death. The man's burning flesh was still in Stone's eyes and nose. When he relayed Jester's strange utterings of sweet, sweet, Stride's face showed surprise and a dawning realization.

Macleod crushed out his cigar as he asked Stride, "Sound familiar, Sergeant?"

"Most definitely, sir."

Stone and Vickersham looked at Macleod expectantly.

"I remember the last name, Stride, but his first name escapes me," Macleod said.

"Armand, sir."

"Yes, that was it. Armand Sweet." Macleod watched the men's reactions before continuing. "We just heard of Sweet a few days ago. Do you recall the three traders we arrested on three different occasions since we've been in the Territories? The ones who were so mysterious concerning where they'd gotten their supply?"

"Yes, sir." Stone and Vic nodded in unison.

"As you know, most of the whiskey we capture comes directly from Fort Benton, no secret about that. But these three traders were vague in their stories and working alone. Two of them couldn't even locate Fort Benton on a map. That's why we thought they were being supplied by someone locally here in Canada."

The four men watched their superior officer closely, Becker with a mixture of awe and wonder. Stone fleetingly wondered what the constable was doing there before Macleod went on.

"After hearing Vickersham's report, I visited our trio of outlaws separately at the hard labor camp. I then mentioned the name Sweet to them in quite a surprising fashion and found their reactions most guilty."

"So," Vickersham said slowly, "this Sweet fellow has been supplying traders on his own."

"Yes. One of the men inadvertently made a mistake and revealed that our man Sweet lives in the foothills northwest of us." Macleod regarded each man pointedly. "Someone needs to go up there and make an arrest."

Becker stepped forward instantly. "Sir, I volunteer!" With his jaw clenched tightly, the scar on his face shone milk-white in the lamplight. When the others looked at him without a word, his face began to flush. "That is . . . if it pleases the colonel . . . and um . . . sub-inspectors. Oh, and the sergeant, sir."

Macleod allowed Becker's painful embarrassment to hang in the air for a while before ignoring him completely. He turned to Stone and Vickersham. "Take six men and bring back this Armand Sweet." The name was spoken almost in a sneer. "I'd prefer to go myself, but I'm in the middle of a report for the government in Ottawa."

Becker, still standing in the middle of the group with no hope of a graceful withdrawal to his original position, waited for someone to tell him what to do.

"Constable Becker," Macleod began, rising to his feet. Without moving a muscle, Becker seemed to shrink back from the colonel. "I don't want to hear of any more mistreatment of prisoners, no matter how vicious you believe the crime they've committed. Do you understand?"

"Yes, sir!"

"We've worked hard to establish the Mounted Police as a fair and honorable organization, both to the lawbreakers and to the Indians in this Territory. I'll not have that reputation tarnished, especially by an overzealous constable."

"Yes, sir . . . I mean, *no*, sir! That is—"

"Dismissed, Constable Becker."

"Thank you, sir!" Becker wheeled and made a hasty exit. The absence of his large physique left a noticeable void in the room.

"That boy's got a long way to go," Stone muttered.

"Stone, I want you and Vickersham to take Becker with you on the arrest patrol."

"Yes, sir," Stone said glumly.

"The boy's officer material, I believe." After sitting down in his chair, Macleod added, "I've never seen anyone so *eager* in my life."

"Not bad with a knife either, Colonel," Vickersham remarked.

"Yes, I've seen Becker's familiarity with that weapon. He can drill the center of a target from thirty feet. And hand to hand . . . whew! There's no match for him." Macleod shook his head in wonder. "No, I'm not worried about Becker's skill in the physical aspect of the job. It's the mental department that has me troubled."

Great, Stone grimaced inwardly. *And it's up to Vic and me to sort that out.*

CHAPTER FIVE

The Sweets

Jenny Sweet watched in mild surprise as a spider landed on the log in front of her. Though she didn't know the proper name for it, she knew the thick-legged creature packed a healthy bite. Raising the ax above her head, Jenny brought it down into the wood with a solid *thunk*, splitting both spider and log. A drop of sweat fell from her forehead as she bent to retrieve one half of the split log and set it end-to-end on the dead spruce stump. *Whistle. Thunk!* The unfortunate spider was already forgotten.

The seventeen-year-old girl attacked the pile of wood as if possessed. Despite her youth, short stature, and slender body, Jenny's movements were deft, powerful, and accurate. The logs split into showers of splinters after receiving direct center hits. She wore no gloves and yet didn't blister or bleed, for her palms and fingers were heavily callused. Rings of sweat formed under the armpits of her well-worn blue cotton shirt as the blade bit into the tenth log.

Her baggy Levi's, hand-me-downs from one of her father's men, were nevertheless comfortable for the hard work. Her father had never bothered to buy Jenny any girl's clothing. Since she'd always been around only men, Jenny had long ago given up wishing for dresses. At twenty strokes, her breathing began to labor in earnest, but she took no notice. Jenny stopped at thirty, not because she was tired, but in order to carry the split wood into the cabin, rekindle the fire, and prepare breakfast for her father and his men before they awoke.

Her face suffused with blood, Jenny piled the wood into her arms. Her short, light brown hair framed an oval, smooth-skinned face with haunted hazel eyes. The area around her left eye was discolored with a bruise.

Jenny vaguely hoped the noise hadn't disturbed her father, Armand, but the wish had no real substance. Jenny Sweet had long ago given up hope for her wishes—any of them—coming true.

Before entering the large cabin, she heard a piercing scream on high and looked up to see a golden eagle soaring in flight toward the mountains. Just before it passed out of sight above the aspens, the eagle dove straight down like a falling dart. Jenny felt a rush of pleasure at the sight but showed no sign of it. Her eyes fell to a spot in the deep woods where she imagined the eagle scooping up a weasel or mouse in its razor-sharp talons. She stood immobile, her gaze glassy, for almost two full minutes.

When she came back to her surroundings, her arms ached from the strain of holding five large logs. Jenny reached for the door, but just before she grasped the knob, it swung open quickly to reveal Sad Sid looking anything but sad.

Sid was the newest of her father's hired men and had an unpronounceable French last name. Armand tagged him Sad Sid, for no apparent reason that Jenny could discern. Anytime he was around Jenny, his eyes flashed with ill-concealed lust. She couldn't remember the last time he'd actually looked into her eyes; his attention seemed to be everywhere *but there*.

"Jenny, Jenny, Jenny . . ." he chanted softly. "Need some help with that load?"

"No." Jenny attempted to get by him, but he reached for the logs against her chest anyway. Instantly his hands were between the logs and her body, and she dropped them as she stepped away quickly. The banging of the logs as they knocked against each other and the doorframe caused Jenny to glance at the door to her father's room. If it woke him up . . .

"Now look at what you've done!" Sid commented with mock sadness.

"Keep your voice down!"

"Oh, so you don't want anyone to know about us, hey?"

"There's nothing to know and never will be. Would *you* like to wake up my father?"

This time Sid stole a look at the door, suddenly anxious. They both stared at the door for a moment, then Sid brought his eyes back around to somewhere below Jenny's neck. "He's still asleep. Plenty of time for us to . . . talk."

Jenny ignored him and squatted down to gather the spilled wood. Out of the corner of her eye she watched his boots as they stepped carefully behind her. When she rose, Sid put his arms around her. Trying to shake him off, Jenny dropped two logs, but she knew she would have to drop them all again to fend him off. The wood clattered to the floor as she spun and grabbed for his throat.

Sad Sid's eyes widened when he felt the strength of her small hands, but he merely tensed the muscles in his skinny neck and laughed. He leaned toward her face, and Jenny felt her arms giving way.

"Jenny!"

Sid and Jenny released each other at once and turned to find Armand Sweet almost upon them. Tall and swarthy-skinned, Sweet looked like a pirate with his long black hair and goatee. His black eyes flashed as he stepped between them.

When the blow came, Jenny doubled over, breathless. After tasting bile, she could see nothing for a moment but a cloud, black and quivering around the edges.

"Never," Sweet roared, "*never* are you to carry on with my men! Or anyone else!"

Jenny's breath came back in gasps. Through involuntary tears, she saw her father's black boots and knew that she would probably be shining them that evening. Finally, she was able to stand straight and found her father in front of her, with Sad Sid watching carefully from behind him. Sid had an odd combination of fear and interest on his narrow face. Jenny could hear Armand's hard breathing over her own panting.

"Do you understand me, girl?"

Jenny nodded slowly, not able to draw enough air to say anything. But there was nothing to say, anyway.

"You've made coffee, I hope?" Sweet asked mockingly.

Jenny nodded again, still unable to meet his dark eyes.

"And you," Sweet said as he spun on Sad Sid, who cringed noticeably. "You'll keep your hands to yourself. I know she threw herself at you, but that doesn't mean you have to take her up on it!"

"Sure, Armand." Sid glanced quickly at Jenny, ready for her to deny her father's erroneous charge, and was surprised at the silence.

Jenny once again picked up the wood and went to the kitchen. Her only protest would have been to slam the wood into the bin forcefully, but she didn't. Childish petulance had gained her nothing in the past but more violence, and the idea of expressing her frustration no longer even crossed her mind. She poured two cups of coffee and set them on the table in the tiny dining area. The pain in her middle had dulled to a sore lump. She could feel her movements being examined with dark, piercing eyes.

"Wake the others, Sid, and hitch up the horses," Sweet ordered. "We've got a shipment to pick up." Sid left the room, and Sweet walked slowly to the kitchen to stand behind Jenny as she kneaded dough for biscuits.

Jenny felt his presence looming over her but went about her business. He would either hit her again, or he wouldn't. It didn't really matter.

"You're just like your mother," he said in a low, seething tone. "I'll not have you growing up to be the harlot she was. So help me, I won't!"

Jenny said nothing but started slightly when she felt his hand in her hair. His touch was gentle, yet she felt the urge to shudder.

"Do you know what happened to your mother?"

Jenny knew, since he'd told her countless times. The grip grew tighter in her short hair, and she smelled his stale breath.

"Answer me!"

"You killed her lover and ran her off."

"That's right. I should've killed her, too. Never forget that."

"I won't."

"You stay away from men. You're too young, and I won't have that in my house."

Jenny laughed with no trace of humor.

"What's so funny?"

"Nothing." Her head was jerked back until she was looking at the ceiling. In a strangely detached manner she saw another spider in the corner. Tiny, delicately spun sacs were dotted through its web, snagged victims that had innocently wandered into the spider's sticky world. Jenny imagined the struggle of the fly or moth as it had suddenly found its wings and legs entangled in the web's silken strands. She wondered if the insects had had a moment of instant clarity and mourned the loss of their freedom.

Sweet was in her vision, upside down, but she kept her eyes on the motionless spider. In a dead voice she said, "I was just gonna say that I *want* to stay away from men."

"That's not what I saw."

"I was fightin' him off, Papa."

"That's what *she* always said! Liar!"

Her hair was released, and Jenny tensed for a blow. Instead, she heard his heavy step recede into the next room.

Jenny served breakfast. She endured Sad Sid's leers, rushed to bring the four men whatever they rudely called for, and cleaned up their mess.

After she watched them ride away down into the forest, Jenny stared blankly at the gap in the trees into which they'd disappeared. When she turned from the window, after what seemed moments to her but was truly five minutes, she went directly to a corner and retrieved a broom. Grasping the handle just above the wire that fastened the straw needles, Jenny squashed the spider against the ceiling corner.

————

Later that day, Stone rode with the small troop of Mounties among the foothills of the Rockies. Brown grass surrounded them, a silent testament to the warmth of the Chinook that had melted the snow. No warm wind in February could touch the snow on the mighty mountains, however. Stone gazed up at the rugged peaks in awe and appreciation. They were similar yet different; some were elegant, some were imposing and brutal-looking. One particular mountain had four straight, deep crevasses running vertically, as if a giant had raked his fingernails down the side. Another summit came to a perfect peak like the point of a spear. The mountains never failed to overwhelm him with their majesty, beauty, and sheer immensity. Some of the mammoth peaks stretched all the way into the clouds.

From his place with Del and Vic, Stone listened to the conversation of Becker, Andy Doe, and Ken Garner behind him.

"You're American, then?" Doe asked.

"Yes," Becker replied. "My father and brother were killed in the war—Pa at Antietam and Joseph at Yellow Tavern."

"What about your ma?"

"She died right after the war in Mississippi."

Stone listened to the painful silence. He knew The War between the States had torn families apart unmercifully, but he'd never personally met any of its victims.

"That's tough, boy," Garner said sympathetically. Gustav Boogaard and Charles Hallman nodded in unison.

"It was hard at the time, of course, but I finally learned that they're all better off with our God in heaven than they are here. *I* can't wait to get there, myself."

Vickersham glanced back at them. Turning around, he gave Stone a strange, quizzical look and spoke so only Stone could hear. "Seems we're always surrounded by Christians, Hunter."

"Yes, it does."

"Coincidence?"

Stone looked at him. "What do you mean?"

"Do you ever . . . think about it?"

"Sometimes."

Vickersham nodded and his eyes went to the mountains.

"Do you, Vic?" Stone watched his friend sway in the saddle, the red officer's plume in his helmet dancing in the gentle breeze. His face was troubled.

"What happened when you nearly died, Hunter? Did you . . . see anything?"

Stone avoided Vic's intense gaze by looking away. For a moment he felt the deep, burning thrust of Red Wolf's knife in his side, and an instant sweat heated his forehead and palms. The smell of wet leaves and rain and smoke hit him, while a vein of lightning split a black sky. He heard water dripping from spruce and cottonwoods in lilting patterns that caused his dry mouth to salivate for a stray drop to fall on cracked lips. He remembered his mouth opening some time later, not in hopes of catching rain, but to strangle a protest against the turn of events that was unfairly about to end his life.

"Hunter?"

"No, I didn't see anything, Vic. Not like you're talking about, at least."

"Do you remember anything at all?"

"I remember the smell of sheets after my mother took them off the clothesline. Clean and white and warm smelling. Summery. It made me think of my mother. She smelled like that all the time."

Vickersham waited a moment, then asked, "Is that all you remember?"

"No," Stone smiled grimly. "That was the good part. The rest of it is pretty dark." Vic said nothing, and Stone listened again to the men talking behind him.

"Where'd you learn to do that?" Garner asked, his voice tinged with anxiety. "A man shouldn't pitch knives in the air while riding a horse! I'm not so much worried about you. I just don't want to see a good mount get cut by accident."

"I won't drop it."

Stone turned to see Becker pitch a short-handled knife with a narrow five-inch blade into the air. The sun scattered sharp reflections from the angles of the spinning, silvery blur, and Becker expertly caught it by the haft as it came down.

"How do you *do* that?" Doe asked in wonder.

"Just practice, I guess. I've always played with knives."

"Didn't your mama ever tell you not to play with—?" Doe realized his mistake and bit off the rest of his question.

Surprising everyone, Becker laughed. "Yeah, she told me a bunch of times, but I was a little stubborn and did it anyway." He pitched the knife into the air again.

"That's enough, Beck—" Stone began, but he was interrupted by a whistling, whirring noise.

"I got him!" Becker yelled, jumping off his horse. "I got him!"

"Did you see that, sir?" Doe asked Stone, round-eyed. "He just got a rabbit with that thing. Just . . . threw the knife and stuck him, pretty as you please!"

"I've never seen *anything* like that!" Vic breathed. "Did you see that, Hunter?"

"No, I missed the show." Stone watched Becker hold up a white-tailed jackrabbit by its long hind legs. Becker had withdrawn the knife and was grinning hugely.

"Get back on your horse, Sub-Constable."

"Yes, sir!" Becker said, still glowing with pride. "How 'bout that, fellas? Got us some supper tonight."

"You can play with your knives on your own time," Stone declared, "but if you slice off a finger on *my* time, I'm short a man."

"Yes, sir," Becker responded, his smile gone. It seemed there was nothing he could do to impress Hunter Stone. He was, however, overjoyed to be riding in the same patrol with him.

"Show-off," Del muttered.

"Hunter," Vic said quietly, "wasn't that a bit harsh?"

"You can pat him on the back if you want to, Vic. I thought it was reckless." Then Stone winked at Vickersham, and Vic smiled.

Doe asked, "Hey, Del, what did you say was the name of these foothills?"

"Porcupine Hills."

"No, I mean the Indian name."

"I cain't pronounce them Indian words! That was Sub-Inspector Vickersham."

Vic half turned and answered, "They are called the Porcupine Hills from the Indian name, *Ky-es-kaghp-ogh-suy-iss.*"

"All that means porcupine?" Del asked.

"No, it means the porcupine's tail."

"I'd hate to hear what they call a rhinoceros."

"Actually—"

"Never mind! I said I'd *hate* to hear it."

"How much farther, Del?" Stone asked. The prisoner that had mentioned Sweet's name to Macleod had told them where Sweet lived in exchange for a shortened sentence. Then, as an afterthought, he'd begged that he be transferred to another prison. The thought of spending time side by side with the man he'd turned over to the Mounties seemed to disturb him. Macleod had refused. The nearest post was the newly established Fort Edmonton, three hundred miles away.

"Should be comin' up on the pass real soon," Del answered. From inside his coat he fished out a plug of tobacco, tore off a corner with his stained teeth, and tucked the wad away in his cheek. He pointed to the east. "Y'all see that smoke over there? That's Miss Reena's Blackfoot village."

Stone looked at the smoke, then back to Del's swollen cheek.

He was reminded of a chipmunk just before the peace of the spring-like day was shattered.

————

Armand Sweet watched the backs of his men as they rode down a pine-studded hill. He insisted on riding behind them because of a paranoid fear of being shot in the back. The men were cutthroats, nothing more, interested only in themselves and making money from the Blackfoot. His eye was trained on Sad Sid most of the time.

Sweet didn't trust Frenchmen. The man who'd been with his wife had been French, as had been Sweet's former employer, who'd tried to cheat him out of his fair earnings. To get his share of the whiskey profits, Sweet had seen no reason not to skim off the top before the Frenchman got his hands on it. When the man had called Sweet on it, Sweet had offered his resignation by pistol-whipping him. Sweet didn't think he'd have the same problem with his present employer, since he'd never met him and probably never would. That was the way Sweet, and apparently his employer, preferred it.

Born literally on the Oregon Trail in 1840, Armand Sweet had lived a life filled with violence since his first steps. The train of pioneers suffered severe hardships on the trail all the way to Oregon, where they were then attacked by Indians. Only two families survived, neither of them Sweet's. A family by the name of Gross rescued the screaming baby from his dead mother's arms. Helmut Gross was a stern father who had never warmed to Sweet. Somewhere during Sweet's early adolescence, Gross decided it was Armand's fault that he had no children of his own, and the beatings began. After a particularly bad episode in which Sweet suffered a broken arm, he left the Gross house and never looked back. Since that time, Sweet hadn't liked Germans, either.

Sad Sid looked around at Sweet—rather sneakily, Sweet thought—and grinned when he found his leader's watchful eyes already on him. Sweet had hired him because the load of whiskey they were to meet was the largest ever—four wagonloads. Sweet hadn't had time to find a man he felt more comfortable with, so he'd settled on Sid. Now he regretted that he hadn't taken the extra time needed. Sweet's other two men, Conklin and Boggs, were sturdy but brainless—just the way Sweet liked his hired help.

"What are you looking at?" Sweet called gruffly.

"Nothing," Sad Sid grinned again. "Just admiring the scenery."

"Well, admire the scenery to the front."

"Sure, boss."

He grins too much, Sweet thought. *Can't stand a man that grins all the time. I thought naming him "Sad Sid" would tone it down, but it hasn't.* Unconsciously, he placed his hand high on his right thigh near his pistol. Sad Sid had done nothing but follow orders for the past four days, but Sweet was more nervous than usual with the huge shipment waiting for them.

After completing the trek down the long hill, the three men in front of Sweet rounded a small bend thick with snow and froze in their saddles like bird dogs on a scent. Boggs was the first to move, and he spun around to give Sweet a disbelieving, openmouthed warning. Sweet spurred his mount ahead and saw a bright splash of crimson in the wooded trail ahead.

Mounted Police. Six or eight of them.

Sweet opened his mouth to order a quiet retreat when his right ear was assaulted by the roar of a gunshot. He started and spun, finding Sid aiming his rifle, the barrel smoking. Sweet was sure his own face registered the same disbelief that Boggs had shown a moment earlier, but for a different reason. "You idiot!" he screamed, then he turned and checked the Mounties. Their horses were milling around in confusion, and one man was writhing on the ground.

As Sweet turned his horse to follow his fleeing men, he chanced one last look at the scarlet riders. Beside the wounded man rested a white helmet with a red plume. He was no longer moving.

Sweet briefly wondered what the plume signified, but as soon as the thought occurred to him, his mind registered the fact that all of the Mounties were still far away, in shock over their fallen comrade, and confused.

Except one. He was charging straight toward Sweet, who dimly heard the thunder of the rider's horse's hooves over the roar in his ears.

A matching blood-red plume waved from the helmet of the charging rider.

PART TWO

A VIOLENT TORRENT

There is a sort of river of things passing into being, and Time is a violent torrent; no sooner is a thing brought to sight than it is swept by and another takes its place, and this too will be swept away.

Marcus Aurelius
Meditations

CHAPTER SIX

The Sick and Wounded

"Reena, it is time for *beba-mokodjibika-gisin*," Raindrop said with a glint in her dark eyes.

"Oh no, not again! I just *had* that a couple of hours ago!" A look of utter dread crossed over Reena's pale face when Raindrop came toward her carrying the medicine.

Raindrop placed one hand on a hip. "Does it help you?"

"You know what it does. It makes me sneeze like there's no tomorrow."

"But does it *help*?"

"Well . . ."

"Here." Raindrop handed her a small pouch.

"This is so disgusting!" Reena reluctantly took the pouch, untied the string at the top, and looked distastefully at the dried and pulverized root inside. The literal translation of *beba-mokodjibika-gisin* was "bear root, it is found here and there." Reena wished fervently that it was only found in South America.

Raindrop stood above Reena, waiting patiently. When she saw Reena hesitate, she made circling motions with her hands. "It will make you better. Take it."

Slowly Reena took out a pinch of the dark powder and stuffed it up her nose.

"Two times."

71

"I know, I know. You'd better stand back." Reena repeated the process with the other nostril, grasped a cloth, closed her eyes, and breathed deeply through her nose. The sneezing began at once—hard, violent sneezes that seemed to begin down at her toes. Between the fifth and sixth one she managed to glance at Raindrop through slit, watery eyes and found the woman smiling her approval. Reena felt a flash of deep, heated resentment, but she knew the Indian woman was only trying to help.

Reena's fever had gotten worse after Hunter's visit three days ago, and a deep chest cough had developed. Raindrop had taken over immediately and practically moved in with her. Two other medicines that Raindrop forced her to take were what she called *o-gite-bug* and *be-cigodji-biguk*. Both, fortunately, were boiled root decoctions that Reena could gulp without really tasting.

Reena had watched Raindrop prepare the bear root one night as she hovered over the fire breathing in fumes of some wet root that Raindrop had placed on the hot stones. Reena couldn't even remember the name of that one, but it obviously contained camphor.

While she'd worked at pulverizing the bear root, Raindrop had talked. "The *o-kyai-yu*, or bear, is the chief of all animals at giving medicine. He is fierce and ill-tempered, but he has shown us kindness in the giving of herbs for healing. No other animal has such good claws for digging roots. He is the only animal that eats roots from the earth, and he is especially fond of acorns and cherries. If a person is fond of cherries, we say he is like an *o-kyai-yu*. If a man dreams of an *o-kyai-yu*, he will be expert in the use of herbs in curing illness."

Reena had nodded weakly at this belief, too feverish to take the natural opening that she had been given to tell Raindrop about God creating the very bears the Blackfeet held in such high esteem. Effectively dealing with the Indian belief in stories and traditions was one of the most difficult challenges of her missionary work.

When Reena had finally finished sneezing, Raindrop nodded with satisfaction and said, "Come. We go to bath."

"But it's *freezing* out there!"

Raindrop bent over and grasped her arm. "Come."

Reena had no choice but to follow and barely had time to throw her fur robe over her shoulders before Raindrop had unlatched the tepee door, and cool air washed over her face. It smelled refreshing, however, and Reena was glad Raindrop had forced her outside. They walked through the village, past colorfully painted tepees and children playing with tops. The toy was fashioned from a thick chunk of birchwood and beveled at the bottom. A boy would spin the top, then see if he could race all the way around the nearest tepee before the top tipped over. Reena watched a boy give the top a tremendous whirl, take off around the tepee, then breathlessly come back to the top. Just before he made it back, the top spun onto its side. His loss meant that every boy playing the game could take a free hit at his arm. Reena winced as she witnessed some pretty heavy blows.

A group of girls stood by watching, but when they saw Reena, they rushed to her side.

"Are you feeling better?"

"Are you ready to teach us some more English?"

"We miss you!"

Reena smiled and greeted each one, then said, "I'm not ready to continue our lessons right now, but if Raindrop has her way, I will be very soon."

"Awww!" was the unanimous reply.

Reena felt better than she had in days. She had had a few small visitors to her tepee while she'd been sick, but she sensed that most of the parents held back their children from visiting One God Woman. The continued distrust from the majority of the tribe was disturbing, but Reena was happy that the children had missed her.

Raindrop shooed the girls away and continued leading Reena to a small round hut built of willow branches and covered with buffalo skins and robes.

Reena stopped abruptly. "You . . . you're taking me to the sweat lodge?"

Raindrop nodded and smiled.

"Who. . . ?"

"Powder Moon suggested it."

Reena couldn't believe it. The sweat lodge was usually reserved for Blackfoot religious ceremonies involving important men.

"Powder Moon says that people have been healed after visiting the lodge, and he wants you to know that he does not mean to interfere with your beliefs in your God. He only wishes to help you."

"That's very kind of him," Reena said, still in shock. "Please tell him of my thanks." Just when she was thinking how discouraging the tribe's behavior had been, the chief proved that Reena's well-being was important to him. When word spread of his concern, the rest of the tribe would *have* to follow his lead. Reena was overjoyed, yet humbled. *Okay, Lord, you've made your point*, she thought with an inward smile.

An ever burning fire was situated close to the lodge, and Reena saw that someone, probably Raindrop, had already placed some stones close to the flame.

"Go inside and take your clothes off," Raindrop ordered.

Reena's eyes widened. "All of them?"

"Of course!"

"Why?"

Raindrop glared at her.

"All right, all right!" The lodge stood only five feet high, so Reena had to duck. It was surprisingly warm inside. In the middle of the tiny area was a small hole in which to place the hot rocks, and thick buffalo robes were spread out on either side. Embarrassed, Reena undressed and slipped under one of the robes. Many skins layered the floor underneath, so she was very comfortable.

Raindrop entered with a basketful of hot, smoking rocks and dumped them in the hole. After leaving again, she returned with a large dipper of water and sprinkled it over the rocks. A thick steam rose from the hole. "It is customary to pray to the Sun now, but you may pray to your God."

"Would you like to pray for me, Raindrop?"

Raindrop shifted her gaze to the fire and shook her head.

"You don't have to be embarrassed with *me*, you know. The only way to learn how to pray is to do it." Raindrop said nothing, so Reena continued, "Please? I feel sort of silly praying out loud for myself." To Reena's surprise, Raindrop whispered a quick prayer.

"Dear God, please help my friend. She is weak and sick, and we need her to help my people understand You better. Thank You, amen." Raindrop looked up through the steam and grinned. "How was that?"

"Very good. Thank you . . . so much."

"It gets too hot in here for me, so I leave. But I will be back every so often to sprinkle the stones."

"All right." Reena spent the next few minutes staring at the closed smoke flap in the ceiling of the tiny hut, breathing deeply of the warm, damp air, and then she began to pray. She prayed for her family in Chicago: her sickly mother, her father, sister Megan, and brother Liam, her ex-fiancé, Louis Goldsen, who'd married Megan, and her lovable uncle Faron somewhere in the Rocky Mountains, his home and haven. She remembered Hunter and Vic and Del. The clouds of steam above her increased, swirling like a warm, incessant fog, and she fell into an unwilling sleep.

"Reena!"

She woke to a gray, misty world, and for an incoherent moment, she thought she was on the banks of Lake Michigan in Chicago playing skip rope with Megan. Her sister was crying while Reena skipped. Crying and crying and . . .

"Reena! Wake up!"

Raindrop was kneeling over her with her laundry. No, it was Reena's clothes, folded neatly. "Whaaa. . . ?"

"Reena, Mounties are here! They are asking for you! One of them is dead!"

Reena's disorientation disappeared in a blink. She snatched the clothes out of Raindrop's hands and, with all modesty forgotten, threw off the buffalo robe and dressed quickly. She had to pause once from the wave of dizziness that hit her when she got up too fast. The clothes stuck unpleasantly to her moist skin, but as she was tying her buckskin dress around her waist she stepped outside. Her head ached fiercely, and she could tell that she still had a slight fever.

The contrast of the hot, steamy air inside the lodge and the cool breeze outside burned her nostrils and made her shiver violently once. *Who's dead? Oh, please, God . . . I don't want to wish anyone to be dead, but please don't let it be Hunter! Or Vic, or Del, or Colonel Macleod or . . . oh, don't let* anybody *be dead! Let it be a mistake!*

"This way, Reena!" Raindrop called and took off at a run in the general direction of Reena's tepee. Following her, Reena found the village deserted, presumably because of the arrival of the Mounted Police. At the edge of the village, a group of forty or fifty people crowded together, with no sign of the scarlet-coated Mounties. A few Indians heard their pounding footsteps and stepped aside as they flew into the middle of the throng.

Reena pushed through the unfortunate ones that weren't aware of her arrival. She received many dark looks and dimly realized that this wasn't helping her image in the village at all. But when she saw the man lying pale and still beside Del and a few other Mounties, she shrieked, "Vic!" and her heart fell. He was covered with a bloodstained blanket, and Reena watched his chest for movement.

"Miss Reena, it's bad, it's *real* bad!" Del said, nearly sobbing.

Reena stopped a few feet from Vic, terrified to ask the question that she dreaded but couldn't avoid. "Is he . . . dead?"

Del blanched and said, "No! Not yet, anyways. Can you help him? It was just too far to go to the fort, and we didn't know what to do, and since you helped Hunter that time, I thought . . . I thought . . . oh, Miss Reena, you've *gotta* help him!"

Reena was stunned to see tears in the man's eyes, but she looked away quickly and knelt beside Vic. "Of course we'll try, Del. Raindrop, get some balsam bark and *gijib-inuskon*. Start a fire by my tepee. Hurry!"

"Miss Reena," Andy Doe said, "it wasn't our fault."

Gustav Boogaard agreed. "We never saw who shot him, and then . . . then . . ."

The men stood around her, helmets in hand, with agonized expressions. Reena realized that they wanted some sort of absolution from her. "It's all right. There was nothing you could do if you were surprised. Hunter wasn't with you?"

"Oh yes, ma'am," Boogaard nodded. "But he took off after them. One minute he was there, the next he was gone. Becker too."

Reena briefly wondered who Becker was, but her attention was on Vic's wound that she'd uncovered. A dark hole high on the right side of his chest oozed blood. "The bleeding's almost stopped. That's good." She stood and said, "Bring him to my tepee."

"Is he gonna live?" Del asked with obvious dread at what the answer might be.

"We'll do everything we can, Del," Reena told him in a soft voice. The scout's pain was disturbing. "But what about Hunter?"

They all looked at her blankly, and she knew they were in some sort of group shock. "Shouldn't someone go help him?"

Eventually their disciplined training took over, and they turned to Garner, who'd recently been promoted to corporal. Garner's eyes lit with understanding. "Yeah . . . Booger, you and Doe get back to Macleod and report this. Me and Hallman will follow Sub-Inspector Stone. Del. . . ?"

"I'm stayin' right here."

The men carried Vic to the tepee and placed him on a raised fur bed across the room from Reena's bed. Vic's face was sweaty and drawn, and he moaned a few times with the movement. After the Mounties left, Del sat beside Vic and watched Reena and Raindrop's movements as they first applied the boiled bark of the juniper and balsam trees to the wound and then a poultice.

"Miss Reena?"

"Yes, Del."

"Would you say a prayer for him?"

"Of course I will. Will you pray with me?"

"Out loud?"

Reena smiled as she finished bandaging Vic's chest. "In your heart if you like."

"Oh . . . yeah." Del snatched off his hat and bowed his head.

Reena prayed: "Dear Father, bless and heal Vic. He's very dear to us, as he is to You. We don't understand why bad things happen, but we trust in You to heal the hurt and wounded if we ask in faith, believing. We *believe* in that healing for our friend and thank You for it. We ask for comfort in this difficult time, and that You place wisdom in our hearts in dealing with our own strife and pain. Amen." Reena looked up, but Del's head remained bowed.

"Don't forget Hunter and the boys," Del whispered.

"And yourself," Raindrop told Reena reproachfully.

Reena prayed that Hunter and the others would be kept safe in God's care as they pursued the outlaws, then reluctantly prayed for her own healing.

"You sick, Miss Reena?" Del asked when she finished.

"Yes, I'm afraid so. Can't you tell by how haggard I look?"

"Haggard? You? I ain't never seen you look anything but beautiful, Miss Reena."

"Thank you, Del."

Without a word, as was the Indian habit, Raindrop left. The Blackfeet were comfortable anywhere, and when they got ready to leave, they simply left.

"She mad about somethin'?" Del asked.

"No, she's not mad. That's just their way."

"They're a handsome people, the Blackfoot."

"Yes, they are."

"Tallest Indians I ever saw. You don't think they're mad at you for us comin' here, do you?"

Reena sighed and shook her head. "I don't think so, but I haven't quite got them figured out yet. They're very private and hard to get to know."

"I don't want to get you in trouble, Miss Reena."

"It'll be fine, I'm sure. They have a great respect for the Mounties. Colonel Macleod is almost like a god to them—a white man who actually keeps his word and has their best interests in mind. They respect that."

Del looked down at Vic when he stirred and moaned. His strange eyes registered a compassion that was alien to his face. Reena was so accustomed to his crotchety but lovable personality that she could only stare in wonder. It had never occurred to her that Del could care deeply for someone, but the evidence was right in front of her. Softly, she said, "I think he'll be fine, Del."

Del nodded but couldn't meet her eyes. "It confounds me. I ain't never seen Vic have a day of sickness since I've knowed him, and here he is, almost kilt. Some people are just *healthy*, you know? They just seem to give off a . . . a . . ."

"Vitality?"

"Yeah, that's the word. Vic woulda knowed it." He smiled, and his eyes brimmed with tears in the soft light of the fire. "He was just talkin' about death the other day. How he was wonderin' what comes after, ya know. Just out of the clear blue sky, he starts wonderin' about it."

"He'd probably been thinking about it for some time, Del."

"Yeah, maybe so. Seemed to be off the top of his head, though. But that's Vic. Always sayin' things to get a reaction outta me."

"What did you tell him?"

Del took a deep breath that caught his throat. "You know stupid ol' me. I tried to laugh it off and told him he was crazy or somethin'. Vic's a deep thinker. I admire that about him, though I'd never tell him that. He's the smartest man I ever met. Got all that English education, and here he is runnin' around a countryside full of men that would just as soon cut your throat for your boots as look at ya." Finally Del met Reena's gaze. "Now what kinda man gives up all that good breedin' and status and chooses this kinda life?"

"A *good* man, Del. A man who wants to make a difference."

"I'll say."

"And you're a good man, too. A good friend."

Del took a cloth out of a bowl of water that Raindrop had brought in and gently began wiping his friend's face. "He's all I got," he whispered.

CHAPTER SEVEN

Capture

Stone rode hard into the foothills. Through the canopy of aspens and birches, the bright sunshine cast strange shadows around him as he raced after the villain who had shot his comrade. He rode breathlessly, his countenance a mixture of fury and determination. Dimly thinking the moisture on his face was melted snow from the trees, he reached up and wiped at it. His white-gauntleted hand came away smeared with crimson.

Vic's blood.

His friend's blood, sprayed and defiled by a coward.

"Of all the people in the world," he muttered aloud. "Of all the people . . ." He whipped Buck's flanks with the reins as they started up the steep hill before him. The vision of Vic suddenly tumbling backward off his horse in a shower of blood was still with him. They'd been only two or three feet apart. Why had the brute chosen Vic instead of him? Stone had taken one look down at his friend and raw instinct took over. He knew that Vic wasn't killed instantly, because he was writhing on the ground. Del had moved deceptively quickly and jumped from his horse to Vic's side. Stone knew there was nothing for him to do except catch the man or men who had committed this wicked deed, so he'd spurred after them immediately. He'd felt a gnawing guilt over his action, but what could he do for Vic that the other men couldn't? He knew now that he should have stayed long enough to issue orders to the men. But Garner would take care of them.

A mule deer and his doe were startled by Stone as he rounded a thicket of brush. Both animals bounded away into the forest with incredibly high leaps. Stone sensed rather than heard movement behind him and veered into a stand of white spruce and fir, decorated with a mixture of horsetails and grouseberry. His breath rasped through his mouth, and Buck stamped impatiently. He slid the Henry rifle from its scabbard and worked a round into the chamber with the lever. Recalling the dim figures he'd glimpsed right after the shooting, he thought he'd seen three or more men. If they'd split up and circled around behind him and had him surrounded . . .

He heard a horse laboring up the hill. *If that's one of them*, he thought grimly, *he doesn't care about making noise*. His fingers tightened around the Henry.

Becker burst into view, helmetless, his brown hair dripping with sweat. Holding his Adams pistol loosely by his side, he showed no surprise at finding Stone. "Sir." He nodded.

Stone thought of admonishing him and telling him to return immediately. He was young, he was raw, and by his recklessness could very well make a mistake and get them both killed.

Becker waited in front of Stone without speaking, his horse stamping impatiently. He'd unbuttoned his tunic to midchest. His face was flushed from riding hard, and the scar looked like a straight flash of lightning against his clenched jaw. He seemed to know what Stone was thinking and understood.

"Let's go," Stone said, turning Buck into the path. Becker was anxious to prove himself, he knew. But in that moment of gauging him, Stone saw a solid will to move on because it was the right thing to do. To Stone, Becker's posture silently said, "A man has been bushwhacked and may be dying or dead. The man or men responsible are close but getting away. Why are we just standing here?" And in an identical situation, Stone would have done exactly the same thing.

The tracks were ridiculously easy to follow; the melted snow had left mud that pointed the way like an arrow. To Becker, he shouted, "There are four of them."

"How do you know?"

Stone gave him a pained look and patiently explained, "Because we're riding over eight sets of horse tracks, four of them heading the way we came, and four of them heading right in front of us. They're backtracking."

"Oh. Yeah, I see it now."

"See it sooner. Keep your eyes open to everything. Assess what you're up against."

"Yes, sir."

"And holster that pistol until you need it. If you happened to shoot my horse, I'd have to kill you."

———————

Armand Sweet recognized the rage building inside him. Dark and white-hot and relentless, it rose from somewhere in the middle of his torso in an almost painful fashion, causing his teeth to grind painfully. His black eyes turned to the object of it. Sad Sid was bent low over his horse, occasionally casting a desperate glance behind him as if a troop of cavalry were on their heels. Sweet's face twisted at the sight of him. Ahead he saw their tracks veering off to the cabin, and he made a decision.

Sweet spurred his horse ahead of the others to the front and side of Sid. In a blurred move, he pulled his huge Colt revolver and swung it with all his might in a savage arc behind him. The solid iron of the barrel and cylinder caught the surprised Sid across the bridge of the nose, and he performed a perfect backward somersault over his horse's hindquarters. Sweet motioned to the other two men to follow and led them, along with Sid's riderless horse, past the trail back to the cabin to higher ground through the spruce trees.

Sad Sid, sprawled in muddy grass and snow, groaned pitifully. A cut over the bridge of his nose leaked blood down both sides of his face—twin crimson rivulets pooling in his large ears. For minutes he could only stare at the evergreen canopy above through blurry double vision. Finally he sat up and managed to gain his feet. Wiping at the blood with his sleeve, he realized that he was on foot but was relieved to see the path that led a short distance to the cabin.

Wearily, with a rising anger of his own, he grinned horribly through the mask of blood and began to make his way to Sweet's cabin.

And Jenny.

———————

Here I am, Becker thought joyously, *riding with him! Actually* riding *with him—just him and me!* Guilt soaked over him quickly when he realized what their mission was: tracking the men that had shot down one of the nicest men Becker had ever known. *Vic may even be dead, 'cause he sure didn't look too good when I left him. That would be the most horrible thing in the world. I don't think he's a Christian, and I didn't get a chance to tell him about the Lord. But how could I? He's an officer, and I'm just a sub-constable.*

Becker watched Stone's broad back in front and concentrated on keeping up. Becker's horse, Egypt, was showing signs of losing strength, while Buck, whose legend nearly equaled Stone's own, ran purposefully with powerful strides. The thought of Stone leaving him behind because Egypt gave out was unbearable. And Stone *would* leave him behind, Becker had no doubt of that. Becker was personally witnessing Stone's bullish, unrelenting pace when his blood was up, which was talked about in whispers at Fort Macleod. He was like a red-eyed cougar on a scent, or a lion on a stumbling gazelle.

Suddenly, Stone stopped Buck.

"What is it?" Becker asked breathlessly.

"They've split up. But I don't think it was voluntary for one of them."

Becker squinted at the tracks but only saw a mess of mud and hoofprints heading in two directions. "Which do we follow?"

Stone didn't answer right away. Becker watched his profile and thought of what a fine-looking man he was. He reminded Becker of his older brother, Joseph, who'd died at Yellow Tavern, Virginia, along with General Jeb Stuart. Joseph had been tall and blonde and determined. It had torn him up to leave his mother and little brother alone near an important river port called Vicksburg, but he'd done what he'd known was right. The Southern army had needed numbers, and he'd understood that. Off to Virginia he'd gone with Becker's father, and the five-year-old Dirk had cried and cried and cried.

Stone broke into Becker's thoughts. "You take the tracks to the cabin, and I'll take the others. Only one man—"

"What cabin?"

Stone looked at him. "The one you'll find if you follow those tracks."

Becker squinted again. "I don't see a cabin."

"It's there, believe me. There's only one man, on foot, so watch yourself when you round a corner. If he's holed up in there, wait for me."

"But if I'm following one man, that means you're . . ." Becker trailed off as he realized that this was exactly how it should be. For Stone to go after just one and send Becker after three would be ludicrous.

"Take him alive if possible," Stone said, then rode off.

Becker watched Stone go and found himself to be terribly uneasy. His chores since joining the Mounties had consisted of the usual "new-man" jobs that nobody else wanted: taking care of horses, helping to build the fort, or hauling water. Now here he was on the heels of an outlaw, maybe a cold-blooded killer, and his stomach rolled uncomfortably as he urged Egypt forward.

Jenny felt unusually tired. Maybe it was boredom, but she couldn't remember the last time she'd taken a nap during the day. In her room, which was tiny but neat, she'd heard a gunshot and figured that her father had gotten a deer. Venison would be welcome, and as she mentally began planning the meal preparation, she fell asleep.

In her dream she stood in a huge, endless field of yellow prickly-pear cactus and scarlet butterfly weed. Jenny could tell it was the middle of summer by the blooms and by the warmth of the sun on her face. Nothing happened at first; she was just content to turn in a circle and admire the beauty and tranquillity of the scene. The plain was pure and golden in its innocence. In her dream, she raised her arms into the sky as she spun around and began to laugh joyously.

Freedom!

Her horse, Splash, whinnied somewhere in the distance. Jenny looked all around but didn't see her. The braying became more urgent, and Jenny woke up to hear that Splash was indeed in distress at the barn. Jenny jumped out of bed, grabbed an old Navy Colt pistol, and rushed outside.

In the small barn, Sad Sid was struggling to bridle the mare, and Splash was having none of it. Sid's back was to Jenny and the doorway, keeping himself between Splash and the only way out. The man and horse performed a strange dance, with Splash skittering away from him whenever he made a move toward her.

"Hey!" Jenny cried, raising the Colt. "What are you doing?"

Sid half turned and said, "I need a horse."

"That's *my* horse! You can't take her!"

"Just watch me."

Cocking the pistol, many questions ran through Jenny's mind. *Why is he bleeding? Where is my father? What happened to Sid's horse?* "Get away from her!" she yelled at Sid.

Sid ignored her and managed to grab a handful of Splash's mane. The black mare with a white-spotted back threw her head around in a near frenzy. "Whoa, girl," Sid coaxed soothingly, "Easy now."

"I ain't gonna tell you again, Sid! Leave her alone or I'll shoot!"

"You ain't gonna shoot me and you know it," Sid countered, slipping the bridle over the horse's nose. "Now point that thing in another direction before you do it by accident."

Jenny felt sick with dread, but her finger tightened on the trigger. Then she heard hoofbeats and relaxed slightly. Her father was coming after all, and he'd stop Sid.

"Get that saddle for me, girl."

"I ain't gonna *help* you steal my horse!"

Sid turned, and Jenny saw real anger in his face beneath the smeared blood. "You get that saddle right now!"

"No."

Incredibly quick, Sid grabbed a branding iron that was hanging on the wall near him and threw it at her. Jenny ducked away, but the iron struck her solidly in the side, and she dropped the Colt. Immediately, Sid was on her. Holding on to the reins with one hand, he swung up his other fist and connected with the side of her head in a brutal blow. Jenny went down, fighting off inky blackness in her vision.

"Hold right there!" a man shouted.

Jenny blearily looked up and saw a big young man dressed in

the uniform of the North-West Mounted Police. He held a pistol in one hand and a huge, wicked-looking knife in the other.

Sid glanced down at the Colt near Jenny and the branding iron at his feet.

"Go ahead," the Mountie said, his mouth twisted in a strange grin. "*Please* go for that gun, partner." The pistol didn't waver in his thick hand.

"Why, you're just a kid! You ain't gonna shoot me any more than *she* was. You're scared to death. I can see it in your eyes."

"My name is Sub-Constable Becker. Yes, I'm young, but I seem to have the advantage here. I'm old enough to figure that out." Becker saw Jenny try to get to her feet. "Step back so I can help this lady up."

"That ain't no lady," Sid snorted.

"I said step back."

"Sure, feller." Instead, Sid dove for the gun.

Jenny heard a brief whistling noise, and then Sid was rolling on the ground, screaming and holding his leg.

"Are you crazy?" Sid shouted. "I'd rather get shot than stuck with a knife!" The haft of the big knife protruded from Sid's thigh. His face, already a mess, grew white with shock beneath the drying blood. "I didn't think you'd do it! I really didn't think you'd do it!"

Becker was suddenly beside Jenny, who was still on her knees. When he gently grasped her arm to help her up, she flinched and jerked her arm away from him. "I'm fine, thank you," she muttered.

"Yes, ma'am." Becker watched her rise, ready to assist if needed, then turned to the moaning Sad Sid. "You're under arrest for suspicion of firing on a Mounted Policeman and assault on this young lady here. What was your name, ma'am?"

"Get this thing outta my leg, please!" Sid begged.

Becker ignored him. "Ma'am?"

"Jenny Sweet."

"Yes, ma'am. Now as for you, sir—did you say Sweet, ma'am?"

"Yeah."

"But that's . . ."

"That's what?"

"Get this sword outta my leg. *Now!*" Sid screeched.

"Shut up," Becker said absently. "Miss Sweet—is it Miss or Mrs.?" He fervently hoped it was Miss. He didn't want to find out that this young, pretty girl was married to a whiskey runner.

"Miss." Jenny kept her gaze on Sid, unable to meet the Mountie's eyes.

Becker took a deep breath and asked, "You're not by any chance related to Armand Sweet, are you?"

Jenny had no choice but to look into his eyes now. "He's my father. Why?"

Sid moaned, "Can't you two get to know each other better later? Get this outta my leg!"

"To answer your question, Miss Sweet," Becker continued, "we were on our way here to arrest your father, when he or one of his men shot my superior officer." He looked down at Sid. "And I hope it was you that did it."

"I don't know what you're talkin' about! Now, help me!"

Becker turned to fully face Jenny, and as he did his boot nudged Sid's wounded leg.

"Owwww!"

"Sorry," Becker said absently.

"Why were you comin' to arrest my father?" Jenny asked, though she knew why.

"I think you'd better get some things together and come with us, ma'am."

"Am I under arrest?"

"Not at this time, and I sincerely hope you never will be."

"Then why should I come with you?"

"Why, you can't stay here alone."

"Why not? I've done it lots of times."

Sid began to moan. Jenny couldn't help but feel a thrill of satisfaction at the man's discomfort. Suddenly Becker turned, reached down and braced a hand on Sid's knee, then pulled out the knife with his other hand. Sid screamed, but Becker calmly placed his hand over the gushing wound. "Would you happen to have some bandages, ma'am?"

"I'll get 'em," Jenny said and started toward the cabin.

"And something for a tourniquet, if you please."

"I just can't *believe* you did this," Sid gasped.

Becker watched Sid's face for a moment, then said, "In my

opinion you deserve much worse."

"For what? I didn't shoot that Mountie. Sweet did!"

"That remains to be seen. I'm talking about you beating on that girl."

Sid turned away and stared at the cabin.

"Here," Becker said as he took one of Sid's hands and placed it over the wound. "I don't even want your blood on me."

————

After they'd patched up Sid and tied his hands, Becker turned to Jenny. "I'd consider it a great favor if you'd come with us, Miss Sweet. I don't feel right about leaving you out here." His blue eyes took in her worn and tattered brown dress, the dark circles under her eyes, and the fading bruise on the left side of her face. He thought she was probably close to his own age of nineteen, but a hardness glinted from her eyes that could make someone mistake her for being older. Maybe it wasn't a hardness so much as finely tuned caution. Whatever it was, Becker would like to hear this girl's story, and he was nearly certain that it wouldn't be good. Right now, he just wished she would look at him instead of at Egypt. "Ma'am?"

Jenny continued staring at the horse, unblinking. Becker waited some more, then began to get worried. "Ma'am, are you all right?" She still made no movement or sound. Becker reached out and touched her arm, and Jenny visibly started.

"Don't . . . don't do that," she said woodenly.

"Do what?"

Her eyes came to his. "Touch me."

"I was just worried, Miss Sweet. You weren't moving and—"

"Just don't touch me."

"All right." Becker watched her, hoping that she'd heard his request and was considering it instead of falling into the strange trance again. Her short light brown hair was tied back from her face with a plain, worn piece of string. Not a ribbon or a pin, just a plain piece of string. Becker wondered if it was by choice or if the bounty from the whiskey running business wasn't that great after all. *Speaking of whiskey* . . . "Ma'am, do you mind if I have a look around the premises?"

The blank look again. "Prem—?"

"The property . . . the area."

"No, I don't mind."

Becker turned to the barn, but then heard her say, "Um . . . sir?"

"Yes, ma'am?"

"I'll go pack some things. I don't mind staying here, but you probably *did* save my life and all. . . ." Jenny was staring at his booted feet. "That Sid's crazy. He's been after me ever since he got here. So . . . I thank you."

"No need for that, Miss Sweet. It's what any self-respecting man would have done."

"Thanks anyway. I'll just go pack while you look around."

Becker watched her go for a moment, then turned toward the barn. Inside was sparse; a saddle with only one stirrup sat in one corner and a few bales of hay and some grain in another. He looked behind the bales and grain, then went around the back and spotted three crates. Retrieving the branding iron, Becker managed to tear off a slat from the top of one of the crates with the handle.

Bottles of dark liquid. Six of them.

What a day! Becker thought. *Vickersham gets shot, I ride with Stone for the first time, save a maiden in distress, make my first arrest, and make my first confiscation. All except for the Vickersham part, that's quite a day's work.* He wondered how to take the crates with him and remembered spotting an old wagon beside the cabin. He hoped it was in working order.

Both axles on the wagon were intact, but a few spokes were missing from the wheels. Becker knew it would be a bumpy ride, and maybe a short one, but there was nothing else to do. He hitched Egypt to the wagon, loaded the whiskey and Sad Sid in the back, and by then Jenny was ready to go. He was prepared to apologize for his discovery, but the girl said nothing. She only looked at the crates for a moment after she'd placed her tattered valise in the back, then she climbed up onto the front seat. Becker noticed that she sat as far away from him as was humanly possible; she may have even been sitting half *off* the bench. Jenny stared straight ahead as they began the journey down the mountain.

Becker's surprise was complete when they found Stone and three men at the place where they'd split up. The men were bound, with Stone holding the reins to all three horses.

"Your mouth's hanging open, Sub-Constable," Stone said with a straight face. "It doesn't become you."

"What . . . how—?"

"They surrendered."

Oh, won't this one be a dandy to tell at the fort? Becker thought.

A dark-bearded man spoke up, his black eyes on the unconscious Sid in the back. "Why should we run when we didn't do anything? There's the man who shot that Mountie."

"You must be Sweet," Becker said.

"I never saw a man more poorly named in my life," Stone commented. "What's in the back there?"

Becker's eyes were on Sweet when he said, "Whiskey. Three crates of it." Sweet's eyes widened slightly. It occurred to Becker that Sweet hadn't even acknowledged his daughter. He hadn't even *looked* at her, or asked what had happened, or asked if she was all right. Becker found himself suddenly despising Armand Sweet. He turned to Jenny and saw that she was no more excited to see her father than he was to see her. *What kind of life has this poor girl had?*

"What happened up there, Becker?" Stone asked. When he'd heard Becker's story, he glanced at the girl sympathetically, then glared at Sweet. "Did you forget about that whiskey, Sweet? Think we wouldn't find it or something?"

"It's not mine. It's Sid's."

"After hearing how he treated your daughter, I can see how a man like Sid could shoot my friend, but let's not get too hasty to blame *everything* on him. We had suspicious cause of you, and only you, when we came up here. You've also told me that Sid's your man. You're obviously the leader here."

"It's Sid's," Sweet repeated stubbornly.

"That's right," Boggs agreed.

"No one asked you," Stone said. "Now, Sweet. Kind of sorry you surrendered, aren't you?"

Sweet slowly brought his bottomless black eyes around to Stone. The two men were only a few feet from each other, and Becker wondered how Stone managed to keep from flinching at the burning gaze locked on him. Sweet was a handsome man, but that was marred by a palpable malevolence. *And poor Jenny was raised by this man*, Becker thought in amazement. *I wonder where her mother is.*

Sweet said to Stone, "I'll bet you're *glad* I surrendered. You would have lost me if you'd followed me into the Rockies."

Stone ignored that and asked, "Do you want to be untied so you can give your daughter a hug? Ask her if she's okay?"

Becker searched for a sly smile on Stone's face, but there was none. Stone was actually *toying* with this dangerous-looking man.

Sweet said, "She looks all right to me."

"Oh, you mean you've looked at her?" Becker asked. "I didn't notice." Becker felt Sweet's dark gaze fix on him, but he managed to avoid blinking, even though he wanted to.

"We don't have time for these stare-downs," Stone said irritably. "Let's move. I have to check on my friend. Sweet, I doubt you're a praying man, but you'd better learn. If my friend's dead, you're going down with Sid. I'll make sure of it."

CHAPTER EIGHT
Travel Plans

Here, Mama," Megan Goldsen said, holding the spoon of oatmeal to Virginia O'Donnell's mouth.

"I don't want any more." Virginia's voice was weak and quiet. The skin on her face and thin, wasted arms was waxen and dry in the dimly lit room. The flesh in her face had sunk in, giving her a cadaverous look, as the internal cancer ate away at her. "I'm just not hungry, darling."

Megan looked down at the barely touched oatmeal in the bowl, wishing she could show how sorrowful she was for her mother, but Virginia would have none of it. Megan had cried once before, and her mother had said, "You stop that, Megan. I'm going to a better place than any of us can imagine." Virginia had never wavered from her faith. Megan had witnessed no self-pity whatsoever, and any crying from Virginia had been because of the cruel pain.

"Megan, you've got to snap out of your doldrums. You're usually so full of life and mischief! Lately you act like a gray old lady who's just lost her cat."

"I'm sorry, Mama."

"What's the matter with you?"

Megan smiled humorlessly and waved around the room. "You have to ask?"

"What have I told you, child? I'm not frightened at all. I'm looking forward to meeting the Lord."

"Well, I just don't understand that, Mama. How can you be sure He even exists, much less has this wonderful place for you after you die?"

"It's called faith, dear. You don't really think there's *nothing* after this life, do you?"

Megan sighed, and the bedsprings groaned as she stood. *Have to start thinking about stopping this weight gain*, she thought morosely. *No wonder Louis doesn't pay me any attention*. Megan was five foot four inches tall, with a figure that used to be curvaceous but now tended toward pudginess. She hated it and hated herself for letting her pride and joy go to the dogs. She'd always known that her sister Reena had been jealous of her figure, and Megan hadn't failed to flaunt it whenever she could. *If you could see me now, little sister. . . .* Instantly, the tears welled right below the surface again, and Megan realized that she wanted nothing more than to see Reena right this second so they could cry on each other's shoulders.

Not trusting herself, Megan started out the door to the kitchen with the bowl. "I'll be right back, Mama."

In the kitchen, Elmira Cotter demanded, "How she doin'?"

Megan burst into tears.

"Whoa, whoa. What all this?" Ellie took Megan into her arms, practically smothering her. Ellie had been the O'Donnells' housekeeper for more than ten years, appearing on their doorstep the day after the Battle of Gettysburg. All of the O'Donnells speculated that she was an escaped slave, but they never questioned Ellie about it. "Whatchoo cryin' for?"

"I want Reena!" Megan howled.

"Reena! What bring all this on?"

"Reena's the one Mama wants to take care of her, not me! Reena's the perfect daughter, and . . . and I'm just a . . . a—"

"Shut yo' mouth, child!"

"It's true, Ellie!" Megan sobbed, pulling back to look Ellie in the face. "It's always been true. Now Mama wants to talk about heaven, and *I* don't know anything about that! But Reena would. They could talk and talk, and Mama would be happier. Mama's about to die, and I can't even make her happy in her last—"

Ellie grabbed Megan's arms tightly. "I don't wanna hear no

more o' that talk! You shut yo' mouth right now. Ellie ain't playin' now!"

Megan looked into the dark brown eyes in astonishment. She'd never seen Ellie so upset with her. "I . . . I—"

"I said shut it!" Ellie warned. "Now, sit down here." She pulled out a chair with red velvet trim and pushed Megan into it. Leaning over directly in front of her, Ellie continued, "I won't hear no talk of dyin' in this house, lest Miss Virginny want to! Ain't nobody mentioned it till you done it just now, and I be puttin' a *stop* to it right away!"

"I'm sorry, Ellie—"

"I ain't finished yet," Ellie barked, but then her face softened, and she went behind Megan's chair and began stroking her long light brown hair. Ellie had loved combing both Megan's and Reena's hair ever since she'd come to them. "Look at this fine hair. You two was always the purtiest white girls I ever saw. Ain't no ar- guin' that."

"Now, Ellie . . ."

"It's true! Hah! You 'member that time you two was fightin'—?"

"*Which* time?"

"You right about that. Y'all was always fightin'. You musta been . . . I don't know, ten or so, an' that'd make Reena nine. Anyways, you was goin' at it like two coons over a head o' cabbage, when Reena—you 'member she was so skinny she always had to hold her drawers up with one hand to keep 'em from fallin' down?"

"Yes, I remember," Megan said softly.

"She was holdin' on to them drawers and flailin' at you with her other hand, and she catch your hair. Took you to the ground with your own hair!"

"She was spunky, that's for sure." Megan felt herself getting drowsy from Ellie's gentle stroking in her hair with her large fin- gers. She hadn't been sleeping well for the past few weeks, and the feeling was warm and fuzzy.

"So then, Reena was on top o' you, one hand with a wad o' your hair, the other one holdin' up her drawers and nothin' to hit you with, so she commences to throw her elbow at your head—the elbow on the arm what's holdin' up her drawers. Then you happen to grab a handful o' *her* bootiful hair, and that's when I put a stop to it."

"It was the first time you ever punished us, Ellie. I remember very well."

"I wasn't *about* to have none o' that purty hair comin' out in hunks all over the place! Both o' you cryin' and spittin' and wailin', why, I picks you up by the scruffs o' your necks, and, Miss Megan, you don't know how close I was to bangin' your heads together! It was temptin' to say the leastest."

Despite her moodiness and depression, Megan had to smile.

"You two was a pair, I'm here to tell the world."

"I guess we were."

Ellie came back around Megan to face her. Her eyes, which had been fiery moments before, were now moist with kindness and empathy. "What you really upset about, Megan? I know it's hard with your mother and all, but you was feelin' poorly and not yourself before Miss Virginny took to the bed."

Megan shrugged without conviction.

"You don't wanna tell me?"

"I . . . I don't really know, Ellie. Louis and I aren't getting along, and—"

The fire leaped into Ellie's eyes again. "That boy been hittin' on you?"

"No, nothing like that. Besides, you know I can hold my own with anyone, with as much fighting as I did growing up. No, it's something else. I can't really put my finger on it."

"You still feelin' guilty 'cause you think you stole him from Reena?"

"How did you know that?"

"Honey, I ain't stupid! Any fool could see how you changed after Reena left. Before, you was a dangerous woman who'd do anything to get what you wanted. That ain't no secret. You had more spirit than a unbroke mare. Then . . . well . . . then you changed."

"I realized what I'd done," Megan confessed, her eyes haunted as she gazed at an oak cutting board by the sink. "I just took him right out from under her nose."

"Now, hold on here. I seem to remember Mr. Louis weren't dragged kickin' and screamin'."

"No, I'd always sensed that he was the same as me—thinking

that high society was something to actually strive for." She looked at Ellie. "And you know something, Ellie? It's very overrated."

"What's 'at mean?"

Megan sighed deeply, more tired than she'd been in years. "It means for all that wealth we have, all the right political connections, and all the high-class parties we attend, Louis and I don't talk to each other. Overrated means you put a high value on something, but when you finally get it, it's a big disappointment. This isn't what I want! Louis and I each have our own little world, our own room. We barely manage to wave to each other every morning, much less talk. That's the extent of our marriage."

"So do somethin' about it! Have a talk with him and tell him how you feel."

"I don't want to."

"You scared o' him?"

"No, I don't want to because I don't *want* to be around him."

"Say what?"

"I don't love him, and I know he doesn't love me."

"That's turrible! How can you live like that?"

"Happens all the time."

"Well, it shouldn't!"

"Oh, Louis is happy, I have no doubt of that. He likes things just the way they are. He has a wife, which is a must in the business world, he has money and power—why shouldn't he be happy?"

Ellie sat down at the end of the table and began paring apples and pears, the activity she'd been doing when Megan had come in. "And what about you?" she asked softly. "Why ain't you happy? You got everything *you* wanted."

Megan didn't answer for a long time. Ellie continued her peeling, carefully avoiding looking at Megan. Finally Megan said, "Everything I *thought* I wanted."

Ellie waited some more. They both heard the passing of an unusual number of carriages outside, signaling the end of the workday in downtown Chicago.

"I have everything I need: clothes, servants, beautiful possessions. I brush elbows with important women and go to tea parties, but those women *hate* me."

"Oh no, child."

"I can sense it. They talk about me behind my back, about how young and . . . and pretty I am, but they despise me. And all the time they're smiling at me and inviting me places and trying to show how much they *like* me! It's unbelievable, and it's sickening. Reena was right when she once told me that I needed to figure out what I really wanted before charging into something that would make me unhappy. So what did I do? I went ahead and charged in and managed to hurt Reena very badly in the process."

"So what you gonna do?" Ellie asked.

Megan gave her a halfhearted smile and stood. "Go check on my mother."

Megan left her mother at eight o'clock that night. She and Louis lived a short distance away on the same street, and their house was situated on Lake Michigan as was her parents'.

A housemaid met her at the huge oak front door and asked if she'd eaten, a slightly accusing look in her eyes.

"I've been with Ellie, Tina. You know she wouldn't let me get away this late without forcing some food down me."

Under her breath, Tina answered, "Bet she *had* to force it, too."

"What was that, Tina?"

"I's just sayin', Miss Megan, that you don't eat right. I'm glad Ellie can force you to eat. I sure can't."

Megan started for the stairs to her room. "Every time I look in the mirror, it tells me I'm eating *too* right."

"I's not talkin' 'bout how much you eatin'. I's talkin' about eatin' all the wrong things. A couple doughnuts in the mornin', piece o' cake at noon—"

"I don't have time."

"You got time to eat that junk!"

"Watch it, Tina." Megan was almost to the top of the stairs, and still Tina wouldn't let it go.

"Sorry, Miss Megan, we just worries about you."

"Thank you, but I'm fine. Is my husband home?"

"Yes, ma'am."

Megan walked down the long hall, passing photographs of family members along the way. Louis's family pictures hung on one side and hers on the other. *Isn't that typical?* she thought to herself bitterly. *Our families can't even mix together, much less the two of us.* Passing Louis's room, she noticed there was no light under the door. She thought about knocking but quickly put it out of her mind. Louis sometimes worked late at night and was probably downstairs in his office.

When she opened the door to her own room she received a shock. Louis was sitting on her four-poster, canopied bed. "Louis!" she blurted, unable to conceal her amazement.

"Hello, darling."

" 'Darling'? This *is* a surprise. I think I'm scared, Louis."

He stood and said, "No reason to be afraid. I'm your husband, for heaven's sake." A few inches below six feet, Louis seemed taller because of his lanky frame. Gold-rimmed glasses were perched on a generous nose in a not unhandsome face.

"A husband who hasn't been in my room for months. What do you want?"

"What makes you think I want anything?"

"The fact that you're here, for one thing."

"Megan," Louis sighed sadly, while coming toward her, "what's happened to us? Why are we complete strangers to each other?"

Megan's shock was complete when he put his arms around her and held her close. Her hands were jammed between them against his chest; she'd had no idea of his intentions, and her impulse had been defense. Tentatively she managed to draw them out and place them on his sides.

"We've let our love burn down to embers, Megan. We've got to correct the situation."

"Correct the situation? You're talking about love, Louis, not some business deal that's gone wrong. I don't think you ever knew the difference."

"And you, my dear? You know all about love, I suppose?" He drew back and smiled.

Megan hated that smile. Jerking her arms from his grasp, she began unbuttoning her dress in the back. "You tried, all right? You can go now."

"Let me help you."

"No! I've done it many nights by myself, so I've gotten to be an expert at it and don't need any help." *Wouldn't you know it*, she thought, *this dress has the most hard-to-get-to and intricate row of buttons of all. I usually have to get Tina's help with it.*

"Don't you even want to talk to me?" Louis asked.

"Sure, Louis. What do you want to talk about? Let's see . . . how many small businesses did you foreclose on today? How's the speculation market? The stock market? Your mistress?"

"I don't have a mistress!"

"So you say. You're either telling the truth, or you're an excellent candidate for a monastery. What about the other questions—foreclosures and things like that?"

"Today's Saturday, Megan."

"It is? I've lost all track of time since Mother's been sick. So you didn't throw any farmers out in their fields today, huh?"

Louis turned her toward him, and his large brown eyes held no rancor for her remarks—only a liquid sadness. "Why are you being so cruel? Can't you think of anything kind to say?"

"Maybe if I try really hard."

"Then would you try? For me?"

Megan stopped unbuttoning and placed her hands on her hips. She was tired, and she didn't understand what he wanted. Why all this out of the clear blue sky? Didn't he know that it would be impossible to magically find whatever it was they had? Sighing, she sat on her dressing table chair and began combing her hair. *At least he's trying,* she admitted to herself. *That's more than I would have done.*

"Is it all that difficult, Megan?"

"Quiet. I'm thinking."

Seeing her half-smile, Louis sat on the chair next to her and waited.

Megan looked at him. "I suppose your hair is still attractive to me. So thick and brown. It's longer now than when we first married, isn't it?"

"Yes," Louis beamed, "but I've been thinking about getting it cut short. I think it's the coming rage."

"Don't you dare! If you want to see a rage, just cut it."

Louis smiled and said, "Now. That wasn't so hard, was it?"

"You try it."

"All right." He rubbed his chin and looked at the ceiling in exaggerated concentration. When Megan didn't find it amusing, he turned serious. "I've missed you, darling. I don't know what's happened to us, and it's . . . hard to see where it all began. Did you love me when we married? I have to know that."

Megan glanced in the mirror over the table and got an idea. Scooting her chair closer to his she said, "Look in the mirror."

Louis turned to face the mirror. "I'm looking."

"That's us, three years ago when we were married."

"Two years, eight months, and four days ago, actually."

Megan rolled her eyes. "I forgot for a moment that you were a banker. Okay, two years, eight months, and four days ago. We look basically the same, except we've established that your hair is longer, and I'm fatter."

"*I've* established no such thing!"

"Thank you, but I *am* fatter."

"Megan!" he sputtered.

"Just bear with me for a moment, Louis."

"If you promise not to make self-deprecating statements like that anymore."

"Okay, I'll be good." Despite herself, and fully aware that all this could be some sort of intricate plan on his part, Megan laughed and actually felt affection for him rising inside her again. The emotion was alien but welcome. It was sort of like the thrill of finding a twenty dollar bill you thought you'd lost forever under the bed. "Look at yourself and tell me—is that the same man who stood beside me on our wedding day? Don't answer right away, just look."

Louis inspected his reflection, his thick eyebrows frowning. "No, that's not the same man."

"Then how can you expect me to be the same woman?"

Louis waved at the mirror. "That's *physical*, Megan. I was asking about your feelings."

"Did you say you weren't the same because of physical things, or because of what's inside you?"

"Because of . . ." Louis trailed off, then smiled. "You've got me. I was thinking that I'm more confident in my career, and more . . . I don't know . . . hard-bitten, I guess is the phrase. But what does that have to do with whether you love me or not?"

"Because I've changed emotionally, too. I don't want this to sound cruel, but I don't even know if I was in love when we got married!" She'd expected him to blanch or be horrified at this statement. Instead, he only stared at her for a long time. Megan held her breath and waited.

"I don't either, Megan," he said softly. "It was a difficult time. Reena was spouting all that missionary stuff all of a sudden . . . I was desperately trying to learn the banking business from your father . . . and then—"

"Then we danced at the spring ball."

"Yes. Then we danced. And everything changed."

"And we deeply hurt a sweet, innocent girl."

"Yes." Louis perked up suddenly. "Why don't we go see her?"

"Who?"

"Reena."

"You want to go to Canada?" Megan felt excited and unbearably childlike.

"Why not?" Louis asked, showing the excitement Megan felt. "We could take the time to get to know each other—I mean really know each other—and see Reena at the same time. There's even some business I could take care of while we're there."

"What business do you have in Canada?"

"There's talk of a railroad across the prairies in the years to come, just like the Transcontinental in the States. It may be an excellent investment opportunity."

Megan's hopes fell when she realized something. "I can't, Louis."

"Why not?"

"Have you forgotten about my mother?"

"Oh yes. I suppose I did. Sorry." Following a short silence, Louis said, "We *could* start on the getting-to-know-each-other-again part right now, though."

Before Megan could ask what he was talking about, he leaned over and kissed her gently but firmly. She made a feeble attempt to pull away, but Louis encircled her with his arms. His lips were warm and eager, and Megan realized how much she missed being close to him. She gave in to what she hoped was a new beginning.

"How about having dinner with me tomorrow night?" Louis whispered, his lips brushing hers.

"All . . . all right."

"We'll go to your favorite restaurant. Your choice. Then we'll come back here, build a fire, dismiss the servants, and—"

"And?"

"And you'll just have to wait and see."

This time, Megan kissed *him*.

———

In his office half an hour later, Louis sat at his fine mahogany desk and stared at the paper in front of him. He'd removed his glasses, and the dim lamplight softened his features so that he appeared years younger than twenty-four.

Picking up the telegram, he read the few words again for the tenth time, then read them again. They hadn't changed since he'd gone to Megan's room. The same old words, same old bad news that gnawed at his insides like a rat on a piece of cheese.

Suddenly, he crumpled the paper and sent it flying across the study. With a clenched fist, he slammed the solid desktop and stood, ignoring the searing pain in his hand. "This has *got* to be handled! Now! Soon!" he raged as he stalked around the spacious room. He kicked the corner of an Oriental carpet and doubled it over. His eyes came to rest on a cigar box, hand-carved in Cuba, and he considered hurling it through the window but managed to stop himself.

Running his fingers through his thick hair, he took many deep breaths, so many in fact, that he became dizzy and had to sit down.

"This will not stop me," he told the room in a determined monotone. "I'll think of something. I swear it."

Louis blew out the lamp and went to bed, only to toss and turn well into the chilly morning.

———

Two weeks later, on March 15, Virginia O'Donnell died of stomach cancer. As fate would have it, Megan had gone home from the deathwatch to take a bath and change clothes when her mother had died. This, more than anything, made Megan cry profusely. She had spent almost a month right by her mother's side, then she died while Megan was taking a short break. Ellie had been there, though, and Jack O'Donnell, her husband. They told Megan that her mother had just stopped breathing in her sleep. It was as simple as that.

The church was full to overflowing on the day of the funeral. Virginia had had few close friends, but she'd been loved and respected by all who knew her. Jack managed to keep an iron-jawed control all the way through to the cemetery. But when he got home, he walked with an exhausted gait to his room and wasn't seen for the rest of the day. Megan had cried a few times on Liam's shoulder during the services, but for the most part she had done most of her mourning in the few days before. Virginia's words had finally sunk in. She'd gone to a better place, and Megan had to believe it for pure self-preservation.

Louis was kind and gentle with her, never leaving her side. He'd made good on his wishes to be closer to Megan. They'd gone to dinner a few times, and by mutual agreement he'd made her room his, too.

Leaving her father's house after the funeral, Megan stared silently out the window of the carriage. Louis watched her, equally wordlessly, with her hand in his. When they arrived at their house, Louis asked, "Please don't take this wrong, dear, but . . . would you be more comfortable by yourself this evening? It won't hurt my feelings if you'd prefer that."

"Of course not. The last thing I want is to be by myself."

They went to bed at once. Megan couldn't get comfortable and shifted, banged on her pillow, and groaned. At last Louis told her, "You're exhausted, Megan. Try to relax your mind and get to sleep."

"I still want to go to Canada, Louis."

"What?"

"You heard me."

"You mean now . . . soon?"

"Yes, very soon. Actually, as soon as possible."

"But . . . what about your father and your brother?"

"They can take care of themselves. And they've got Ellie. Reena has no one. At least, no one that we know of."

"You're going to wait to tell her in person? Do you think that's fair?"

"What do you mean?"

"I mean a telegram would reach her faster than we would. Shouldn't she know as soon as possible?"

Megan sighed and threw the covers off of her legs. "I can't decide. Which do you think is best?"

Louis was silent for a long moment. "If it were my mother, I'd hate to think that I'd gone a full month after she'd died without knowing about it. Wouldn't you?''

"Like I said, I can't decide. I'd sure hate to get the news when I'm all alone, though.''

"Reena's a strong girl. And you know that she has people to help her. It's Reena's way.''

"Unlike me, right? I'm not strong, and I don't have a friend in the world.''

Louis put his arms around her and searched her eyes in the dim light. "That's enough. You've had a hard time of it, and you need rest. Tomorrow, if you're sure, I'll begin making arrangements.''

"Go ahead, because I'm sure.''

Louis fell asleep on her shoulder, with Megan absently stroking his thick brown hair.

CHAPTER NINE

Love Rejoiceth in the Truth

Two days after Vickersham's shooting, Reena and Vic were visited by Colonel Macleod, Stone, and Becker. Reena was still unaware that her mother had died a week earlier. The Blackfoot Indians treated Macleod with respect, offering him berries and fruits as he rode into the village. Their faces reflected pleasure tinged with awe. Following protocol, Macleod first visited Chief Powder Moon, while Stone and Becker went to Reena's tepee. Both of them were anxious to see Vic.

"Reena!" Stone called from the tepee flap.

Del answered the call, looking tired and old. "Hunter! Boy, ain't it great to see you! Come on in, boy."

"Where's Reena?" Stone asked. He would have expressed concern over Del's obvious exhaustion, but he thought it would only embarrass the man.

"Well, she couldn't very well stay here with us two, so she's stayin' with Raindrop. I think she's teachin' the young'uns right now."

Stone tried to hide his disappointment but wasn't sure he succeeded. He and Becker stepped into the tepee.

"Becker," Del greeted shortly.

"Hello, Mr. Dekko."

"He's in and out of it, mostly," Del informed them as they went to Vickersham. "Right now he's out."

Stone knelt beside Vic and placed his hand on Vic's bare arm. The skin was hot to the touch. Underneath the faint smell of woodsmoke, Stone detected a darker, more somber scent: the odor of sickness. He knew it well, for he'd smelled it on himself before. Gently he uncovered the wound, peered at it, and grunted.

"What?" Del asked worriedly. "What is it?"

"That's the exact same spot I shot Red Wolf. High on the chest."

"What's that mean? That mean he's gonna die?"

Stone gave him a reassuring smile. "No, Del. Red Wolf died by hanging, not from the wound. He would have lived, just as Vic will."

"Phew! Don't scare me like that! You get these looks on your face sometimes, Hunter, that scare me to death."

Becker asked softly, "Has he improved much since you brought him here?"

"He's better than he was, that's fer sure. I swear, Hunter, I thought he was dead, sure as the sunset. Bleedin' all over the place, barely breathin'. What's the story with them fellers what done this? You kill 'em?"

Stone's face tightened. "No, I didn't kill them." He was well aware of his reputation in the Mounties of being hard-nosed and getting the job done—any job—but he resented the fact that some of the men saw him as the Grim Reaper of outlaws.

"Okay, okay. Don't get all riled. I's just askin'."

Stone heard a rustle behind him and turned to find Reena entering. Her black hair was tied back from her face, revealing the lovely curve of her jawline. Stone's heart tapped a beat faster as all three men came to their feet.

"Hunter! I thought you'd be here when I heard Colonel Macleod had come."

"Hello, Reena." She was wearing one of her cotton dresses instead of the buckskin she favored. Stone wondered if she wore that when she taught the children, in order to achieve a separation between teacher and student.

"Hello," Reena said to Becker. "I don't think—"

"Hi, ma'am, my name's—"

"Take that helmet off, you dummy," Del growled behind him.

"Oh yeah." Becker removed his helmet and introduced himself.

"They told me you were pretty, Miss O'Donnell, but . . . but . . . I don't—"

"Oh, fer cryin' out loud!" Del sighed. "Put a round in yer chamber 'fore you fire off with that mouth, Becker!"

"Thank you, Mr. Becker." Reena blushed, then she turned to Stone with a smile. "I didn't know I was a topic of conversation at the fort."

Stone shifted his feet and glared at Becker. "Neither did I."

"But I didn't mean . . . I was just trying to pay the lady a compliment, sir!"

"It's all right, Mr. Becker," Reena laughed. "No harm done."

"Thank you, ma'am, and please call me Dirk."

Stone stepped to Reena and took her arm, leading her beside the sleeping Vic. "Tell me about him."

"He's stable. The bullet went through clean. He lost a lot of blood and he's battling a fever, but it'll only be a matter of time before he's up and around."

"Can we move him to the fort?"

"I wouldn't advise it." Reena looked at each man in turn as they stared down at their friend. "Come on, gentlemen. I just told you some good news, and you all look like you're at a funeral!"

Stone smiled and said, "You're right. It's just . . ." He heard a commotion outside and told Becker, "Go let the colonel in."

"Just what, Hunter?" Reena asked quietly, looking up to his eyes.

Stone was suddenly very conscious of how close she was to him. But then again, he was *always* aware of her when she was around. As she searched his face, he found himself unable to speak. She was the most beautiful woman he'd ever seen, and he could smell the clean scent of her skin and hair.

"Hunter?"

"Permission to enter, Miss O'Donnell?" Macleod roared from the flap.

Reena's eyes moved away from Stone, and she said, "Of course, Colonel."

Macleod stepped through the flap, then straightened himself to his customary erect posture. His dark eyes scanned the interior of the tepee before they came to rest on Reena. "Ah, you're as lovely as a field of lilies, as always."

"And you're still a flirt, Colonel," Reena smiled.

"Blame these old Scottish bones, my dear." Macleod removed his helmet, revealing his rapidly receding hairline, and his gaze went to Vickersham. The good-natured grin vanished instantly. "Oh, there's my boy."

"Reena says he'll be fine, sir," Stone said.

"That's excellent news, Stone, but I don't like the idea of him being in this condition in the first place. The cowards!" He knelt beside Vickersham and, just as Stone had a few minutes before, laid a hand on his arm.

"You've caught the men who did this?" Reena asked.

"Stone and Becker arrested them the very same day, I'm glad to say. The one who did this, name of Sid something-or-other, is going back to Ottawa for a very long vacation in one of our fine penal institutions. The other three are serving time at the fort on whiskey possession charges."

"Don't forget the assault case, sir," Becker added.

"Yes, I remember, Becker. In due time." Macleod glanced at Stone and said with amusement, "You're being observed, Sub-Inspector."

Stone was shocked to find Vickersham staring right at him. "Vic!" he exclaimed, kneeling down and taking his hand. "Hello, friend."

Vic's throat clicked as he tried to swallow. His sharp, handsome features were layered with a sheen of sweat.

"Get him some water, Del." Del brought a cup of water to Stone, who carefully poured it into Vic's mouth. Vic closed his eyes gratefully.

"Better? Can you talk?"

"How long?" Vic rasped.

"Three days ago, pal."

Reena handed Stone a cool, damp cloth. "Put this on his forehead, Hunter."

Stone carefully wiped Vic's face and placed the cloth on his forehead. "It's good to see you, Vic. I'm glad you're going to be okay."

Vic shook his head and squeezed Stone's hand. "It's good to see *you*. And you, Colonel."

Macleod was grinning from ear to ear through his full beard. "I'm here to take you back, lad. Are you fit for duty?"

"Absolutely, sir."

"He's not going *anywhere*, Colonel Macleod," Reena stated firmly.

Macleod glanced up at her, then back to Vickersham. "Seems I've been overruled, son. I recognize a higher authority when I see one. I suppose you'll just have to stay with this pretty lady awhile longer. Sorry for the horrible sacrifice."

"Anything for the Mounted, sir." Vic smiled weakly.

"That's my boy."

Reena said, "Would you gentlemen allow me to give Vic his medicine and check his poultice before he passes out from talking too much?"

While Reena tended to Vic, the men moved to the other side of the tepee and Del asked Macleod, "That Sid feller been moved to Ottawa yet?"

"Not yet. He's scheduled to—" Macleod broke off and glanced at Del sharply. His beetle brows came together as he said with a knife-edged voice, "Dekko, your loyalty to your friend is quite admirable, but your thinking and reasoning are not so commendable at this time."

"I's just curious," Del shrugged.

"Get it out of your mind, Del," Stone said gently. "You'd gain nothing from it, and it's not a justified revenge since Vic wasn't killed."

"Justified revenge, Stone?" Macleod questioned. "Who are you to decide what punishment is justified or not?" His eyes narrowed. "Have you been having the same thoughts?"

Stone was silent, but Becker said, "Excuse me, sir, there isn't anyone who *hasn't* considered . . . the . . . um . . . act. Every man at the fort is—"

"I don't care for that sort of vigilante attitude among my men! Justice *was* served under the very law we are here to uphold, and I'll not have it questioned by *any* man! If there are some who feel that it is too lenient, then they're welcome to find a new career! Is that understood?"

"Your voices are carrying, gentlemen," Reena called, not even bothering to turn around. "These tepees are remarkable for their ability to hold in sound—and voices."

Macleod glared at the three men in turn. "Now, see what you've done? You've upset Miss O'Donnell!''

Stone didn't dare tell him that the only voice that was carrying was his own, and Reena wasn't upset, she was simply amused.

"I'm not upset, Colonel. Just concerned."

"As well you should be, miss. As well you should be." Macleod continued glaring at them, then turned to Reena. "Miss O'Donnell, since you've given the order that Sub-Inspector Vickersham isn't to be moved, I'll make my way back to the fort. Is there anything at all that you need for his care? Medicine? Bandages?"

"I still have plenty left from the supply the men gave me when they brought Vic in. If I *do* need something, I'll let Del know, and he can come for it."

"Very well. I must thank you on behalf of the North-West Mounted Police. I don't know if Vickersham would have lived had they brought him all the way back to the fort."

"Don't mention it, Colonel. And have a safe trip back."

Macleod turned to Stone. "Are you coming, Sub-Inspector?"

Stone detected a glint in the man's eye and knew that Macleod understood. Macleod seemed to understand everything around him, no matter how trivial it might be. "I'd appreciate the colonel's permission to stay in the village for the night . . . to supervise Vickersham's progress . . . and to . . ."

"Never mind, Stone. Permission granted, but I want you back at the fort by midafternoon tomorrow."

"I'll be there, sir. And thank you."

Macleod faced Del and asked, "Dekko, aren't you a bit tired of keeping watch over Vickersham? Don't you need a break since Stone's here now to take care of him?"

"I'm fine, sir. I ain't leavin' him."

Macleod stepped closer to Del, and as he talked his eyes cut over to Stone. "I think you need a break, scout. You look a bit exhausted."

Del didn't get it. "I said I'm fine, sir, I just—"

Macleod sighed and whispered, "Dekko, you're stretching my patience to its breaking point. You *do* need a break so that *Stone* can help *Miss O'Donnell* take care of our man. Now, don't you *agree* with me, Dekko?"

"Oh, without a doubt, Colonel, when you put it that way. I have been feelin' a bit tired and all. A break is probably exactly what

I need." He glanced over at Vic forlornly.

Stone understood Del's anguish and suggested, "Sir, Del can stay if he wants to—"

"No, Del *can't* stay if he wants to. He needs a break. How much sleep have you had, Dekko?"

"Oh, I've had enough to—"

"Watch yourself, Dekko. You're talking to the Assistant Commissioner of the Mounted. I wouldn't want you to lie to me."

Del looked down at his worn boots, then back to Macleod, but his eyes only came as far as the golden buttons on his tunic. "I ain't hardly slept at all, Colonel."

Macleod's face softened as he smiled, and he put his arm around Del's shoulders. "Del, I hope that someday God will bless me with a friend as faithful as you."

Later that afternoon Stone explored the Blackfoot village. The people were fascinated by his uniform, and the children couldn't resist reaching out and touching the bright red fabric. One boy ran his hand down the yellow stripe on the side of Stone's blue trousers, his eyes large with awe. Stone greeted them and smiled and even shook hands with a few of the stony-faced braves.

While in the Assiniboine camp after he'd nearly been killed, Stone had admired their neatness and responsible orderliness. Not so with the Blackfoot. He sensed that their tattered clothing and the shabby condition of the village were no fault of the women and children. Rather, he suspected that the responsibility lay solely with the whiskey-craving braves. Once they got a taste of whiskey and liked it, there seemed to be no limit to what they would do to get it. Horses that were invaluable to the Indian way of life were traded for bottles of the vile stuff, as were their fine furs and carefully detailed crafts.

"Give an Indian some whiskey," a Hudson's Bay Company employee had told Stone once, "and there's gonna be trouble."

Stone had looked at him wryly. "How's that different from white men?" The man hadn't liked Stone's comparison, and on his way out of the trading post with his supplies, Stone heard, "Injun lover." He hadn't bothered to set the man straight; a mission to change the collective minds of men who thought that way would have taken the rest of his life, with little to show for it.

The Cypress Hills Massacre, in which dozens of Assiniboine had been killed by drunken white men, had been the tragedy that had finally forced Parliament to organize the Mounted Police. Stone had no illusions concerning the "difference" between a white drunk and a red one. It was the same as someone saying they liked green apples but despised red ones. An apple was an apple.

The growl of a mongrel dog brought Stone's attention back to his surroundings. The animal was black and gray, with one useless eye that was void of color. Stone gave him a wide berth. *Even the Blackfoot dogs look meaner than the Assiniboine dogs,* he mused.

Stone made his way back to Reena's tepee. Inside, she was reading to an apparently sleeping Vic.

" . . . and though I give my body to be burned, and have not love, it profiteth me nothing. Love suffereth long, and is kind; love envieth not; love vaunteth not itself, is not puffed up, doth not behave itself unseemly, seeketh not her own, is not easily provoked, thinketh no evil; rejoiceth not in iniquity, but rejoiceth in the truth; beareth all things, believeth all things, hopeth all things, endureth all things. Love never faileth." She looked up when she felt Stone's presence. "Oh, hello, Hunter. How long have you been standing there?"

"Only a few moments. Those are wonderful words," he said as he sat down beside her and leaned against the backrest.

"Yes, they are. They are also very *important* words. They teach us how to love. I read to you like this when you were wounded."

"I remember." He ran his hands through his thick blond hair. "You look tired, Reena. Why don't you let me sit with him the rest of the night?"

"Do you know how to love, Hunter?" Reena asked directly.

He searched for teasing in her face but found none. The question caught him by surprise, and he hesitated before answering slowly, "I have loved before."

"You're talking about Betsy, right?"

"Yes."

"But she loved you back. That was easy. What about the man who shot Vic? Do you love him?"

"No."

"According to God's Word, we're supposed to."

"Then you should try really hard to love him, Reena. I'd prefer not to."

"In my true, human nature I'm not capable of loving someone like that. I have to depend on God and the Holy Spirit to fill me with love *for* him."

"Would you like to hear what that lovable man did to an innocent seventeen-year-old girl?"

"What are you talking about? What girl?"

"Jenny Sweet, Armand Sweet's daughter. He's the one we went up there to arrest in the first place. He's a real lovable fella too, but that's another story. When Becker arrested Sid, he was happily beating the stuffing out of sweet Jenny Sweet. I mean *beating* her. Dr. Nevitt, the fort's physician, examined her and found bruises all over her body—some of them fresh, some of them fading—but all of them bad."

"Sid did that?"

"I think her lovable father had a hand in it, too."

"Why are you making fun of me, Hunter?"

"I'm not, I—"

"Yes you are! I'm just trying to teach you God's Word because I *thought* you had an interest in it."

"Hey, hey," Stone said soothingly, sitting up and taking her hand. Her lips were drawn into a straight line, and she wouldn't meet his eyes. "Reena, I know what you're trying to do, and I appreciate it. I *do* want to learn, but don't you see I'm nowhere near the place where I can love these disgusting characters I see every day? That's the point I was trying to make, and maybe I was belittling. I apologize."

Reena met his gaze and nodded slowly. "I'm sorry, too. It's just . . . just that I—"

"What? What's the matter?"

"Oh, Hunter, I just want you to develop a love for God so that we . . . so that we could . . . oh, what am I saying? Forgive me, I don't know what's gotten—"

Stone moved closer and placed his hand on the side of her face. "Shhhh. It's all right. I understand, and I feel the same way." She was staring at his mouth, and he couldn't resist. He kissed her, met no resistance, then crushed her lips to his. She returned the passion and energy of his kiss, her arms encircling his neck as they both yielded to their loneliness and mutual need for closeness. Stone had a sudden thought that he felt needed saying *immediately*. *It can wait . . . it can wait . . . no, it can't.* "Reena," he whispered, his lips brushing hers as he spoke. "I have to say something."

Reena gave a slight shake of her head and kissed him again. Then she stiffened, as if to realize what she was doing, and pulled back a few inches. "What is it?" she asked, a bit breathless.

He touched her cheek gently and said, "I have to tell you that I don't want to use God to win you. We've both agreed that it wouldn't be right for you to . . . have a relationship with me since I'm not . . . Anyway, I don't want you to think that since I haven't rushed in and become a Christian that I don't lo—care for you." He blushed furiously at his mistake and went on quickly, hoping she didn't catch it. But he could tell she did by the widening of her eyes. "I'm still searching for . . . for answers. And to ask to be saved with any other motive than wanting a relationship with God would be . . . a terrible thing to do, wouldn't it? Does that make sense?"

To his surprise, she kissed him again. But this time it was incredibly gentle and *loving*. When she drew away, her eyes were moist. "It makes perfect sense, my darling. God wouldn't want that, and I wouldn't want that, and you wouldn't want that." Then she whispered, so low that Stone had to strain to hear her, "I'm not afraid to say it: I love you, Hunter Stone."

Stone's heart began to hammer so fast he was afraid it would be damaged.

"I've loved you since the summer I took care of you. You made all the hurt I suffered over Louis go away, even though you didn't know it. I realized then that there were far more honorable men in the world than he. Thank you for that."

Feeling remarkably foolish, Stone sensed his own eyes burning with tears. Her words were wonderful and uplifting, but it was her face that moved him so powerfully. He recognized the look of true love—he'd seen it on Betsy's face so many times—and Reena's held it now. The thought of Betsy sent a bolt of sorrow through him, but he dampened the old familiar pain at once. This was a happy moment, and he had had very few of them.

"You don't have to say anything, Hunter. I can see you struggling with a reply."

Stone's mouth worked, but no sound came. Was it too soon

after Betsy's death? Did the fact that his mind had gone to Betsy's face in the middle of this tender moment mean that he wasn't ready to say the words?

"Would you hold me for a—"

"I love you, too, Reena," he blurted and was aware of sweat breaking out on his palms. "I never thought I'd say that to another woman again. But you are everything to me."

Reena closed her eyes, and one solitary tear dropped from her lashes. Stone drew her to him and cradled her head against his shoulder as he leaned against the backrest.

For a long time they watched their friend sleep deeply and the cook fire die a slow death.

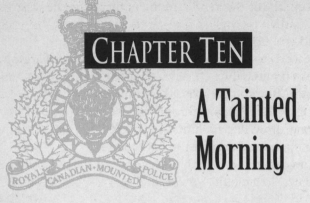

CHAPTER TEN

A Tainted Morning

Shifting gray clouds overhead gave the promise of rain. Becker found himself glancing to the skies often, silently willing away the moisture until he could get Jenny to the Blackfoot camp.

She was riding Splash to his left. She wore black denim pants and a white cotton shirt. A blue ribbon was tied in her hair. Though still pale and withdrawn, Jenny seemed to be more rested and alert than when he'd found her. Maybe being away from abusive men, if only for a few days, was just what she'd needed.

They passed a large growth of bulrush, and Becker pointed. "What kind of bird is that?"

Jenny followed his finger to the nest close to the top of the vegetation. The pointed head of the bird stood out clearly as its high monotone song rang out. Jenny looked at Becker strangely and answered, "That's a waxwing."

"That's right! They look sort of like a kingbird, except a kingbird has a smooth head and white throat."

"If you say so."

"What are those two flying over there?" he pointed again.

"Do you think I'm stupid? They're swallows. You can tell by their scissor tails."

"Ah, but what *kind* of swallow? There are many different kinds—"

"Who cares?" Jenny retorted sharply. "Why are you askin' me

116

all these questions? Are you testin' how much I know?"

"No, not at all!" Becker assured her, surprised at the sudden anger that had surfaced from nowhere. "I was just trying to make conversation."

"You think I'm dumb because of the way I talk, don't you?"

"Absolutely not!"

"You talk funny, too. You don't sound dumb like me because you use big words. Where are *you* from?"

"Mississippi, in the United—"

"I know where Mississippi is!"

"Miss Sweet—"

She held up a hand. "Call me Jenny. We both know I ain't a miss."

"I disagree with that statement. Wholeheartedly."

"There's another one of them words. Where'd you learn to talk like that?"

Becker could feel himself blushing. "I didn't really *learn* it, actually. I just . . . just have a love for books, and I guess if you read enough, it sort of sticks with you, you know?"

"Now you're tryin' to talk like me."

"What?"

"Never mind. Leave me alone."

Becker was totally confused. Her aggressiveness had turned him defensive in a matter of moments. However, he also felt guilty for being exposed. He'd noticed her mountain-woman accent and had taken for granted that she *was* poorly educated, if educated at all. He still doubted that she'd reached very far in school, but she was by no means dumb.

After her statement of wanting to be left alone, she moved Splash a few yards ahead of Becker and Egypt. He watched the smooth way she rolled with the movement of the horse. She looked so tiny sitting in the saddle, but her riding ability shone through despite her size.

Becker had talked to Dr. Nevitt after his examination. A cold, blue rage had burned through him for the rest of that day. Word had spread through the fort, and Becker heard many men talking about "wanting to spend a few minutes alone with the whiskey runners."

Becker shared a room with three other men, and they'd all

agreed to let Jenny have it. She'd stayed inside all day the first day and come out at dusk to breathe some fresh air. Being the only woman at the fort, many men had been waiting to see her. Suddenly there'd been fifty men milling around the yard, every one of them trying desperately to find some reason to be out there at that moment. Though they tried to be circumspect in getting a look at her, Jenny couldn't stand the scrutiny and vanished back inside.

"She think we're going to bite her?" Andy Doe had asked after watching her disappear.

"I think she probably *expects* us to bite her," Becker had answered. "Wouldn't you, if you were her?"

"I guess so. That's real sad." All the men in their small group had cast dark looks at the jail across the yard.

Loud rumblings of thunder rolled over the prairie Becker and Jenny were crossing. Jenny slowed her horse, and Becker saw her glancing warily up to the sky. "I've got slickers for us," he told her.

"I don't like lightning. Never have." She looked at him and seemed to square her shoulders a bit. "Why do I have to go to these Injuns?"

"Because you're too young to be on your own."

"You tricked me, didn't you?"

"No, I didn't trick you. I really wanted you to come with me because I didn't want to be responsible for leaving you alone on that mountain. If I'd known you were just seventeen, I wouldn't have given you a choice."

"And how old are you?"

"Nineteen. Twenty in four months."

"So you call *me* young?"

Becker thought he might have seen a teasing light in her eyes—maybe. "I learned a lot in just two years. You will, too."

"What did you learn from seventeen to nineteen that made you an adult?"

He thought a moment before answering. "That people aren't always what they seem to be. That not all Yankees are liars and thieves. That a beesting really hurts." He looked off in the distance to a stand of cottonwood trees. A sparrow hawk circled above it, the smallest of falcons. "And never to underestimate a man because of his size," he finished quietly.

Jenny kept her eyes on him. "Does that last thing have something to do with that scar on your face?'' she asked softly.

His head came around quickly, and his eyes were wary.

"Was he smaller than you? Is that why you say that?'' she asked.

"Actually he was bigger than me, and needless to say that's pretty big. That's why I underestimated him. I didn't think a man that large could be as quick as me. I was wrong.''

Jenny stared at the scar until he looked at her, then she averted her gaze quickly. They rode in silence for a while until Jenny asked, "Why you call your horse Egypt?''

"Because I'd like to go there sometime and see the pyramids. Wouldn't that be something to see?''

Jenny didn't answer, but to Becker's relief she didn't laugh, either, like everyone else he'd told.

"You ever see a shooting star?''

"Only a few times. Why?'' Becker was thinking that this was a very odd girl and wondering if she wasn't slightly brain damaged from a well-placed blow to the head.

"Not shooting stars in the *sky*. The *flower*.''

"No, I haven't. Are they pretty?''

"Pretty! They're so beautiful! When they're bloomin' they're purple—sometimes they seem kinda pinkish-purple—and they have gold at the bottom of the bloom, the prettiest gold you ever saw. And down at the root are these big leaves that sorta make a homey little nest for the whole thing.''

Becker watched in amazement as the girl became animated. When she smiled—for the first time he could remember—he saw twin dimples that added to her charm. As he observed her, the light slowly faded from her face and the strange blank look returned. "Miss Sweet? Ma'am?'' He didn't want her to go into the trance again.

"What?'' she asked, as if nothing had happened.

"It sounds like a very pretty flower. Will you point it out to me if we come across one?''

"They don't bloom till June. Bloom till June, that rhymes, don't it?'' More thunder made her cringe again.

Becker moved Egypt closer to her—as close as he dared without scaring her—and told her, "Don't worry. We'll beat the rain. It's not far now.'' She looked at him uncertainly. "It'll be fine.'' He smiled.

As they rode, he thought about scars. Maybe the ones that didn't show were worse than the ones that did.

———

When Reena woke that day, she remembered what had transpired the night before, and her heart skipped a beat. Even before she opened her eyes she thought, *I can't believe I said that! I must really be feeling lonely to do something that bold.*

Washing her face and getting dressed in a sort of daze, she stepped out of Raindrop's tepee into the cloudy day and woodenly made her way to her own. *What do I say now? What if he's thought about it and regretted the whole thing? How embarrassing!* She stopped in her tracks and stared at the tepee. The last place she wanted to go was her own home. Even the happy painting of children playing on the outside, carefully drawn by Raindrop, wasn't enough to encourage her to approach.

"Reena? What are you doing?"

"Oh, good morning, Raindrop. I . . . I don't really know what I'm doing."

Raindrop's moon face showed concern. "What's the matter?"

Reena sighed deeply. "I'm afraid to go home, actually."

"Afraid of the Stone Man?"

"No . . . yes . . . oh, never mind! It's too complicated to explain right now."

"There he is." Raindrop pointed.

Stone had stepped outside the tepee to empty a water pan. He was shirtless, dressed only in his blue pants and suspenders. Smooth, rippling muscles in his torso flexed with every move. "Oh, my," Reena muttered.

"He is strong!" Raindrop exclaimed.

"Obviously."

"Come. I will go with you."

Reena jerked her arm out of Raindrop's grasp. "No."

"You cannot stay away from him forever!"

"I can try!" Too late Reena realized how their voices were carrying, and she saw Stone turn to them. "Now you've done it! He's seen us!" She planted a huge smile on her face and waved at him. He lifted a hand tentatively.

"Now we go," Raindrop said firmly.

Reena obediently followed. Stone watched them approach, and before she knew it she was babbling. "Morning, Hunter! Beautiful day, isn't it? Well, not exactly beautiful, really, since it looks like rain, but we need some rain. I can't remember the last time it rained, can you, Raindrop?" She giggled, feeling hopelessly out of control. "Raindrop, do you remember the last raindrop?"

Stone and Raindrop stared at her, then exchanged curious glances. "Reena, are you all right?" he asked.

"Sure! I'm fine. Aren't you?" Reena smiled brilliantly.

"Yes . . . um . . . would you like to come inside?"

"Yes, I would. I'd like that. To check on Vic and all, you know."

Stone continued staring at her for a long moment before ducking inside the flap. Reena saw the suspenders tighten against his broad back and wondered why they didn't rip apart.

"He woke up once during the night—" Stone began.

"Hunter, put your shirt on," Reena said.

"I'm sorry. Did I offend you?"

"Offend's not a good word for it. Distract . . . maybe?" Feeling impossibly foolish, Reena felt herself blushing like the dawn. Hunter was still looking at her with the same strange, contemplative inspection. Reena began to get angry. *Why doesn't he help me stop acting this way by making me more comfortable? He's watching me like I'm a lunatic!*

Stone suddenly smiled weakly as he removed the suspenders from his shoulders and began putting on his shirt. "As I was saying, he woke up once, and we had a nice little talk. I do think the fever's gone."

Reena knelt down beside Vic and felt his forehead. His eyes opened at once. "Hi, Vic."

"Good—what time of day is it?"

"It's morning."

"Then, good morning, Reena."

"Sleep well? You sure look better."

"I slept fantastically. Hunter woke me with his snoring, but I forgave him."

"Hunter snores?" Reena asked, looking at Stone.

"My head's a little stopped up."

"Nonsense!" Vic argued good-naturedly. "He snores like a hibernating bear."

"You *are* feeling better, aren't you?" Stone asked. "Your mouth is, anyway." Vic's eyes were clearer, and his face had color in it for the first time since he'd been shot.

"I fix something to eat," Raindrop announced and left with a long look at Reena.

"How did you sleep, Hunter?" Reena asked.

"Well enough. You?"

"Fine."

She watched for some sort of emotion on his face, but he wouldn't meet her eyes. A halfhearted roll of thunder outside was followed by the tapping of light rain on the tepee. Reena busied herself by checking Vic's bandages. The fluid that had leaked into the bandage had dried, and as she nervously lifted it, she promptly dropped it right back on the wound.

Air sucked in through Vic's teeth.

"I'm sorry!" Reena cried.

"Let me help," offered Stone.

"I've got it!" she replied, more rudely than she'd intended. The tension between them was humming through the air. Vic *had* to feel it.

"Well, if you don't need my help anymore, I guess I'll get back to the fort," Stone said.

"Maybe you'd better."

"Whoa, wait a minute!" Vic cried, his eyes going from one to the other. "What's going on with you two? Have I missed something?"

"No!" Stone and Reena answered in unison.

"Sorry I asked."

"I'll go saddle Buck," Stone said tightly. He grabbed his coat and hat and left.

Reena began preparing a new bandage with shaky fingers, her mouth tight. *What in the world happened? I ruined everything by telling him I loved him!*

"Reena?"

"Never mind, Vic. Maybe I'll tell you about it later."

"All right."

Stone stuck his head back in. "Your guest is coming," he said curtly, then disappeared.

"Oh, I forgot!"

"Who is it?" Vic asked.

Reena told him about Jenny Sweet. Hunter had explained to her the night before that the Mounties didn't really know *what* to do with her, and until they could decide, Jenny needed to stay with *someone*. "I don't really know what I'm supposed to do with her, but I couldn't exactly say no." She hurriedly finished tending to Vic's wound and got to her feet.

"Go stop him, Reena," Vic said softly. "You didn't mean what you said, and neither did he."

"Just stay out of it, Vic, okay?" She began tidying up the tepee for her visitors.

———————

"Sub-Inspector? Where are you going?" Becker asked. They'd arrived at the edge of the village and met Stone leaving it.

Stone passed by on Buck without stopping. "Catch up to me, Becker. I've got to go."

"Yes, sir."

With round eyes, Jenny watched the big man ride by. Unmistakable fury burned in his strange gray eyes. She looked at Becker questioningly, but he only shrugged. Jenny felt a strong reluctance growing inside her. "I don't think I wanna do this."

"Why not?"

"I wanna go to my cabin."

"Well, you can't. We've already talked about that."

"You can't stop me. I can go after you leave."

Becker stopped her horse, and now she saw the beginnings of anger in *his* face. "Why are you talking like that? Miss O'Donnell's a kind lady. Give her a chance."

"I don't know nothin' about Injuns! What am I supposed to do here, wrap myself in a blanket and smoke pipes?"

Becker let go of Splash's bridle, his face as cloudy as the sky. The scar on his face shone like the edge of a knife. "Fine. Go, then."

"What?"

"I said go!"

"But Colonel Macleod said I had to—"

"I'll square it with Colonel Macleod. I'll tell him you knocked me in the head and took off, or something."

"He wouldn't believe that!"

"He might." Becker looked at her appraisingly. "You've got a lot of anger in you. You could probably take me."

Jenny was sorry she'd brought the whole thing up. This young man was only trying to help her, and she kept treating him badly. But the thing of it was, she couldn't help it. Something inside her just *wanted* to be rude, and she couldn't stop herself. She was tired of men and their bossy ways. All of them.

"I'm waiting," he said.

"I'll stay," Jenny whispered.

"What was that?"

"I said I'll stay."

"Good. It'll be—" Becker suddenly turned and called after Stone, who didn't hear. "I forgot to tell him," he muttered.

"Tell him what?"

"About this telegram for Miss O'Donnell. I wonder if he knows what's in it?"

———

Jenny's first reaction after meeting Reena was to fluff her own hair. Reena's was incredibly vibrant and beautiful, and Jenny felt as if she were wearing a dirty mop on her head. The lady tried to put Jenny at ease at once.

"Jenny, this is Sub-Inspector Vickersham."

The man had a nice smile, though he was obviously very weak. "Sorry you got shot," Jenny mumbled.

"Thank you, Miss Sweet, but you're not the one who shot me."

"No, but I shoulda kilt that man *before* he shot you." Jenny received stunned looks and wondered what was wrong. She was only trying to make him feel better.

Becker cleared his throat. "Um . . . Miss Sweet also had a few problems with that Sid fella, Sub-Inspector. Severe problems."

"I see," Vic said thoughtfully. "Well, Miss Sweet, I'm certainly glad you didn't kill Sid, and I'm sure *you're* glad you don't have it on your conscience."

Jenny shrugged and said simply, "Wouldn't bother me."

Becker smiled at Vic's disturbed expression. Putting on his hat, he told him, "Miss Sweet's full of a lot more surprises, sir. I've got to be going and catch up with Sub-Inspector Stone. He sure was in a hurry." He noticed the look that passed between Reena and

Vic but didn't comment. "Miss Sweet, it's been a—"

"Ain't you got something for Miss O'Donnell?"

"Oh yes, I almost forgot! A telegram came for you by way of Fort Benton." Becker fumbled in his pockets for the paper.

"Where's it from?" Reena asked in a strangely hollow voice. "I've never gotten a telegram before. That's usually bad news, isn't it, Vic?"

"Not all the time, Reena."

Jenny saw her look at the piece of paper as if it were a snake. Maybe it *was* bad news, and then it would be Jenny's fault for reminding Becker of it. She crossed her fingers behind her back until she felt pain in them.

Reena reached out slowly and took the telegram. It was thin blue paper and wrinkled from much handling. One corner of it was actually torn. The wax sealant on the corners of the opening was black. Reena turned it over and over in her small hands, and for a moment Jenny thought she would turn and drop it in the fire instead of opening it. But then she did open it, and her lips moved very slowly as she read. Jenny could hear her all but inaudible whisper, but she couldn't understand the words and didn't think she *wanted* to understand them from the pasty color Reena's face was turning.

"Reena?" Vic asked, his forehead wrinkled with worry. He tried to sit up but failed. "What is it?"

The blue paper began shaking in Reena's fingers, and Jenny looked up and saw an astonishing amount of tears running from her eyes in so short a time. Her teeth were gritted together, and Jenny just had time to notice how white they were before Becker stepped between them.

"Miss O'Donnell?" Becker asked, taking her arm.

"Becker, help her down. Now!" Vic yelled hoarsely.

Before Becker could move, Reena's legs gave out completely. With a swift, smooth movement, Becker scooped her up in his arms. The telegram fluttered to the ground beside Vickersham, who picked it up and read it.

His rich brown eyes came up slowly to rest on Becker. "I think you'd better go and fetch Sub-Inspector Stone."

PART THREE

OF YOUTH
AND YOWS

Youth means love,
Vows can't change nature,
Priests are only men.

Robert Browning
The Ring and the Book

CHAPTER ELEVEN

Let Loose the Tears

Nine-year-old Reena made her way through the large house, crying for her mother. On the front of her blue dress was a huge spattering of mud. Her hands were coated with the mess, and her face was streaked brown where she'd wiped at her tears.

"Mama! Mama!"

"Reena! What's all that screeching about?"

She turned to find her father's head craning around the doorjamb of his office. When he saw her dress, his face blanched and his eyes narrowed. "How many times have we told you not to play in your Sunday dresses?"

"I wasn't playing, Da, I was—"

"Stop that wailing this instant and go wash yourself!"

Reena's mouth worked, but no sound came out. Shoulders slumped and rounded, she started upstairs.

"And stay in your room until I come for you!"

Head drooping even lower, Reena climbed the stairs slowly. "Why, oh why, oh why, doesn't he ever give us a chance to explain?" she muttered piteously.

"Reena!" her mother exclaimed, horrified.

Reena looked up at her—her mother's young, pretty face and long honey-colored hair piled on top of her head in a beautiful chignon taken up in a gold net—and burst into new tears. "Mama!" She bounded up the last few steps and raced to her.

"*Reena, wait! Wait!*" Virginia managed to catch her right before the soiled garment collided with her own peach-colored dress that she'd purchased only that week. Holding her daughter at arm's length, she asked, "*What happened?*"

"*Oh, Mama, it was that Tommy Flagg! He . . . he . . . I—*"

"*All right, calm down, dear.*" Virginia put her arm around Reena's shoulders and guided her to the bath. "*You can tell me about it while you get cleaned up.*"

Off came the dirty dress and undergarments, and Virginia started wiping Reena's face with a damp towel. "*I hate boys!*" Reena announced vehemently. "*They're mean and dirty, and they smell bad!*"

Her mother smiled. "*I thought you were sweet on Tommy Flagg.*"

"*I ain't sweet on—*"

"*Don't say ain't.*"

"*Sorry. I'm not sweet on* anyone, *ever again! I'm not even sweet on Da anymore.*"

Virginia stopped scrubbing immediately and lifted Reena's chin. "*I'll not hear that sort of talk. I don't care if you* are *mad or upset.*"

"*Yes, ma'am,*" Reena said glumly. "*But why won't Da even give us a chance to talk or explain ourselves before he jumps us?*"

"*Here, wash those grubby hands in our new sink.*" The O'Donnells had been one of the first families in Chicago to have running water installed. It had been done a year earlier, but Virginia insisted on saying "new sink" anytime she found the chance. It remained the one prideful thing in her life.

When Reena was through, her mother wrapped a towel around her as they walked to Reena's room. "*Your father isn't very patient sometimes. He takes things in with his eyes, then starts talking before he's thought things through. It's no reason not to love him, Reena.*"

"*Aw, I still love him. I'm just mad at men in general.*" Reena saw her mother attempt to cover a smile and wondered what was funny about what she'd said. Grown-ups were weird sometimes. She continued with her story: "*Tommy was throwing mud at Choo-Choo. You know Choo-Choo, don't you?*"

"*Yes, I know Choo-Choo. I'd prefer to call him Randall, like his mother intended.*"

"*His* mother *calls him Choo-Choo!*"

"*Oh, my. Well, go on.*"

Reena sat on her bed while her mother placed the dirty clothes in the English Victorian wardrobe. It was tall mahogany, flanked by serpentine-fronted doors. Once Reena and Megan had hidden from their father inside it a few years before. When he'd found them, they'd been extremely sorry they'd ever thought of the idea. "So Tommy's throwing mud balls at Choo-Choo, and I'm walking by, and one of the balls hits me—splat! Then I start screaming at Tommy, and both of them are laughing at me—even Choo-Choo, and he's got mud on him from head to toe. All you could see was white teeth and a pink tongue! Then Tommy stops laughing, and he starts to come toward me looking sorry, but I ran away."

"So it was an accident."

"I don't know if it was or not."

Virginia sat beside Reena and folded her dainty hands in her lap. Reena loved her mother's hands even more than her hair.

"Tommy likes you, darling. His mother told me that he even drew a picture of you and put it on his bedroom wall."

"He did?"

"That's what she said."

"I didn't know Tommy could draw. It probably looks like a gargoyle, and it's got my name over it. Great."

"Mary says it's very well done. It even surprised her.*"*

"What does it matter, Mama? I still got smashed with a mud ball by him!"

"It was an accident, *Reena. You said so yourself." Virginia smiled and tucked a stray strand of Reena's hair behind her ear. "And besides, even if it wasn't an accident, he got your attention, didn't he?"*

"Oh, he did that, all right! But why would he want me to be mad at him?"

"Boys are different, dear. I've been telling both you and Megan that for a long time, and neither of you believe me yet. They want to be noticed. *The more you notice them and think about them, the happier they are."*

"Is Da like that, too?" Reena asked in disbelief.

"Men are the same as boys in a way. They want to be admired instead of noticed. But, then again, your father likes for me to notice him, too."

Reena shook her head sadly. "This is too confusing."

Virginia laughed and took Reena in her arms. Stroking her raven-black hair, Virginia whispered, "You'll figure it out someday."

"I think she's coming out of it," Vic said.

Reena sighed contentedly. The only thing better than looking at her mother's hands was having them smoothing her hair.

"I never *seen* nobody pass out before."

"Mama?"

"Yes?"

"When I find the boy I want to marry, will you like him?"

Virginia chuckled softly and said, "I would hope so."

"I really want you to meet him and like him. Do you like Tommy?"

"Yes, I like Tommy."

"Do you think I'll marry him?"

"You're nine years old, Reena. There's plenty of time to find the right man. And when you do, I'm sure I'll approve of him."

"You've got to be at my wedding, Mama. Promise me."

"I promise, dear," Virginia whispered. "I promise."

"Reena?"

She opened her eyes. She wasn't in her comfortable, cheery bedroom. She was in a dirt-floor tepee with the skins of animals for walls. The dried tears on her face weren't for Tommy Flagg. And worst of all, she wasn't in her mother's arms with slender, white fingers coursing through her hair. Her back hurt, her head hurt, and her heart hurt. She just wanted to go back to wherever she'd been moments before.

"Reena? Are you all right? Can you hear me?"

She turned her head and saw Vic looking at her with deep concern. Something was strange about him. His face was more full, or his—suddenly Reena realized that she was lying beside him and seeing his face at a totally different angle than she was accustomed to seeing it. "Vic? Oh, Vic, she's dead! I'll never see my mother again!"

"I know, my dear. I'm sorry." He swallowed with difficulty as he reached out and touched her hand.

Reena moved her gaze to the smoke hole in the top of the tepee. "I want to go home, Vic. I want to see my father. I want to eat tomatoes, and Ellie's flapjacks, and . . . and anything that hasn't just been shot the day before."

Vickersham said nothing, but she felt him squeeze her hand.

"I'm tired of living in dirt! I'm tired of living around people who hate me!"

"They don't hate you, Reena, they—"

"I'm tired of living alone! What if *I* died? Who would care?"

"*I* would care."

Reena felt as if she should get up, but the need wasn't strong enough to make her bother to try.

"Becker's gone after Hunter. They should be here any minute. Is there anything I can do for you, Reena? I suppose that sounds ridiculous considering my circumstances."

"Can you pray?" She looked over at him and saw his face fall. "I'm sorry, Vic."

"Here's some water," Jenny called, entering through the flap. "Oh, she's . . . I mean, you're awake." She went to Reena and offered her a clay cup. "Brung you some water."

It was as good a reason to sit up as any, so Reena did. "Thank you." She sipped the cold liquid gratefully. Her mouth was dry, and her head thumped with a painfully regular rhythm.

"You sure scared us," Jenny commented. "We didn't know what to do 'cept lay you down and wait. I'm real sorry, ma'am . . .'bout your ma and all."

"Don't ma'am me, Jenny. I'm not much older than you. Please call me Reena."

"All right."

"And thank you."

"Sure."

Reena saw Jenny open her mouth to say something else, then close it, then open it again. "Is there something else?"

"I'm just real sorry. I lost my ma, too. But she didn't die. She just took off to get away from my pa. So I think I kinda know how you feel."

"Yes, you probably do."

"Reena," Vic said, "about what you were saying—"

"I meant it. I meant every word. I'm so tired."

"I know you're tired and saddened, but I hope you don't make any rash decisions at this time. Your sister's coming *here*, you know. To see you and help you through."

"Don't start trying to make sense right now, Vic. Give me a chance to be an irrational woman and cry and dream, all right?"

"Of course," he smiled.

"In the meantime," Reena said, rising to her feet and swaying for a moment, "I'm going to start packing."

———

When Hunter took Reena in his arms, her whole body shook as she cried.

Not the soft, gentle crying that produces rolling tears and leaves nice even tracks like rain on a windowpane. Reena sobbed uncontrollably against the wool of his tunic. Her small hands gripped the fabric and twisted. She felt a fingernail break but didn't care.

Jenny and Becker quietly left the tepee. Vic stared at the ceiling, wishing mightily that he could leave too. He'd never seen such an outpouring of emotion and sincerely hoped he never would again. At first he was embarrassed for her and for Hunter, who merely stroked her back as she wept. Then Vic saw the cleansing effect it was sure to have. No longer ill-at-ease, he watched his friends struggle with comfort: one wishing to give it, and one wishing to receive it. He wished he could join them.

Stone didn't try to calm Reena. At one point, she drew back a fist and planted it solidly in his chest. He expected more outpouring of her grief in this fashion, but it didn't come. The muscles in her back were tight and wiry under his hands. Her hair smelled like honey, and he idly wondered what she washed it with.

"I want to go home!" she wailed. "I want out of here!"

Stone brought a hand up and pressed the side of her face against him. He didn't want her to go back to Chicago, and he didn't want to hear that kind of talk anymore. But he said nothing. He only made soothing noises that sounded hollow even to himself.

Later, after she'd calmed down and sat by the desk she had purchased at a nearby trading post, staring at the floor, he left the tepee.

Reena's vocal sorrow had drawn a large group of Blackfoot outside the tepee. Their faces were curious but understanding. Their own women mourned in much the same way. Stone spotted Raindrop, and after explaining what he wanted, she led him to Powder Moon. The old chief had cataracts, and while Stone talked and Raindrop translated, Stone looked into those milky eyes and wondered if he was being heard but not seen. The old man's eyes never went to his face. Powder Moon nodded slowly when Raindrop finished, then he spoke.

"He says he is sorry for her heart," Raindrop translated. "And he says that One God Woman will need more than one god to help her at this time. She will need the spirits of her ancestors to guide her to what is the right thing to do."

Stone looked deeply into the strange, chalky eyes, hoping that the old man could see him as he firmly shook his head. "No, she will not. You do not know her God, so you do not understand." He glanced at Raindrop. "You tell him that, word for word."

An hour later he led the small party out of the Blackfoot village with a borrowed wagon for Vic to ride in. Stone struggled with feelings of anxiety. If Reena were in her right mind, she wouldn't be doing this. She was leaving a job undone, a mission uncompleted, and would probably regret it later. But those were the least of her worries. He knew that people were sometimes forced to choose self-preserving actions that went against their nature. This could be mistaken for selfishness, but was far from it. He understood that better than any person alive.

So he took her away.

The sharp crack of a bullwhip startled Megan. The bullwhackers had been silent for a time, and she'd grown accustomed to the sleepy swaying of the wagon. Now they were at it again.

"Get up thar, you old heifer!" called one of the bullwhackers, a big mountain of a man. This was the first sentence she'd heard from him that didn't contain a choice selection of purple language. Megan couldn't guess *what* his partner was saying.

The Frenchman shouted at the animals, then looked over at Megan as he cracked his eighteen-strand snake whip and grinned hugely, revealing a total absence of teeth. He had dark swarthy features and a bushy black beard. His affection for Megan was obvious, though as far as she could tell, he couldn't speak a word of English.

Megan and Louis were traveling parallel to the bull train in a wagon. Megan hugged herself and shivered. "I'm cold, Louis."

"Shouldn't be far now."

"That's what you said yesterday. Why won't you give me your coat?"

"Then what would I wear?"

Megan sniffed and said, "You're such a gentleman."

"Megan, we're both wearing coats, and yours is thicker than mine. I'd freeze to death if I gave you mine."

"You should have thought about this weather back at Fort Benton. Then we wouldn't be cold."

"I can't think of everything, dear."

Megan glanced at him. He was wearing a brand-new slouch hat that looked so strange on him that she nearly did a double take every time she looked at him. All his life he'd worn bowlers, and right now he looked as out of place as a bear at the Queen's Ball. Her smile faded, and she said irritably, "Why did you buy that ridiculous hat?"

"What's wrong with it?" he asked defensively.

"Never mind, Louis. Find a mirror somewhere, and then you'll know."

Louis snorted, pushed his glasses farther up the bridge of his nose, and replied, "You're such a polite lady. Keep your opinions to yourself."

Megan said nothing and kept her eyes straight ahead. Louis's grand idea about falling in love with each other again had failed. As their journey north had dragged on and on, from rail to stagecoach to ship, they'd both gotten tired and irritable. With no solid foundation of love to fall back on, they'd taken their frustrations out on each other in every way. If it weren't for Reena, Megan would have turned back days ago.

Megan could see from the corner of her eye that the Frenchman was staring at her again. She sighed deeply. "*Why* must we travel with these clods?"

With exaggerated patience, as if speaking to a slow child, Louis answered, "Because they know the way. Because of Indians. Because I have equipment on one of those wagons that's important."

"What equipment?"

"Business."

Megan turned and looked at the four wagons being hauled by the team of twenty bulls and oxen. All the wagons were loaded down with goods stacked seven feet high. She figured the total load must be in the tons. With this ponderous train, they were making only about seventeen miles a day. Her eyes accidentally came to rest on the Frenchman, who was gesturing frantically at her.

"*Le fort!*" he called excitedly, pointing ahead of them.

Megan scanned the flat plain in front of them and saw nothing. She turned back to him.

He held up two fingers. "*Le fort!*"

"What's he going on about?" Louis asked.

"I think he's saying the fort's two hours ahead. Or two miles." She inspected Louis accusingly. "Or two days."

Louis gave her a heated glance and whipped the horses viciously with the reins. "Look, I'm tired of your complaining, Megan. Part of the reason we're making this trip is for you, remember? To see your beloved sister. So why don't you get off my back?"

"And what's the other part, Louis? What's this mysterious cargo you've got over there? I thought you were only coming up here for speculation on the railroad, which the man we talked to in that restaurant in Bismarck said wouldn't even be constructed until the '80s! Is there something you're not telling me?"

"No!"

"I think you're lying!"

The backhand was swift and well aimed. Megan had no idea that Louis was so quick. Even as her cheek stung like fire, she was on the move. "How *dare* you!" she screeched. As she knocked off his silly hat and grabbed him by the hair, she moved to her knees on the bench seat to establish a better angle.

"Megan!"

She held on to the handful of his long hair and began hitting him in the face and head with wild blows that somehow managed to get her point across. He dropped the reins, reached for his glasses, and jerked them from his face before groping for his vest. Megan was a tenth of an instant faster, and her hand reached the derringer before him.

Scooting across the seat as far away as possible from him, she pointed the tiny pistol his way with a shaking hand. She heard raucous laughter coming from the bull wagon behind her, then applause. Not daring to turn around, she awkwardly cocked the derringer and said, "You've gone too far this time, Louis!"

"I wasn't reaching for that gun!"

"I wasn't talking about the gun. I was talking about you hitting me! But now that you mention it, I think you *were* going for the gun! *Another* lie!"

"Megan, please. Let's calm down here. Your hands are shaking so much you might accidentally pull the trigger!"

Megan's mouth was bone-dry. She licked her lips and moved the aim of the gun just to Louis's left. An accidental shooting would be horrible, and she would have to live with the guilt of it for the rest of her life. Megan had never held a gun before, though she knew to cock it from watching her father handle them. She didn't know which of them was more terrified at the moment.

Louis noticed the horse team beginning to veer away from the bull wagons and quickly grabbed the reins to straighten their path. "I'm sorry I hit you. I've never done that before."

"I know you're sorry, and I know that it'll never happen again. Right?"

"Why do you bait me, Megan?"

"Answer my question!"

Louis sighed and ran a shaking hand through his hair. Then he put on his glasses before looking at the derringer and saying, "Put that away, please."

"I'm waiting, Louis."

"All right, it'll never happen again! Now please put it away!"

"Are you saying it'll never happen again *because* I've got this gun, or—"

"I'm saying it because I mean it! Now put it away!" Small beads of sweat had formed above his upper lip and on his forehead despite the cool air.

Megan uncocked the derringer carefully, noticing Louis wince as she did so. Placing it in her purse, she said, "I'll hang on to this, if you don't mind. There's no telling what we might run into out here, and I sure can't depend on you to protect me since you were about to use it on me."

"I wasn't going to use it, Megan, I was just—"

"You were just what? Tell me."

"I wasn't even *reaching* for it, I—"

"Oh, shut up, Louis. You can't even keep your lies straight." Megan placed her purse on the other side of her, away from Louis. Her heart was still racing from the idea of actually holding a loaded gun on another human being, even though he was trying to hurt her first. Despite her shock and fear, she felt a strange sensation from the very *power* of it.

"Megan, darling, I'd feel better if the gun were in my safe-keeping. You have no experience, and they're very dangerous."

"What's your experience, Louis?"

"Target practice."

Megan waved to the grinning bull handlers, adjusted her bonnet, and said, "I think I'll take some target practice after we reach the fort. Do you think that's a good idea? That I learn how to protect myself?"

Louis swallowed and kept his eyes straight ahead. "Yes, it's probably a—"

"Good idea," she finished for him. "I thought so."

They drove on in silence for a while. Louis looked as if he'd swallowed a whole plum; his Adam's apple worked up and down frantically. Megan felt a pang of sorrow for him, then remembered the burning on her cheek.

With exaggerated calmness she told him, "Don't you ever lay a hand on me again."

CHAPTER TWELVE

Sisters and Adversaries

The next day, Stone showed Reena the small village that had sprung up around Fort Macleod. The day was warm and bright, and Reena was wearing a peach-colored dress with double skirt and tunic-style bodice. Her bonnet was matching in color, ornamented with myrtle-green leaves and a full rich bow at the back. She'd bought the outfit before coming to Canada and knew it was probably out of fashion, but it was her best dress, and she wanted to at least *look* nice, even though she was basically miserable.

" . . . and over here," Stone continued, "we have Dan Horan's shop. He claims he'll make any design or fit of shoes or boots."

Reena saw a small building with huge front windows displaying Horan's stock. In one window hung a hand-painted sign that claimed: "Repairs of all kinds done neatly and with dispatch. D. Horan."

Stone went on. "Near the back in Mr. Horan's shop, you'll find Paddy Hannafin, barber. Proud owner of the dullest razor west of Ottawa."

Reena attempted a smile for him but succeeded only in briefly turning up the corners of her mouth. Stone was trying to cheer her up, and she appreciated it, but on the whole she wished she were alone. The danger of tears spilling over at any moment was still with her.

"I sense that my audience is becoming bored with all this,"

Stone said with raised eyebrows. "I guess that means I won't get that tour guide job for the town of Fort Macleod."

"I'm sorry, Hunter. I'm just not in the mood to laugh."

"Does that mean maybe at a different time you'd find me charming and humorous?" He was still smiling, unwilling to quit without a final try.

Reena looked at him seriously. "That's exactly what it means. Any other time . . ."

"Peanut brittle or taffy?"

"What?"

He gestured to the next building that proclaimed:

A. La Chappelle
Tobacco and Candy
Billiards

"Peanut brittle or taffy? Or how about a praline?"

"No, I'm really not—"

"All right. I see I'll have to pull out the grandest of the grand: a honey popcorn ball."

"Why don't you go ahead and have something, and I'll pass?"

"Because I don't want to be the only one with sticky stuff all over my face. Come on."

The store smelled more of rich tobacco than candy. In appearance, Tony La Chappelle seemed Italian rather than French, but his accent was unmistakably Gallic.

"Sub-Inspector Stone! Where did you find zuch a pretty lady in dis barren land?"

"Tony, this is Miss Reena O'Donnell."

"*Mademoiselle*, it ees my pleasure." La Chappelle stood about five feet nine inches tall, with a stocky build, black hair, and handlebar mustache. His forearms were furry with hair, Reena observed as he pulled down on a handle and began twirling a long strand of taffy around a stick.

"For you, *mademoiselle*, with Tony's compliments."

"Why, thank you, Tony," Reena said, taking the stick.

Stone shook his head. "You *are* a charmer, Tony. Even I couldn't get her to say she wanted anything."

"Zat ees because you are not handsome like me, Sub-Inspector." Tony smiled.

"Maybe you're right. I'll have some brittle." Stone led Reena to a small table for two by the front window and held out a chair for her. "So, what do you think about our local whiskey trader turned legitimate?"

"He was a whiskey trader?" The taffy was delicious, and Reena's mouth watered for more. "I hope you don't mind my not waiting."

"Be my guest. Yes, Tony was one of the top whiskey traders in the Territory when we came here. He was also the unluckiest, since we caught him first. He saw the potential for more people to flood in here and opened this billiard parlor."

"I'd say he's pretty enterprising. Where are the tables?"

"Through that door back there." Stone pointed to the door that was guarded by a pair of wood-carved soldiers in bright blue uniforms. They stood about four feet high.

"Who are those soldiers supposed to be?" Reena asked.

Bringing Stone's peanut brittle on a plate and two glasses of water, Tony answered, "Napoleon's soldiers, *mademoiselle*. The greatest fighting men ever in ze world."

"Except for the Confederate soldier," Stone murmured as he took a sip from his glass.

Tony winced and put a hand to his forehead. "*Why* must we have dis conversation every time you come in here, Sub-Inspector? You know you can never ween dat argument!"

"I don't have to win, Tony, because I've already won. It's the documented truth. The Southern soldier could march farther, faster, and on less food than any man in history. Then when the fight began—"

Tony vigorously shook his head from side to side while Stone talked, his eyes closed in exasperation and stubbornness. "No, no, no, no, no—"

"Gentlemen, please!" Reena begged with her first smile in two days.

Tony grinned instantly and bowed to Reena. "For you, my pretty *mademoiselle*, I weel either withdraw or cut dis villain's troat for his heresy. His fate lies in your exquisite hands."

"Why don't we let him live today?"

"As you weesh," Tony smiled, withdrawing back behind his bar.

"Quite a character," Reena commented around another bite of taffy.

Stone nodded but didn't answer right away because his mouth was full of brittle. He watched a bull wagon train pull into sight on its way to the fort before saying, "There was a time when that charming gentleman *would* have cut my throat for challenging his beloved Napoleonic soldier. Back when he was full of whiskey all the time."

Reena heard the rattle of wagons and the shrill cries of men urging animals to do their bidding. The long line of yoked bulls and oxen began passing slowly by, and her eyes widened. "What in the world is that?"

Stone explained the way supplies were brought to the fort from Montana Territory. The four wagons filed by as he finished, ". . . and sometimes there are eight or ten of these coming in loaded down. It looks like this one's alone—"

"Megan!" Reena suddenly shrieked.

Stone started and looked around, but he only saw a lone wagon passing by behind the bull train.

"Megan!" She screamed louder this time and was out the door before Stone could even rise. Once outside, she screamed again, "Megan!"

The woman in the wagon jerked her head around, then jumped down from the seat, catching her dress on the brake. Reena ran toward her while Megan helplessly pulled and yanked on the hem of her dress. A ripping sound split the air just as Reena reached her and threw her arms around her.

"Reena!" Megan said breathlessly. "I can't believe it's . . . it's you!"

Reena squeezed her sister as hard as she could and felt helpless tears coming. "Oh, Megan, I'm so glad you came!" Reena sobbed. "At first I wasn't sure if . . . if this was a good idea, but now . . ."

"I know, dear. It's all right."

"Let me look at you!" Reena cried, pulling back to arm's length and wiping her face.

"No!" Megan replied. "I want more hugging!"

The sisters hugged each other in the middle of the street while Louis stopped the wagon and stepped down. He approached to a distance of ten feet away and watched the Mountie come toward them from a billiard parlor. Louis nodded, but the Mountie wasn't looking at him; he was watching the women.

"*Now* can I look at you?" Reena asked. Giggling, they separated and inspected each other.

"You're still too tall," Megan said critically, but with a smile.

"And you're still too short."

"I'd still kill for your hair."

"And I yours."

They stared at each other for a moment longer, then laughed and embraced again.

Megan saw Stone standing near them and whispered, "Oh, my. Does he belong to you? Tell me he does!"

Reena spotted Louis over Megan's shoulder, and her elation slowly died. She'd wondered how she would react when she saw him, and now she knew. She felt hurt and sudden loathing. He smiled shyly, obviously uncomfortable, and Reena felt the bad feelings slowly fade. Louis was a part of her past, but now he was married to her sister. There was nothing to do to change that. *And*, she thought with a satisfied feeling of strength, *I wouldn't change it if I could*. "Hello, Louis," Reena greeted him quietly.

He whipped off the slouch hat and wrung it in his hands as he spoke. "Hello, Reena. You're looking as if this country agrees with you."

"It does."

"Reena!" Megan whispered urgently.

"What?"

Into her ear Megan whispered, "Is this gorgeous man in uniform yours?"

Reena chuckled and pulled away from Megan as she introduced Stone.

He half bowed and said, "It's a pleasure Mrs. Goldsen. I've been looking forward to meeting you."

"The pleasure's mine, Mr. Stone."

"Well, come on," Reena said, looking around at the small number of people on the boardwalk who were watching them curiously. "We can't just stand out here in the middle of the street. Let's go have some taffy."

Never in her musings had Reena thought that she would actually smile this day, much less laugh. As she took her sister's hand and looked into her sea-green eyes, she thanked God that He had sent Megan her way just when she needed her. The spring day suddenly seemed pretty, instead of just another day to struggle through.

Tony La Chappelle's eyes lit up when the four of them entered. His customers were few, but he knew in his French heart that more would grace his establishment in the future.

Reena turned to the men. "Why don't you boys stay here by the window while we have our girl talk in the back?"

They looked at each other quickly, then back to Reena with slightly stunned expressions. Louis gave a half nod, and Stone said, "All right." The two men selected a larger table for four, instead of the cozy two-seater Reena and Hunter had taken before.

Reena had made the proposition without thinking. Now she realized that she'd just asked her ex-fiancé and the man to whom she'd recently confessed her love to pass the time of day together after having just met. Hunter knew about Louis, and Louis clearly suspected the truth about Hunter and Reena. *What have I done?* Reena wondered, but then Megan was pulling on her sleeve.

"Come on, little sis. I want to hear everything."

Megan and Reena seated themselves by the wooden French infantrymen, where Reena had a clear view of the men. Stone was sitting with his legs crossed, chatting with Tony, while Louis faced the window as if the other two weren't there. Reena hoped that Hunter could somehow be polite to Louis. She felt a hand on hers.

"How are you doing, Reena?" Megan asked, concern filling her features. "When did you get the news?"

"Two days ago."

Megan made a disgusted sound deep in her throat. "News travels so slow to these out-of-the-way places. I'm sorry."

"It's not your fault. I'm sort of glad it took that long, since you arrived so soon after I learned of it. I was in pretty bad shape when I first heard. How did Da take it?"

"Very well, actually. Mother had been . . . failing for some time. He had time to prepare for it, I think."

"And Mother? Was she. . . ?"

"Oh, Reena, she was so gallant! Even to the last she kept her senses, and through the pain she stayed cheerful."

"Did she suffer much?" Reena asked, afraid of the answer.

" I don't think so. The medicine helped her a lot. She couldn't have hidden a great amount of pain." Megan felt a twinge of guilt for telling a small lie to Reena, but to tell the whole truth would do nothing but grieve her more.

"I'm glad," Reena said.

Megan carefully arranged the white cloth napkin in front of them into a small, complicated peak. "So you're not . . . upset with me anymore?"

"Of course not! Didn't you get my letter a year ago?"

"Yes."

"And why didn't you answer it?"

Megan sighed and said, "I just thought it was best to leave it as it was for the time being. That was one reason, and another was that I really didn't know what to say—'Thanks for not hating me for stealing your fiancé?' "

"You could have said anything you wanted. I would have been happy just to get a word from you."

"Then I'm sorry. It was rude of me."

Tony came by, and though Reena was aware that she was ravenously hungry all at once, she declined more taffy. Megan ordered some, and after Tony left with politeness and compliments galore, Reena asked, "How are you and Louis doing?" She glanced to the front and saw that the two men were actually saying words to each other. Hunter was sitting with his legs crossed, his black boots brilliantly reflecting the sun shining through the window, and his hands laced in his lap. Though he looked at ease, Reena sensed that he was trying *too* hard to be relaxed. *Keep your head, Hunter. Don't beat up my sister's husband.*

When Reena became conscious of her thought, she was filled with shame. Most women would give anything to have a man who cared enough to make her enemies his, and who would take her word without question. However, Louis really wasn't an enemy, for Reena had forgiven him in her heart long ago. But Hunter was inexperienced in the ways of forgiveness, and he was reacting the only way he knew. He would attempt to be polite to someone he held in contempt. He didn't know Louis and might have liked him had he had the chance, but he knew how Louis had treated Reena, and that was enough. Poor Louis could probably never do anything to become friends with the man he was sitting across from.

Reena became aware that Megan hadn't answered and turned to find her staring at her taffy stick. "Megan? Did you hear me?"

"Yes, I heard you."

"Well, maybe another time." Megan's silence and demeanor told more than words could say. Her normally lively eyes had dulled, and her youthful face suddenly looked older. Reena decided to change the subject. "Tell me about Mother, Megan. I want to know all about her final days."

Stone couldn't believe that Reena had actually suggested that he and Louis chat together. Didn't she know how he felt about Louis? *She must not be thinking clearly yet. Oh, well, I guess I have to make the best of it.*

Luckily, Tony came over, and Stone managed to avoid talking to Louis for the time being.

Tony was full of news that Stone had missed while he was at the Blackfoot camp. Trouble had boiled over into violence at a Cree camp on Wolf Creek north of them. A brave had gotten drunk, accused his best friend of being with his wife, and then attacked him. The man accused defeated him handily since he'd been sober, but the accuser had gone to his wife and killed her. A troop had been sent out at once under Inspector Crozier of F Division. Before he could be captured, the Cree had committed suicide—an unheard of practice among the Indians. "Ze whiskay," Tony said solemnly. "Ze whiskay."

At a Blood Indian village—the Bloods were part of the Blackfoot nation—a woman had fled from her husband, who was the son of the tribe's medicine man. The Mounties, Colonel Macleod in particular, detested getting involved in such matters, but instead of merely running away, the woman had taken one of her husband's ponies. The Indians had no notion of communal property, and to put matters in perspective, Macleod had reasoned that at least the Bloods had recognized the Mounties' authority and asked them to fetch her rather than taking it upon themselves to do so.

"Why was she running from him?" Louis asked. It was the first time he'd spoken, and Tony looked at him as if he were seeing him for the first time. Stone thought Tony sensed the discomfort in the air between the two men.

Tony glanced at Stone before answering, as if silently asking if he should indeed speak to this stranger with the funny accent. Stone kept his face neutral, and Tony shrugged, saying, "She did not like him."

"Was he a drunk, too?"

Tony again glanced at Stone as if to say, "Am I expected to answer *two* questions from this stranger?" Receiving no facial advice from Stone, Tony answered grudgingly, "I am sure dat I don't know, *monsieur*. Mebbe you should ask de squaw." With that, he marched back behind his counter in a quiet huff, angry that his gossip had been interrupted.

Stone covered a smile and took a sip of the cider Tony had brought them. It was hot and tangy.

"What got into him?" Louis asked.

Setting down his cup, Stone looked at him. Now he knew how Tony had felt. A direct question had been thrown his way, and he didn't even want to talk to the man asking it. He faced the window, watching a tired-looking woman emerge from the I. G. Baker Store across the street. Her clothes were gray and drab, her bonnet a drawn capote that once was pink satin but now had faded to nearly white from the sun. Her face appeared older than her years under the shade of the small brim. She'd probably been wearing the head covering while working in the fields of her farm. He wondered how long she'd held on to the twenty-years-out-of-date but pretty hat before she'd resigned herself to knowing that she'd have to use it for practical purposes rather than ornamental ones. Stone figured the first day she'd worn the hat as she'd planted beans or plowed behind a mule must have been a very sad day indeed. He watched her as she quickly and deftly stacked the goods into the back of a wagon. He could tell she had done this many times before.

"So you're not talkative, either," Louis commented. His eyes, too, went to the woman.

"What do you do for a living, Mr. Goldsen?"

"I'm in banking and investments."

"Sounds lucrative."

"Just like anything else, I suppose. Some days are better than others."

A teenage girl came out of the store with her arms filled with supplies, and the bonneted woman helped her load them into the wagon.

"May I ask you a question . . . what was it . . . Stone?"

"Sub-Inspector Stone."

Louis inclined his head, mock-impressed. "Sub-Inspector Stone, then. May I ask you a question?"

"You seem to be full of questions."

"I'm a curious man."

"Go ahead." Stone knew what was coming.

"Are you and Reena . . . ah . . . connected in some sort of way?"

Stone kept his eyes on the window, and another teenager—a boy this time—came out of Baker's with still more supplies. Maybe the woman wasn't as poor as Stone had first thought. She had enough goods to last for months.

Looking directly at Louis, he said, "Are you asking if my debits equal Reena's credits on the balance sheet?"

"Ah, *touché!* But that's a bookkeeper's business to which you've so poorly referred. My business is speculation, investment, and profit. Much higher ideals—and income, I might add—than a bookkeeper's."

"I'm impressed," Stone said, sounding anything but. "Tell me, Mr. Goldsen, does your wife share your ambitions? She doesn't seem like the type."

Louis quickly glanced back to Megan, then a light dawned on his face as he returned his gaze to Stone's. "I see," he said, nodding slowly. "In other words, if I mind my own business, you'll mind yours. I'm impressed, Sub-Inspector. The bulls are pawing the ground before the charge. I believe I have underestimated you."

"I would imagine you do that a lot."

"Storekeeper!" Louis suddenly called out. "Don't you have anything stronger than this cider?"

Stone smiled, imagining the look on Tony's face behind him.

"I weesh I did, boy. Then I could give you some, and the Sub-Inspector would arrest you."

Louis leaned toward Stone. "What's he talking about? Is hard liquor illegal here?"

Stone gazed back out the window. The bonneted woman whisked back inside the store, and a half-minute later she marched out with three more children and a toddler. That made six children. No wonder she had purchased so many supplies. Stone made a mental note to ask Baker's proprietor, D. W. Davis, if the woman had a husband.

Stone turned slowly to look at Louis. "What are you doing here, Goldsen?"

"We're dropping the courtesies now?"

"I ask again. What are you doing here?"

Louis's eyes were concealed by the sunlight reflecting from his glasses. His mouth, which was barely wider than his nose, turned up in a smile. "Why do you ask me that?"

"You said you're a banker. I take that to mean you're fairly well educated and up-to-date on international matters. Therefore, you *know* that whiskey is illegal in the North-West Territories. What kind of game are you offering here?"

Louis sat back. The smile was gone, and his Adam's apple worked in a hard swallow. "Game? I don't . . ."

Stone sat forward at an angle where he could see Louis's eyes. They were wide and brown and alert, like those of a trapped animal. Stone knew the type; he'd seen them in Ottawa when he'd been bounty hunting. They were born with a silver spoon tucked neatly in their mouths, and nothing in the passing years had failed to pry the spoon from them. Whatever they wanted, they got. They were as addicted to Papa's purse strings as an opium addict is to the pipe. If Papa strayed too far, the tendency was to lash out at the people around them, usually hardworking servants trying to feed their families on meager wages. They were sent to the best schools with no fear of failing, for they *would* pass and receive a diploma, even if they didn't attend class. Then, as if from some obscene birth, they sprouted their own purse to hold and fondle and protect. Nothing mattered but that appendage, and keeping it fed and full.

To Stone, all of that was disgusting enough. The worst part—the part that scraped against him like a sand burr in a sock all day—was the arrogant attitude that went along with it all.

He was sitting across from that attitude right now, and his patience had worn thin. "I don't know what you're doing here," Stone said with an unmistakable edge, "but I know what you're *not* here for: your lovely wife, Reena, a vacation, or the fresh air. And I really don't think you came here to see me and insult me or my friend over there. So why don't you save me a lot of trouble and tell me why you're here?"

Louis looked over at Tony so he wouldn't have to look into

Stone's cold gray eyes. Tony, within earshot, lifted a hand and wiggled his fingers in greeting.

"Watch yourself, Mr. Goldsen," Stone warned calmly, leaning back in his chair to stare out the window again. "Because I'm sure going to be watching you."

"Wait a minute!" Louis whispered urgently, "I haven't done anything wrong here!"

"Not yet, you haven't, except for baiting the first man you met here, who happens to be an officer of the only law in this territory. If it were me, I'd consider that a big mistake. But you're your own man, aren't you?"

"I'm . . . I'm sorry, Sub-Inspector, I didn't mean—"

"Actually, I'm glad we had this little talk," Stone said casually, picking lint from his trouser leg. "It makes the rules clear. I like that—a clearly drawn set of rules—don't you?"

"Well, I—"

"I live by a code, Mr. Goldsen. A code based on honor, justice, and the law. There are no gray areas in that arena, just black and white. I'm comfortable with that." Stone paused, and when Louis didn't reply, he said, "If your actions here, whatever they may be, hurt Reena as you hurt her before or in any other way, you'll answer to me. Is that a clear enough rule for you?"

Louis began nodding but didn't answer right away.

"Or how about this: if that happens, I'll close your account. Is that a banker's reference, or did I insult you with bookkeeper's talk again?"

"No, that's a banker's reference," Louis replied, trying to smile.

"So there are no gray areas here? Only black and white?"

"Absolutely."

Stone drained the tepid cup of cider. "Good. Then you've had a very productive day, getting to know the natives and all that." He heard the ladies approaching behind him and turned with a smile. He saw at once they'd both been crying and knew they'd probably been talking about their mother.

Reena took a deep breath and tried to return his smile. "So, have you boys been getting along all right?"

They both stood, and with a look at Louis, Stone said, "I think we understand each other completely."

CHAPTER THIRTEEN

A Dry and Thirsty Land

Stone escorted Reena to the fort while Megan and Louis settled in at Baker's boardinghouse. The house had been built by Donald Davis, I. G. Baker's proprietor, for the Baker employees. Stone thought Davis must have been thinking big expansion, because he'd built a huge eight bedroom house for only three employees.

As they approached the gate they noticed a crowd of Mounties standing around the entrance. Some of them were casually clad in shirt and suspenders, and all were staring anxiously toward the horizon across the Old Man's River. That is, they were until Reena came into view. They'd seen her before on the day she, Vic, and Jenny had arrived, but they still couldn't help staring at her.

Stone spotted Boogaard in the crowd and asked him what they were doing.

Boogaard pointed, and Stone could just make out a wagon and riders in the distance. "That's the mail, according to Wicks," Boogaard told them excitedly. A constant source of grumbling, the mail delivery to Fort Macleod had been, at best, unreliable. Any news of incoming mail brought anticipation like no other event at the fort. Boogaard turned to a tall, sad-looking man next to him. "If you're lying, Wicks, we'll soak your head. You know that, don't you?"

"I'm not lying," Wicks said defensively. "I saw the bags myself. There must have been forty of them."

As one, they turned and faced the horizon again, wistfulness etched on their faces.

"That's a sad sight," Reena commented as they passed through the gate. "Can't Macleod do anything about the mail service?"

"Macleod's a competent man, but even he can't change the postal delivery."

"Speaking of Macleod," Reena said, seeing him walking toward them.

Macleod tipped his hat to Reena, then said to Stone, "You and Stride get a detail together. We've got three more deserters on our hands."

"Three more?" Desertions had occurred regularly from the time of the March West, but the numbers had been high of late. "Who are they?"

"Hallam, Foster, and Mack. They were last seen heading north up the river. I want them found, Stone."

"Yes, sir. I don't know two of them, but I didn't know Mack was unhappy."

"It's not your fault, Stone. One or more of them stole two hunting passes from my office, and I'll have to make an example of them. So ignore the hunting passes they're carrying; they're not legitimate. Good day, Miss O'Donnell," he said brusquely, then passed by them toward the gate. Apparently he'd heard of the mail and was as anxious as the rest of the men.

"Well, there goes our dinner together," Stone said to Reena.

"You have to leave now?"

"I'm going to wait until that mail gets here to break the bad news to a few men. You're going to see Vic?"

"Yes."

"Tell him hello for me."

"I will." Reena watched Stone go to his quarters before she crossed the yard to the infirmary. The sound of a harmonica sailed on the air in a lonely lilt. She knocked on the door and heard a hoarse answer inside.

Vic was alone in the room, lying on a cot by the back window. The late afternoon sun cast light on his pale, damp face. His legs were over the side of the cot awkwardly.

Reena rushed over to him. "Vic? What are you doing? Where's Dr. Nevitt? And Del?"

"Gone with a scouting party north," Vic panted. "I wanted some water, but . . ."

Reena gently placed his legs back on the bed. "Where's your attendant?"

"I . . . I don't know. I remember someone saying something about the mail, then I fell back asleep."

Pouring Vic a glass of water, Reena fumed, "Does this whole fort stop functioning when there's a rumor about the mail coming?"

"Pretty much," Vic said, smiling. He drained the glass, and Reena filled it again from the tin pitcher. "I don't blame the boys, Reena. They miss their families."

"Well, don't you try getting up again. Bang on the wall or throw something through the window to get someone's attention." She paused as she set a wooden chair beside the cot. "Or better yet . . ."

"What?"

"Better yet, I'll take you to the boardinghouse where I can watch over you."

"No, no. That's too much—really."

"Nonsense! You're not going to get better without *constant* care, Vic, and everyone's too busy chasing the Pony Express, or whoever delivers up here."

"Macleod would never clear it."

"Yes, he would. I'll make sure of it. Besides, it would actually be a favor to me, Vic. That way I won't have to come to the fort every day."

"You don't have to—"

"Yes, I do. I feel responsible for you."

"Why?" Vic asked, almost laughing.

"Will you do it, or not?" Reena asked in a playful, stern tone.

"Yes, nurse."

"Then that's that. Have you eaten, or did some urgent matter like a card game keep them from cooking for you?"

"Actually, I am a bit hungry."

While Reena prepared venison cutlets, corn, and rolls, Vic fell into a deep sleep. Instead of waking him when she was done, Reena moved the chair by the window and opened her Bible. She alternated between reading a few lines from the Psalms and gazing out the window at the sun creeping toward the mountains.

Vic slept for nearly two hours. The attendant returned, clutching a handful of letters. The knives in Reena's eyes caused him to apologize sheepishly, place the letters on a table by the door, and quickly take his leave. Reena was tempted to look at the return addresses of Vic's correspondents but managed to keep to her seat.

Some time later, she glanced over at Vic and was surprised to find him watching her. "Good afternoon," she said.

The setting sun cast an orange tint on his face, making him appear more healthy than he was. "I feel like I've been asleep all day."

"Only for a couple of hours."

"What are you reading?"

Reena looked down at the Bible and read, " 'I will lift up mine eyes unto the hills, from whence cometh my help. My help cometh from the Lord, which made heaven and earth.' "

"Where is that?"

"Psalm 121. Beautiful, isn't it?"

"Very. Did David write that?"

"No, it's anonymous."

"Would you read me one of David's?"

"Of course. I'll read you my favorite, as a matter of fact." Reena looked at the spectacular view out the window before turning to Psalm 63. The clouds above the mountain where the sun had hidden itself burned a molten gold. Above them floated clouds of pink rose and deep lavender.

Vic said softly, his voice tinged with awe, "These fellows that stay in the infirmary are fortunate in two ways: they get out of work details, and they get to enjoy this magnificent view every evening. I'll have to remember that."

"It *is* incredible."

They watched until the clouds turned ash-colored, and when Reena turned to Vic, she saw a tear rolling down his cheek to the pillow. "Vic, are you all right?"

"Read to me, Reena. Just read."

Reena lifted her Bible and began reading. " 'O God, thou art my God; early will I seek thee: my soul thirsteth for thee, my flesh longeth for thee in a dry and thirsty land, where no water is . . .' "
She read the whole psalm and couldn't help but hear Vic sniffle

once. When she finished, she didn't want to face him for fear of embarrassing him.

He sniffed again, then asked, "What was that about the shadow of His wings?"

" 'Because thou hast been my help, therefore in the shadow of thy wings will I rejoice.' "

Vic swallowed with a click, and Reena gave him some water. He drank gratefully while Reena lit an oil lamp. The soft glow was enough to reveal a haunted look in Vic's face. When he spoke in a whisper, he kept his eyes on the lamp. "I was so frightened, Reena. So frightened. I don't *want* to die. But then, who does? Do you?"

"Of course not, Vic. But I'm not afraid to die."

"See? That's how I wish I could be. More like you and Hunter."

"Hunter?"

"Yes. That man has no fear of anything on this earth or anything *not* on this earth."

"All of us have fears, Vic. Even Hunter."

"He sure doesn't show it."

"You can be unafraid of death, too," Reena said quietly. "It's very easy, ridiculously easy. Just come under the shadow of His wings." Vic said nothing, but now he was staring at her. She saw tiny pinpoints of light reflected in his dark eyes. "You know, Vic, that your soul is that dry and thirsty land where there's no water, don't you? But water *is* available for those who want it."

Vic was silent for a long time. "I do want it."

"Then pray with me. Ask Jesus into your heart."

"I . . . I . . ." His mouth continued working, but no sound came forth. Then he managed to say, "I can't."

"Sure you can!"

"Not right now, Reena," Vic said firmly. "Do you think the food's still edible?" His manner was jovial, the issue dismissed as suddenly as it had come.

Reena couldn't help thinking that a great chance had been lost, but she didn't know what she could have done differently.

———

The next day Reena arranged with Macleod to have Vickersham moved to the boardinghouse. Macleod took her request personally. "Do you believe that our facilities aren't enough for Vickersham?"

"No, not at all, it's—"

"Speak freely, Miss O'Donnell."

"Very well. It's my opinion that Vic needs constant care, and the duties of the fort might . . . distract the men from giving him what he needs."

Macleod's eyes narrowed. "What happened? Was Vickersham left unattended for an extended period?"

The last thing Reena wanted was to get anyone in trouble, so she had to choose her words carefully. "When I arrived yesterday, he was alone, hungry, and thirsty. But the attendant was just excited about the mail, Colonel, and he *did* return, so please don't say anything to the man. I wouldn't want him to be disciplined because of me."

"Oh, he'll be disciplined, Miss O'Donnell, you may be sure of that."

"*Please*, Colonel Macleod. For me?" Feeling guilty about using false charm, she nevertheless smiled and batted her eyes, just once.

By his knowing smile, Reena could see that Macleod knew what she was doing. But he pretended to consider her request seriously for a moment before saying grudgingly, "Very well, ma'am. Just this once I'll let a known lack of discipline go unpunished. All of these favors will, however, cost you dearly."

"Sir?" His words sounded ominous, but there was a definite twinkle in his eyes.

"The Police are throwing a party in a week. I'll expect a dance from you—that is, if you dance. I wouldn't want to compromise anyone's principles."

"And I get to take Vic with me today?"

"You drive a hard bargain, Miss O'Donnell. That's why I feel no guilt over my blackmail."

Reena laughed. "I'd love to have a dance with the most famous Mountie in the Territory."

"I'm not so sure that Stone doesn't hold that title, but I'll take the compliment when flung at me so baldly."

Macleod offered to make all the arrangements for Vic's transport. Reena considered stopping by to see Vic, but knowing Macleod's attitude about getting things done, she decided she'd better get back to the boardinghouse and ready things for her patient.

She felt tired and drained. The previous few days had been difficult, to say the least, and when she'd gone home after taking care of Vic the night before, Megan had wanted to talk. Talk they did, right up until three in the morning. The news of Louis and Megan's troubles had surfaced. Reena, though sorry for Megan, wasn't surprised by Louis's total attention to business and everything else but his wife. After going to bed, she'd prayed and thanked God that He had seen fit not to test her faith by having her marry Louis.

Megan had made an interesting comment. "Louis is up to something, Reena. I don't know what it is, but why would he come here? At first he talked about railroad investment speculation, but I heard the rails won't be constructed through the Territories until well into the 1880s. What else could he be doing up here?"

Reena had had no answer for Megan, and as she walked along in the cold morning, she still couldn't think of anything. But Louis was the least of her concerns.

Armand Sweet hammered the nail into the board viciously. "I'm sick and tired of building these stupid storage sheds," he grumbled darkly to Boggs. "Why can't those Mounties do some work for themselves?"

"Why should they? They've got us—free labor." Boggs was sawing a plank siding board and taking his time about finishing it.

"I don't want to hear a word out of a man who's going free tomorrow. I'm just talking to hear myself speak."

Boggs and Conklin had received much lighter sentences than Sweet since it had been established that the whiskey was found at Sweet's cabin. The Mounties didn't feel they had anything on which to hold the two men. *Besides*, Sweet mused, *it was me they wanted all along.* This thought made him snicker. *So they have me, but only for another month. Then they'll see they should have kept me longer.* This reflection made him laugh.

"What's so funny?" Boggs asked. He'd finally finished the plank, and with a furtive look at the Mountie guard, he slowly started on another.

Sweet stopped his hammering and looked over at Boggs. "I don't want you to stray far when you get out, Boggs. I've got big plans for us."

"Yeah, your big plans landed us here."

"Fine," Sweet hissed. "Then you'll miss out on a lot of money, and if I ever see you again, I'll kill you. How's that big plan?"

"Settle down, Sweet! I was just joshin' you!"

"I ought to take this hammer and adjust your thinking right now." Sweet turned to the Mountie, who was sitting on a bay mare keeping an eye on the twenty or so prisoners. As he watched, the Mountie turned the mare to the top of a small hill and yelled a challenge to the other side. A man appeared on horseback, his hands raised. They talked for a few minutes, then the Mountie turned and pointed directly to Sweet.

"Hey, Boggs! Who's that?" Sweet watched Boggs squint at the horseman. He had forgotten for a moment that Boggs was extremely nearsighted. "Ah, never mind, you blind rat! Why don't you get glasses?"

"I look stupid in glasses."

"And you look so intelligent without them." Sweet saw the man ride down toward him. He was unaccustomed to riding a horse, that much was certain. *Some Easterner probably*, he thought and spat.

"Mr. Sweet?" the rider asked. "May I have a word with you?"

"What for? Who are you?"

"It would be worth your time, I assure you." He looked around the work area. "Unless you have more important things to do."

"Very funny."

The man dismounted and waved to the Mountie, who waved back. After tying his horse to a nearby sapling, he nodded for Sweet to follow him. "Let's go for a walk."

"You got a gun?"

"No, I'm unarmed."

"Well, that's a fool thing to do—go to a prison camp without a gun."

"I don't think you have reason to harm me, Mr. Sweet."

"I ask again, who are you?"

The stranger cupped his hands to his mouth and blew on them. "My, it's cold."

"You get used to it. I'm still waiting for you to answer my—"

"Why don't you shut up and let me ask the questions?"

Sweet stopped and almost hit the arrogant man. Then he remembered the Mountie and checked to see if he was watching, which he was, of course. "I don't think you know who you're talking to, mister, but let me tell you it's a big mistake to get on my bad side."

The man had an arrogant smile to go with his attitude. "You're Armand Sweet, a whiskey trader who receives his whiskey in big shipments from Chicago by way of boat on the Milk River. That route is the safest possible because you bypass Fort Benton. You also got caught. That's *your* big mistake. Now, since that's established—"

"Who *are* you?" Sweet asked, but a bit more politely this time. This man knew things that even Boggs and Conklin didn't know. The only other person that knew was . . .

The stranger studied Sweet with that superior smile of his. As he saw Sweet figure it out, the smile grew. "Now do you know who I am?"

Sweet looked around to the Mountie quickly, then back to the stranger. He couldn't believe this man was actually *here*! "Yes, I know who you are now. We finally meet face-to-face."

"Yes, finally. I *am* your employer after all—at the moment, anyway."

"What's that supposed to mean?"

The man reached in his coat pocket and produced two slim cigars. He gave one to Sweet, lit it for him, then held the match to his own. "It means that these shipments must *never* be traced back to me. If you're going around getting caught, that worries me. Are you sure you're up to the job?"

"I've been up to the job going on two years now without getting caught."

"Yet, here you are, working like a common slave."

Sweet inhaled deeply and let the smoke escape from his nose. The tobacco was, predictably, excellent. Taking a step closer to the man, he said, "I've made a lot of money for you. I'd think you'd be more grateful."

"I *have* been grateful. Now, I'm just nervous."

Sweet smiled at the first realization of his upper hand. "So you think I'm going to tell them who you are?"

"It had crossed my mind."

"Why would I give up the best money I've ever made? That is, if I'm still employed. If not . . . well, that's another matter."

The stranger's eyes cut over to the Mountie, who was slowly walking his horse in their direction. "Look, we're running out of time. I was supposed to be asking you directions to somewhere since you know the territory." He drew deeply on the cigar. "As you know, the largest shipment yet is on its way. I'd already ordered it sent before I received the news of your capture. It'll be at the usual place next Wednesday."

"I don't get out for another month."

"Then maybe you'd better explore other alternatives. If you're not there, I'll find another man to take your place. By the time you start screaming my name, I'll be back in the States, and this would have to be my last shipment. It's your choice."

"I'll be there."

The Mountie arrived and said, "You got your directions yet? You're really not supposed to be talking to the prisoners, you know."

The man touched his hat brim. "You've been most kind to allow it, sir. I'll be on my way now." With a nod to Sweet, he left.

"Get back to work, Sweet," the Mountie ordered.

"Yes, *sir.*" He smirked with a mock salute. *These morons are so proper and superior. I could take any of them, anytime.* His smirk disappeared. *Except for the one with eyes of no color. He might be a problem. What was his name? Stone! Yes, I think we'll see each other again. In fact, I'll make it a point to pay him a visit.*

Resuming his hammering, Sweet began to whistle.

Boggs looked at him as if he'd lost his mind.

———

Late that afternoon while Megan was trying to take a nap, she heard heavy boots in the hallway stop outside her door. A note slid through cleanly underneath, and the boots walked away.

Feeling both curious and tentative, she moved to the door and stared down at the paper for a while before retrieving it. *Your goods are stored in the shed behind the house.*

"What goods?" she said aloud, then remembered the business cargo Louis had mentioned was on the bull train. "His cargo is my cargo," she muttered, putting on her shoes.

The house was utterly silent as she tiptoed down the stairs. Outside, she went around the back of the house and peered cautiously about. Satisfied that no one was around to question what she was doing there, she entered the storage shed.

Inside, the building was dark and nearly empty. A few carpentry tools lay scattered around. A bureau cabinet stood in one corner beside a set of bedsprings propped against a wall. Boxes lined one wall, but two wooden crates sat in the middle of the shed as if just placed there.

"That must be the mysterious cargo," Megan whispered to herself. She wondered how she was going to break into the crates without leaving evidence of entry. Carpentry tools came to mind, but on a whim she tugged on the lid of one crate and was shocked when it swung upward smoothly on hinges.

Her heart accelerated instantly when she saw the unmarked gallon jugs. Unmindful of her dress, she knelt down on the dirt floor and took a deep breath. She watched her hand go toward the cork stopper of one of the jugs as if it had a mind of its own. She couldn't stop the hand, it just *went*. The cork popped out easily with a soft pop.

Megan bent over slowly and smelled the lip of the bottle. At once, she gagged and coughed violently at the vile odor rising from the opened jug. When her eyes cleared, she found that she was standing in a newly formed shadow thrown from the doorway to the shed.

"Not the finest of whiskeys, but the Indians love it," Louis remarked in a jovial tone.

CHAPTER FOURTEEN

The Black-and-Blue Lady

Jenny could feel the cabin in the foothills drawing her. She sat on a small hill south of the fort and watched the Mounties on parade. Occasionally her eyes lifted to the mountains in the distance, and she imagined saddling Splash and riding to them, and home.

The Police were performing complicated drills on horseback with colorful flags and guidons whipping in the wind. She liked the Mounties—they'd all been very polite to her—but she just didn't belong here. People were everywhere, around her all the time, and the only way she could be by herself was to stay in her room at the boardinghouse or walk outside of town as she had this day.

Reena was very nice to her and always tried to carry on a conversation, but she was very busy . . . and sad. Jenny always felt as if she were imposing on her mourning and on her time. Reena's sister was pleasant but sort of distant, as though she was also very sad about something. Something besides her mother's death. Something deep down that nobody knew about.

And then there was Dirk Becker. Jenny hadn't seen much of him because he had his duties at the fort. Disturbingly, she found that she missed his company, even though she hardly knew him. He was the first man she'd ever met who didn't want something from her—to cook for him, or clean, or . . . *anything*. And the way he'd handled the evil Sid had sent a thrill through her. She'd never had anyone take up for her before, and she hadn't realized until just last night right before she went to sleep that the word for what he'd done was *concern*. He'd been *concerned* about her. She'd even whispered the word over and over, tasting first the hard *c* and then the soft one, letting them roll off her tongue like honey. It was a nice word.

Dirk was a man, though, and she was certain that somewhere deep inside him was a monster waiting to show itself. She felt guilty thinking about him that way, but it had to be there. It was in every man she ever knew. Even if by some miracle there wasn't a blackness inside him, he wasn't for her. He was smart and handsome, despite the scar, and full of *concern*. He would never want her. No one would want her.

The sound of children's voices broke through Jenny's reverie. She turned and saw four children coming up the hill toward her. One of them, a boy of about eight, twirled a metal hoop on a stick. The youngest of them was a girl who looked about five, though Jenny couldn't be sure. She'd never in her life spent time around children, and as they came toward her, she thought of running away. Kids were completely strange to her and might as well have been from the moon.

"Hi," said the boy with the stick. He was obviously the leader.

Jenny didn't answer. Her eyes followed the stick, and she expected him to suddenly swat her with it. He merely seemed curious about her, but one never knew.

"What's your name?" he asked.

Jenny glanced at the half circle they'd formed around her. She felt crowded and stifled the urge to back away.

"Cain't you talk?" The stick stopped spinning as the boy considered this phenomenon.

"Y-yes."

"So what's your name? Mine's Timmy, and that's Joey, Margie, and that little one down there's my sister Lydia. She follows us around a lot."

Jenny looked at Lydia, who clutched a doll dressed in tattered clothes and had one arm missing. The little girl wasn't even paying attention to Jenny; she was watching the Mounties.

"You sure you can talk? Is there somethin' wrong with your head?"

"My . . . my head?"

"Yeah." Timmy made a horrible face and twirled a finger beside his own head. "You know. Stupid." They all laughed except Lydia.

"I ain't stupid!" Jenny shot back, leaping to her feet. She was satisfied to see them step back as one with fearful faces.

"Sorry!" Timmy said immediately, his eyes round.

"He was just joshin', lady," Margie said. "He likes to josh." She had red hair, freckles, and warm brown eyes. On second glance, Jenny thought that she might be the oldest instead of Timmy.

"Hey, I'm almost as tall as you are!" Timmy crowed. He stood up as straight as he could, his momentary fear already forgotten.

"Yeah, I'm short, but I ain't stupid," Jenny said. "And my name's Jenny Sweet."

Joey's eyes widened as he pointed and said, "Hey, you're—"

Margie whacked him in the chest. "Shut up, Joey."

For the first time, Lydia tore her eyes away from the Mounties on parade and looked at Jenny. The young girl's blond hair whipped around her face. She had a deep crimson birthmark on her left temple.

"I'm the what?" Jenny asked. They looked at one another, then everywhere but at Jenny. "Come on, I'm the what?"

Lydia said, quite clearly, "You're the Black-and-Blue Lady."

"What's that supposed to mean?" Jenny asked with dread. She already knew what it meant, and she could feel her face blushing. "You mean everybody in this place is talkin' about me?"

"It don't mean anything, ma'am," Timmy said.

"Yeah, it's nothin'," Joey chimed in.

"The Black-and-Blue Lady," Jenny said distantly. "So all this time, everyone's looked at me and laughed behind my back, huh?"

"Oh no!" Margie cried. "Not everybody knows, and the ones who do don't laugh. They feel real sorry for you."

"If not everybody knows, then how do you know? You're just kids."

"We hear lotsa things. Big people don't think anything about talkin' in front of us. They think we're deaf or something, like we're not even *there*!"

"You don't *look* black-and-blue," Lydia commented. "You look just like us."

"She *is* just like us," Timmy told her. "She just had a few bruises when she got here. Horse prob'ly threw you, huh?" he asked Jenny.

At that moment Jenny realized that they knew a horse hadn't thrown her. Their interest in her answer intensified dramatically, as if the last thing they wanted to hear was the truth: that sometimes big people weren't kind and nice and responsible. Sometimes they were mean and took it out on their kids. The ultimate horror of their world was standing right in front of them.

"Yeah," Jenny whispered and tried to smile. "A half-broke horse threw me into some boulders. I had bruises all over me."

The children didn't sigh with relief, but their faces clearly showed it.

"I got throwed one time," Timmy announced proudly. "Into some blackberry brambles."

Margie giggled suddenly. "We could have called you the Scratch Boy!" All the children, even Timmy, laughed heartily at this. Even Jenny had to grin.

"Would you like to see our fort?" Lydia asked. Without waiting for an answer she reached across and took Jenny's hand. "It's very nice. Not as nice as that one"—she pointed to Fort Macleod—"but it keeps the rain out."

Jenny allowed herself to be led down the other side of the hill toward a stand of aspens and cottonwoods. Timmy began spinning the hoop on the stick again while doing a strange little hop and skip. Joey and Margie drew close to Jenny and chatted about the fort and their planned improvements to it.

"She'll *see* the fort," Lydia interrupted. "Let's talk about *her*."

Joey and Margie looked at Jenny expectantly.

For a while, Jenny forgot about the cabin in the mountains, and she was no longer afraid of Timmy's stick. In fact, she wished to try the hoop sometime.

That afternoon, Jenny talked more than she ever had in her life.

Megan stared at Louis's outline against the bright light behind him. At last, she said through numbed lips, "Louis, what have you gotten yourself into?"

"*Us* into, you mean?"

"What are you talking about? I don't know anything about this!"

Louis stepped inside the shed and shut the door until only a thin line of sunshine showed along the edges. Taking off his hat, he laughed deep in his throat. "You sure know how to spend the money I make off of it. And believe me, there's a lot to spend."

"But this is . . . this is . . ."

"Illegal?"

"It's not only illegal, it's *wrong*!"

Louis laughed again, clearly enjoying himself. "Of course it's wrong. Why do you think it's illegal? Megan, you're so naive."

"And you're an idiot! How could you do this?" Megan began to get to her feet because she was tired of looking up at him and his arrogant smile. She felt hands on her shoulders, and then she was sitting on the dirt floor. "How dare you! I told you never to lay a hand on me again!"

Louis balled his hands into fists and placed them on his hips. He was no longer smiling. "Let me tell you how it's going to be from now on. You're my wife. You do as I say, or I'll divorce you. Now we both know that a divorce would separate you from your beloved upper ladies' circles in Chicago. You'd be an outcast."

"I don't care about that anymore!"

"Shut up, *dear*," he sneered. "I'm not through talking. Wait until your husband is through, and if I ask for your opinion, you can speak."

"This is insane!" Megan cried, beginning to rise again. She saw him swing from the corner of her eye and just managed to avert her head enough to catch the blow on the side of her head instead of her face.

"You will keep quiet!" Louis roared.

Megan's world had somehow turned into a nightmare. How had this happened? The side of her head throbbed as she gently massaged it. The thought of attacking him with her fists and fingernails crossed her mind, but she knew that despite his lithe build, he was still stronger than she. Frustration and anger coursed through her, and tears of humiliation gathered in her eyes. The dim light around the doorframe shone like prisms as she considered making a run for it.

"Don't even think about leaving until I've had my say," Louis growled.

Megan crossed her arms over her raised knees and rested her head on them. He could hit her again for not facing him, if he wanted to. She just didn't care anymore. She watched tears fall in a steady flow onto the skirt of her dress.

"Now, if you're thinking about reporting me to that oaf Stone, or anybody else, including your sweet little sister, just remember that I'll drag you down with me. I'll say we're partners in this enterprise, and that we're up here to expand our business. Trust me, they'll believe me."

Megan heard the rustle of clothing and felt him very close to her. It was all she could do to keep from scrambling away in revulsion.

"So you just have your little visit with Reena, and I'll take care of what I need to do. Then we'll go home and resume our happy little lives. Right, my dear?"

Megan lifted her head and hoped the contempt and loathing she was feeling showed through as she locked eyes with him.

Louis merely smiled. "You may speak now."

"What if you're caught by accident, or by doing something stupid? Would you drag me down with you then?"

"Of course! We're husband and wife. We share everything."

Megan's eyes narrowed. "What's happened to you, Louis? What happened to make you this way?"

Louis stood and corked the whiskey jug. Brushing off his hat, he answered, "Life, my dear. Just life." He went to the door, then turned and added, "I'm a good businessman—no, a superior businessman. It's too bad you don't recognize that sitting there in your fifty-dollar dress. Maybe someday you will."

The door creaked slightly as he left, and Megan blinked from the bright light. She considered the crates for a while. An iron-headed mallet stood amidst the saws, hammers, and nails by the wall. It would smash the jugs nicely.

Then she remembered his threat and knew there was no one to turn to for help. Louis would only beat her, or worse. His sudden freedom with his fists could escalate into something worse.

Megan shuddered and rocked back and forth, thinking.

But there were no options.

"Megan, I want you to meet Vic after supper," Reena said around a mouthful of buffalo steak. After almost no appetite for days, she'd awakened from her nap ravenous. Mrs. Howe, the boardinghouse cook, obviously knew her craft. The steak was tender and delicious.

"I'm a little tired tonight, Reena," Megan said. Her plate was virtually untouched. To make the motions of eating in order to put off any comment from her sister for as long as possible, she slowly cut up her steak into tiny pieces.

"Come on, you've got to meet him. He's a wonderful man—"

"I'm sure he *is* wonderful, but I'm tired, all right?"

Both Reena and Jenny stopped eating and looked at Megan in surprise. Reena took in the shifting of food on her sister's plate. It was something Megan had done since childhood when something was bothering her. If Reena or Liam hadn't been hungry as children, they simply sat and stared at everyone else and pouted. Megan would always try to make a show of eating, even if she wasn't. Then Reena noticed a smudge of dirt below Megan's left ear.

Jenny said, "You know, you two don't look *nothin'* alike from the front, but from the sides you look *just* alike. Amazin'."

Reena smiled at her briefly, then asked Megan, "What did you do this afternoon?"

"Nothing. I went for a walk."

"Did you pick flowers or something?"

"Why?" Megan asked defensively.

"Because you've got dirt on your neck."

Megan snatched up her napkin and scrubbed all over her neck. "I don't know, sort of dusty today, I guess."

"I didn't notice any dust when I was—"

"Reena! Just drop it, all right? I'm fine."

Lips tight, Reena resumed eating. Megan was so *closemouthed* about herself and always had been. She was stubborn, too. If Megan and Hunter had been thrown together in romance and marriage, it would either have been the worst relationship imaginable, or the best in history, considering how much they were alike.

The thought of Hunter caused Reena to say another quick prayer for him. Vic had told her that most of the men received the easiest and safest duties, while Hunter always got the demanding, difficult, and dangerous ones. "It's only because he is what he is, Reena," Vic had said. "The best we have."

Reena had grinned and shot back, "Yes, and I see who's always with him on those patrols—you, Vic."

"Played with some kids today," Jenny informed them, breaking into Reena's thoughts. Jenny looked down quickly, as if actually starting a conversation was the last thing she wanted to do.

"Oh, really?" Reena asked. "Who were they?" From what Reena had learned, Jenny probably hadn't had much dinner conversation in her life.

"Well, I didn't really *play* with 'em. They just showed me their hiding place and showed me how *they* play." She told Reena their names and suddenly realized that she didn't know their last names.

"Kids," Megan said in disgust. "They should be seen and not heard. And I'm not so sure about the seeing part."

"Megan!" Reena exclaimed. "That's horrible!"

Megan just shrugged.

"Why don't you like kids?" Jenny asked.

"They just seem to be loud and . . . and boisterous—"

"What's that mean?"

"Boisterous? It means rowdy or stormy. That's a good word for kids—*stormy*. They're like a tornado moving through the room."

"Maybe you just ain't been around 'em much. I hadn't been around any till today, and I had a great time with them."

"Good for you, Jenny. I mean that."

Mrs. Howe sailed into the dining room through the swinging door that led to the kitchen. "Save room for blueberry pie, ladies!" She set a bowl of lemon water down in case they needed to wash the fresh honey that came with the bread from their fingers. Slightly plump, her salt-and-pepper hair was cut short. She had a wide nose and very bad teeth.

"None for me, Mrs. Howe," Megan told her.

Mrs. Howe put her hands on her generous hips and stared at Megan's plate accusingly. "Well, you won't *get* any pie until you've eaten something off your plate! What's the matter with you, child?"

"Nothing. It's all very good. I'm just not hungry tonight."

Mrs. Howe's dark eyes went to Reena and Jenny. Then she performed the habit that disgusted Reena: she sucked her teeth. She apparently was unable to say two sentences without it. "You two aren't having any troubles by the looks of those swiped-clean plates. You want me to divide Mrs. Goldsen's pie between you?"

Reena smiled at Jenny and answered, "I think we've had enough, thank you."

On her way back through the swinging door Mrs. Howe muttered, "I should say so!"

Jenny leaned toward them and said in a whisper, "Mighty pudgy lady to be talkin' about what *we're* eating."

From the kitchen came the musical call, "I'm much slimmer than I used to be!"

They looked at each other in shock, then burst out laughing.

"How'd she hear that?" Jenny asked in embarrassment.

After Reena and Jenny had their pie and groaned with pleasure from their full stomachs, Mrs. Howe brought Reena Vic's supper plate. "You tell that handsome Englishman he'd better watch out. It's been three years since my Edgar's passed on, and I'm about through with my mourning."

"I'll tell him, Mrs. Howe."

"Seems like every day there's more women moving in, and I don't like competition."

"Well, there *are* about one hundred forty other men in that fort," Reena said lightly.

"Yes, but I want that one. I just *love* to hear that man talk. I could sit around all day and night and listen to him read poetry to me. *Love* poetry, mind you." Mrs. Howe giggled like a little girl.

Vickersham looked up when the door opened and saw a woman with Reena. She took his breath away. She was, quite frankly, the most beautiful woman he'd ever seen.

"Hi, Vic," Reena said. "We're not bothering you, are we?"

"No, no. Please come in." He watched the woman, unable to tear his eyes away from her. For some reason, which he couldn't begin to understand, he'd always been attracted to blondes. Something about the way the sunshine leaped from their hair. He was hypnotized.

"This is my sister, Megan."

"Hello," Megan smiled.

Even her voice was beautiful—husky yet melodious. Vic wanted to hear her say more.

Vickersham was propped up on three pillows, wearing a blue nightshirt and covered with blankets. He stifled the urge to draw the covers to his chin. "This is quite a surprise to have *two* lovely ladies in my room. How will this look?"

Reena looked at Megan accusingly. "There would have been just me. I had to drag my sister here."

"You didn't want to meet me, Mrs. Goldsen?"

"It's Megan," she said, glaring at Reena, "and I'm delighted to meet you. I've just had a long day, but I thought it was time we met."

"Please sit down. Do we have enough chairs, Reena?"

"I'll go get another one down the hall."

Megan sat in the Victorian walnut armchair by the window. "How are you feeling today?"

"Better, thank you. I can't wait to get out of bed, though."

"It must be hard."

"Is your husband accomplishing what he came up here for? Reena told me about his business interests." He was sorry he asked, because her face fell and she quickly looked out the window.

Megan sighed and gave a small chuckle that was totally humorless. "Oh, he's accomplishing things all right."

Vickersham knew better than to ask what that meant, and then Reena was back with another chair. "Reena, is Del back yet?"

"Not yet. If he were, he'd be right here, I'm sure."

"Who's Del?" Megan asked.

Vickersham told her about him. Megan nodded and smiled in all the right places while he talked, but he had the idea that she wasn't really listening to him. He wanted very badly to ask her to confide in him, for she looked completely lost, distressed, and sad. Reena, too, was watching her very closely, no doubt aware of the same vibrations that Vic was receiving.

They talked for an hour. It was the most enjoyable hour Vic had experienced since his wound. Despite Megan's distracted air, she was polite, funny, and intelligent. A few times he caught her looking at him as Reena spoke, then she would glance away quickly. He didn't know what the looks meant and didn't care. It was enough just to be noticed by such a lovely woman.

When she said good-night, she shook his hand and smiled. He enjoyed the memory of her for a while after they'd gone, but gradually he became haunted by it. She was a married woman, and he had no business thinking as he was.

It took Vic a long time to fall asleep that night.

CHAPTER FIFTEEN

Turquoise Joy

Three days after Megan discovered Louis's illegal dealings, Armand Sweet sat listening to his jailers. His cell was tiny and contained only a small bunk and a discarded washstand stripped of its drawers. Until two days ago he'd been able to play checkers with Boggs in the next cell by placing the board between them and reaching through the bars to move the tiles.

Now Boggs was gone, and Sweet was left alone with his thoughts, his extreme boredom, and his jailers. One of them was named Huson, the man who'd lent Sweet the checker set, and the other was Fuller. They were out of Sweet's sight by the front door, but he could hear them clearly.

"There is no way," Huson said in a lofty tone, "that I'm on guard duty Monday night. No way on this earth. That's the night of the Police ball. Every female within fifty miles will be here wanting to talk to a Mountie."

"Look at the assignments, Huson!" Fuller said with obvious mirth. "Whose name is that right there?"

"It's a mistake."

"That ain't no mistake, you moron! Macleod just handed it to me."

"That's *Colonel* Macleod to you," Huson told him petulantly.

Fuller started laughing, and Sweet heard a slapping sound that

must have been Fuller pounding on his thigh with glee. Sweet began to smile himself.

"Hey, wait a minute!" Huson shouted over the gales of laughter. "I believe you owe me some money, Fuller."

The guffaws ceased at once. "Uh-uh. Forget about it!"

"Yeah, I seem to remember you borrowing five dollars against
payday, and payday was four days ago. Have I been repaid? No, I
don't think I have—"

"I had to give almost all my money to pay my tab at Baker's!
You know that, Huson."

Huson's voice suddenly developed an edge. "I'm calling in my
marker—now."

"I don't have it! I just told you—"

"So you're not going to pay me in cash? I'll have repayment in
another way."

"Never!" Fuller shouted. "*You've* got guard duty, not me! It
says so right there on those orders from *Colonel* Macleod."

Sweet was struck by an idea so crystal clear he bolted upright
on his bunk. The thought of escaping had entered his mind many
times, but only as musings; he'd never seen any sort of chance to
make a break for it until now.

"You listen to me—" Huson began.

"Sub-Constable Fuller!" Sweet shouted.

"What do you want, whiskey man?"

"A word with you, if you have the time."

"I'm busy."

"Believe me, sir, it'll be worth your time." Sweet listened hard
as he went to the bars of his cell. He heard a deep sigh, something
slam on the desk, and then booted feet coming toward him.

Fuller appeared—all five foot six of him—and asked, "What do
you want?" His baby face showed anger and sulkiness over Huson's
upper hand.

"Mr. Fuller, how would you like to borrow five dollars?"

"From you?"

"Yes."

"Where'd you get five dollars?"

"Do you want it or not?" Sweet asked curtly. The boy was beyond stupid, and Sweet had no patience with stupid people.

Fuller's face revealed a sudden dawning, and he said eagerly, "Yeah, I want it!"

"Shhh. Hold it down. I don't want Huson to find out about this, or he'll be all over me." Sweet reached into his pants pocket and brought out some bills.

"Where'd you get all—?"

"Never mind! And keep your voice down! I want you to *casually* glance over and see if Huson's watching you."

Fuller did so and said, "No."

"Here." Sweet shoved the five dollar bill into his hands and said, "Now listen to me very carefully. I want you to put Huson off for a while, leave, then come back and give him the money. That way he'll think you borrowed it off of someone else, and you get to go to the ball."

It took a few moments for Fuller to digest this complicated information. Finally he smiled and said, "Hey, thanks, Sweet!" He turned to go, then stopped abruptly. "Say, why you doin' this? I thought you liked Huson."

"I do. But I like you better, Fuller. Huson can be a pain sometimes. You just found out how big a pain he can be, huh?"

Fuller's face split into a grin. "Yeah, I did. Thanks again."

Sweet stretched himself out on his bunk again. He didn't hear the rest of the conversation between the Mounties. He didn't even curse as his feet hung off the end of the bunk as he'd done every day since his incarceration. He just lay there and smiled.

"Jenny, where are you going?" Reena called from the parlor of the boardinghouse. She and Megan were sitting on a sofa drinking tea.

"Um . . . out to " Jenny mumbled, confused. She'd thought no one but Mrs. Howe would be up so early in the morning. She was dressed in Levi's, a simple cotton shirt, and boots.

"You're going to see the kids?" Reena smiled.

"No, I was just going for a walk," Jenny answered, her eyes shifting away.

Reena knew that her walks always ended up with the children. Jenny was slowly healing from her bruises, both inside and out apparently, by spending time with the kids. Her color was better, and though she was still extremely shy around any adults, she was conversing with Reena and Megan more and more. Her conversation was limited to talking about the children, but at least she was talking.

Megan stood and replaced her teacup on the saucer. "Not today, Jenny. We're going to find you a dress for the ball."

"Uh-uh, I'm not going." Jenny actually took a step back toward the door as if ready to bolt.

"Please?"

"I . . . I don't know how to dance. I don't know how to be proper like you folks. I don't know how to *stand* when I'm—"

Reena saw pure panic, went to Jenny at once, and said soothingly, "Wait, Jenny, it's all right. No one's going to *make* you go. We just thought it would be nice for all three of us to dress up and do something different. There won't be another party for months, maybe a year."

Jenny watched her warily, glancing at the door a few times. Reena looked at Megan for help.

"Listen, Jenny," Megan said, "I want some company at the ball. I don't want to just stand around and be uncomfortable."

"You don't get uncomfortable, do you?" Jenny asked in surprise. "You're a real lady. I'll bet you've been to a hundred balls."

Megan smiled. "I've been to a few, yes. But I don't know anyone else here except you and Reena. I'll feel alone if you don't come with us."

Jenny relaxed a bit, but then squinted her eyes at them. "Wait a minute, you've got each other. You don't need me."

Megan laughed and said, "It's not a matter of *need*, Jenny. It's that we *want* you to go with us. You know, just us girls having a night out on the big town."

"Ain't your husband gonna be there?"

Megan seemed at a loss for words for a moment, then she said, "Louis is a busy man. He hasn't said whether he's going or not. But even if he goes, he doesn't like dancing that much. He'll probably just stand by the punch bowl with the men."

Reena didn't comment on the lie her sister had told; unless things had changed dramatically, Louis *loved* dancing. Reena was dying to ask Megan what was going on, but whenever she began probing about it, Megan looked so hurt and ashamed that Reena always let it drop. She asked Jenny, "So, will you come with us?"

Jenny bit her lip as she thought about it. "You won't leave me alone? Even for a minute?"

Reena remembered the dance she'd promised Colonel Macleod and the hope of one with Hunter. Before she could begin structuring an answer, Megan beat her to it.

"I'll stay with you as long as you want."

Wringing her hands briefly, Jenny said reluctantly, "Well . . . all right, I'll go." Then, very shyly, she asked, "Will Dirk Becker be there?"

"Of course he will," Reena told her with a small smile. "And you probably won't have to go looking for him. He'll be watching for you."

"Do you think so?"

"Oh yes."

The blush left Jenny's face as she grinned.

"So we're all set, then?" Megan asked. Without waiting for an answer, she passed by Jenny on her way out of the room. "Let me get my coat and we'll go."

"Go where?" Jenny asked.

"To I.G. Baker's and see if Mr. Davis has anything decent in stock for you to wear."

"But what if he doesn't? Does that mean I don't have to go?"

Megan stopped before she reached the stairs and turned to Jenny, her face softened and a little disappointed. "Jenny, dear, you don't *have* to go. We want you to think of it as something to look forward to, not to dread!"

"I'll look forward to it." Jenny nodded. She swallowed, and Reena thought she looked as if a judge had just pronounced a prison sentence on her.

The day was cold and blustery. Reena shivered in the deep-blue fur-lined cloak she'd borrowed from Megan and pulled it tighter around her. Megan, too, was uncomfortable in her gray wool coat as they neared Baker's store.

"Doesn't it ever get warm here?" Megan asked in irritation. "It's almost April and it's still freezing!"

"Be warm tomorrow," Jenny announced.

"How do you know?"

"Chinook comin'."

"What's that?"

"It's a warm wind that blows in over the mountains and warms things up a lot. See it over there?"

Megan followed Jenny's finger and saw what seemed to be a line of thick white clouds hovering over the mountains. The sky was otherwise empty.

"It'll blow in tonight, and tomorrow will be so warm you won't even *wear* a coat."

Megan looked at Reena. "Is she serious?"

"Every word's the truth. You've never seen or experienced anything like it."

Just before they reached the store, Jenny suddenly yelled, "Hey!" and began waving to a group of children crossing the street. They waved back but seemed unsure. "Come here! We're goin' shopping!"

The kids looked at one another uncertainly, except for a little girl holding a doll. Reena thought she was adorable, even though she was dressed in tattered clothes. She looked like a street urchin straight out of Dickens. Reena suddenly realized that the children probably would have run to Jenny if she and Megan weren't with her.

"Why aren't they in school?" Megan asked Jenny.

"There ain't a school to go to. Their mammas teach them some, but—" Jenny waved again. "Come on. What's the matter with you?"

The children bolted behind the livery stable, except for the little girl. She continued watching Jenny, appearing tempted to join her.

"What an adorable little girl!" Megan breathed.

Reena recalled Megan's comment about children a few days earlier and said teasingly, "Well, you've seen her now. Surely you don't want to hear her, too."

"I was just . . . having a bad night when I said that, Reena. I've never been around children much. In fact, hardly at all."

"Me neither," Jenny said, "and I didn't know what I was missing. They're fun, and they say the funniest things. But they're funny in a strange kind of way, you know?" She paused and motioned to the girl again. "It's like they see the world different than us."

"What's her name?"

"Lydia." Jenny raised her voice and called, "Lydia! Come into the store with us!"

Lydia glanced around to the other children, who were peeking around the corner of the stable. Then she smiled at them, waved, and started toward the women. A hissing sound came from the livery, and Reena saw the oldest boy gesture frantically for Lydia to join them. Lydia ignored him.

"What's that on her face?" Megan asked.

"A birthmark."

"No, I see that. What's on her cheek?"

"Prob'ly dirt," Jenny answered nonchalantly. "She misses a spot every now and then if they can catch her."

"Catch her?"

"She hates baths. But don't worry, she don't stink."

"Good heavens!" Megan uttered, then she squatted down and held out her arms. "Come here, Lydia. My name's Megan."

Lydia regarded her shyly and cautiously, but edged toward Jenny. She gripped the one-armed doll tightly. When she saw Megan take out a lace handkerchief and lick it, she *ran* to Jenny with a horrified expression.

"I'm just going to wipe your face, darling!"

Jenny told the girl, "Let her clean your face. It's dirty, and that's not good for a proper young lady like you." Lydia shook her head against Jenny's legs. "Go on. She's a nice lady."

Lydia reluctantly released Jenny's legs and obediently went to Megan, who said softly, "That's a good girl. You don't like being dirty, do you?"

Lydia shook her head and grimaced as the kerchief scrubbed lightly at the smudge.

"If you don't like being dirty, why don't you like taking baths?"

"Get cold. Don't like being cold."

"Isn't there a stove in your bathroom?"

Lydia shook her head. When she felt that enough cleaning had been done, she went back to Jenny. She didn't clutch desperately at her, though; instead, she regarded both Megan and Reena with large blue eyes.

"Would you like to go in the store with us and look at dresses?" Reena asked. "Maybe we can find one for you."

Lydia shook her head uncertainly and glanced at Jenny, who said, "Her pa would have a fit. He's a proud man."

Reena asked, "What does your father do, Lydia?"

"'Bout what?"

"I mean, what does he do for a living?"

"He's a farmer, but our crops got blowed away the end of last summer by a tornado. So'd our barn."

"What did he do for money?"

"Went trappin' all winter, but he don't know how to trap."

Reena smiled her best smile at the girl and offered, "Why don't you come with us? Maybe you'll see something you want that your pa won't mind us getting you." She saw Jenny react at the edge of her vision, but Reena held out her hand, and Lydia hesitantly took it.

Over Lydia's head, Megan whispered, "That's horrible! We've got to do something."

Reena just winked at her.

The I.G. Baker Store was large but still crowded with merchandise. The rows of shelves and tables were stuffed to overflowing with every item imaginable. Farming implements lined the walls, hanging from nails and hooks. On the tables were hats, every article of men's clothing, what looked to Reena to be a mile of barbed wire snarled together, saddles, harnesses, and hardware items. The shelves bore groceries, household needs, and odds and ends from baskets to weather vanes. Reena saw a gleaming brass microscope with a sign that informed her: "A Henry Crouch microscope—all the way from England! $9 or let's trade something!"

The proprietor, Donald Watson Davis, was an American born in Vermont. He'd been a quartermaster in the U.S. Army during the war. It was there that he learned what people wanted and needed and how to get it. His face was kind but reserved, from what Reena could see. A black beard totally covered the lower half of his face, so all that was visible was a lower lip. His head was perfectly round, but he was of average build and height.

"Morning, ladies," he greeted, with no trace of an Eastern accent. His voice was curiously flat and disinterested, as if he'd just walked up to them and said, "Ecclesiastes."

Megan asked, "You have ladies' dresses, Mr. Davis?"

He nodded. "This way."

They followed him toward the back of the store, and Reena watched Lydia to see what interested her. With large eyes she surveyed the myriad of goods, but nothing seemed to catch her attention enough to make her stop and inspect it. Either that, or she was too frightened to touch things.

Lydia did pause at a black fan with circus scenes on it but very briefly. It wasn't until she saw the cradle that she came to a dead halt. Hearts decorated the wood, and it swung freely on an arch-shaped base. A bright amber blanket rested invitingly inside. Reena felt Megan beside her, and they exchanged glances.

"What's that say?" Lydia asked Jenny, pointing to a sign below the cradle.

Jenny stared at the sign for a long moment.

"Jenny? What's it say?"

"It says . . . ." Her voice trailed off, and she turned to Megan and Reena helplessly. Her face colored just as Reena realized why Jenny was momentarily at a loss for words. Megan, however, recovered quickly.

"It says, 'Chestnut and Cherrywood, Just Waiting for Your Baby!' Do you like that, Lydia?"

"It's the most prettiest thing I ever saw!" Lydia breathed. Then, as if dismissing the cradle entirely, she turned her back on it. "Ain't you gonna look at the dresses?"

Reena understood that she hadn't forgotten the cradle. She just knew it was something to be admired, then left alone. It was out of her reach, and she would never own it, so why torture herself? The same thing would apply if Reena were shown a room filled with gold dust. The sparkle and shine and wealth would be impressive but unattainable in real life. The thought that the little girl couldn't even *dream* saddened Reena.

D.W. Davis stood patiently by, and when Reena nodded to him, he gestured and said, "This way, please."

Reena took Megan's elbow and felt her tense. "Wait a minute, Reena. She *wants* that cradle—"

Through tight lips Reena whispered, "*Go*, Megan. Not now."

"But—"

Reena gripped her sister's arm harder and practically pushed her after Davis.

Around a corner, unseen from the interior of the store, was the ladies' shop. Two racks of dresses in the center of the small room were surrounded by tables holding neat rows of hats, gloves, undergarments, and accessories. Davis had much more than Reena had imagined he would.

"This is it?" Megan blurted.

Reena flashed a smile at Davis before saying, "Megan, this isn't Chicago. We're in the middle of Indian country, remember?"

Davis cleared his throat. He plainly thought that he had an impressive stock for a shop in the middle of nowhere, and his feelings were hurt. Reena didn't blame him. "I'm going to try to keep up with modern style. These were purchased last winter, and I don't have the capital to reorder, especially since I've sold barely four dresses since I've opened."

"I understand, Mr. Davis," Megan said smoothly and in an apologetic tone. "May we look around?"

"Of course." Davis withdrew to the other part of his store, still slightly miffed.

Megan began inspecting dresses with alarming quickness and expertise. Every once in a while she grunted, and once she uttered, "Oh, my," in surprise with a trace of disgust. Before Reena knew it, Megan had breezed through one whole rack. "Let's hope the other rack is more promising," she muttered to no one in particular.

Reena moved to Jenny and Lydia, who were at the undergarments table. Jenny slowly lifted a black corset that was the longest one that Reena had ever seen.

"What's that do?" Lydia asked.

Jenny turned to Reena and gazed in amazement at her torso. "You really wear this?"

Reena felt herself blushing. "No, I . . . well, not right now . . . I *have* before—"

"Why?"

"To . . . um . . . accent the figure, Jenny. You know . . ."

Jenny shook her head and examined the corset with a curled lip. "No, I *don't* know. If I put one of these on, I'd feel like a wagon-harnessed heifer."

Reena laughed and said, "That may be true, but a heifer would probably be more comfortable in its harnessing than you would be in that."

"Am I gonna have to wear—?"

"I'm afraid so."

Jenny swallowed and decided she wanted a second opinion. To Megan she called, "Do I really have to wear one of these tomorrow night?"

Megan's eyes lit up when she saw the corset. "Of course, Jenny! That's probably the most fashionable item in here. See how long it is, Reena? England has decided that we need to have long slender figures this year." She looked down at her own full figure and sighed. "That's going to be quite an undertaking."

Jenny inspected Reena critically, making her blush all the more. "You mean me and Megan gotta wear one, and you don't?"

"No, I'm afraid I will too, Jenny."

"But you're already long and slender."

Reena shrugged and said, "I know. It's not fair, is it?"

Megan strode over to them holding a turquoise dress. "This is nearly hopeless, girls. Flowers, flowers, flowers all over these ball dresses! That was 1873—two years ago!"

Reena covered a smile. To Megan, two years in fashion might just as well have been twenty.

"Anyway, this is the only dress that I think I can—"

"It's beautiful!" Jenny exclaimed, throwing down the corset. She reverently ran her fingers over the silk dress.

"This is just an evening dress, Jenny, but we can—"

"I don't care what it is."

"Megan," Reena said, "it doesn't *have* to be a ball dress."

"All right, all right," Megan said impatiently "Now let me show you, Jenny. We'll have to bring the hem up, but don't worry, I have to have that done all the time. The color will bring out your eyes, and the bodice high behind and square in front is perfect for you I'll have to do some minor alterations to bring out the slim look and replace those silly flowers on the shoulders—"

"I *like* the flowers." Jenny took the dress out of Megan's hands and held it up to herself. To Reena and Lydia she asked shyly, "How do you think I'll look?"

"You'll be the prettiest lady there!" Lydia sang out.

"She's right, Jenny. I don't know if I want to be around you after all."

"What do you mean?" Jenny asked with panic in her voice.

"It's humor, Jenny. I meant that you'll be much more beautiful than I, so—"

Jenny made a scoffing noise, but Reena could tell she was pleased. She couldn't take her eyes from the dress. Suddenly she said, "I'll work for it, Megan. I'll pay you back every cent. How much is it?"

Megan shot Reena a quick, nervous look, but told Jenny, "This is my treat. I don't want to hear any more about it."

Jenny shook her head in wonder and hugged the dress to herself. Reena had never seen so much life and joy in her face before.

"It's *real* pretty," Lydia repeated.

Jenny moved behind the little girl and held the dress up to her chin. Reena heard Jenny whisper, "I'm gonna give it to you when you grow up, Lydia. Just remember that."

Lydia's face beamed.

CHAPTER SIXTEEN

The Pioneers of a Glorious Future

Stone just made it back on the day of the ball. The three deserters had been easy to track, but they'd made better time than he'd expected of them. Once his patrol caught up with them, they were half-frozen, very hungry, and only too happy to surrender. They made a pitiful effort to explain their absence away with the hunting passes, but when Stone offered them something to eat in exchange for the truth, they dropped their lies at once.

When they got back to the fort and Stone had turned the men over to Macleod, he found Del eating with a group of Mounties. The day was warm from the Chinook and getting warmer. Most of the men who weren't setting up for the ball in the courtyard were lounging around throwing catcalls at those who were working.

"Hey, Hunter!" Del shouted when he saw him. "How 'bout this weather, huh? Just perfect for a dance, don't you think?"

"It's nice, all right." Stone nodded to the other men and accepted a plate of fried prairie chicken and corn. Sitting beside Del, he said, "Looking forward to it, are you?"

"You bet! Ain't you?"

"I'm too tired to find the energy to anticipate."

"You sound like Vic with them big words."

Stone took a bite of chicken and moaned with pleasure. "You seen him yet? When did you get back?"

"Yesterday. And yeah I seen him. Even laid up, he's still a smart aleck." Del's eyes danced with glee. "Told me I'd have to do-si-do with all the gals for him in his absence. Don't that beat all?"

"Isn't there any way he can come?"

"Nah, still too weak." He looked at Stone and told him, "You'd better get cleaned up. It's only a couple hours away."

"I think I'll take a quick nap first." To his surprise, Stone found that he'd wolfed down most of the meal quickly without even realizing it. Around a mouthful of corn, he asked Del, "When are you going to get ready?"

Del looked down at his dark blue trousers, which had a hole in the knee, and his lavender shirt which sported a few stains of some sort. "I *am* ready!"

"Del, you have to wear something nice."

"What's wrong with this?"

"It's not nice."

"Now, come on, Hunter. Even if I did get all dandied up, what gal would want to dance with me, anyway?"

"I'm sure you'd find some takers, Del."

"Bah! You can fool yourself, but don't try foolin' me." He stood and stretched. "But just on the *off* chance that you may know what you're talkin' about, I'll put on my best duds. You comin'?"

"No, I'll sit here a minute."

"Suit yourself."

Stone ate another piece of chicken while considering the decorations for the ball. If weather hadn't permitted, the ball would have been held in D.W. Davis's huge barn. Now the plan was for the fort to host it, as Macleod had hoped. Inside every enlisted man's quarters there was much activity also, because the settlers who attended would be sleeping in the Mounties' cabins. The Mounties would be bunking outside in the courtyard. For once, the men didn't complain as they secured their quarters; their mood was too high and expectant.

All across the courtyard between the walls of the fort, ropes had been strung on which to hang lanterns. The yard would be well lit during the celebration. On the inside of the front gate was a huge hand-painted banner proclaiming, "THE PIONEERS OF A GLORIOUS FUTURE." Stone smiled to himself. It was an optimistic and, hopefully, prophetic motto.

Scarlet and white streamers draped from the ropes and over

every door in sight. In the middle of the yard a huge bonfire was being prepared, and Stone thought the heat from the logs, if they all were lit at once, would drive everyone out of the area. The cook fire by the mess room had doubtless burned nonstop all day, preparing the menu of buffalo hindquarters and tongues, haunches of venison, saddles of antelope, prairie chickens, wild geese, cakes, plum puddings, and mince pies. Stone wondered if Macleod, in his unfailing optimism, had overestimated the numbers that would attend. If he had, the Mounties would be eating leftovers for days to come.

Satisfied that everything would proceed safely without him, Stone rose and made his way to the officers' quarters. His two-day-old beard itched and chafed, but he didn't trust himself with a razor until he'd had a little sleep.

With a heavy sigh, not bothering to remove any clothing except his scarlet jacket and boots, he climbed into his bed. Despite the shouts and racket and laughter all around the fort, he was asleep in less than two minutes.

———

The western sky, painted orange and deep red, cast a glow over the fort that was almost surreal. Stone, Del, Becker, and Macleod sat with several other men outside the officers' quarters and watched the arrival of settlers and a few curious Indians. Stone had slept for the full two hours until the appointed time for the ball to begin. Del had rousted him out of his bunk, and he'd hurriedly taken a bath and shaved, afraid he'd miss Reena's arrival. As it turned out, he needn't have bothered.

"Fashionably late," he muttered to himself as he watched a man dance a jig to a lone young violinist. The boy was probably his son since the man's steps unfailingly tapped in time to the complicated tune.

"What was that, Stone?" Macleod asked. His hair was oiled, and he was resplendent in his dress uniform that included his saber. All the officers wore their sabers.

"Oh, nothing, sir. Just thinking out loud."

"That can get a man in trouble, Stone. I'm surprised you do it."

"Only when I'm waiting for a lady, sir."

"Then I suppose you do it quite often, if my experience with females matches yours." Macleod dug inside his tunic and produced a cigar. With relish and taking his time, he smelled the length of it, thumbnailed a match to life, and lit it. "I'll certainly be glad when my wife joins us here."

"When will that be, sir?"

"Another year at least. But I plan to make a trip to Ottawa before then. Police business, you know," he winked.

"Of course."

Dirk Becker, facing the front gate while Stone, Del, and Macleod watched the courtyard, suddenly leaped to his feet. His face registered total astonishment. Stone followed his gaze and got to his feet, too.

Reena, Megan, and a woman he didn't recognize stepped gracefully out of a carriage. Where the carriage had come from, Stone didn't know and didn't care at the moment. Reena was absolutely stunning in a bottle-green, off-the-shoulder dress. He'd never seen her shoulders before, and the orange glow from the sunset made them look incredibly soft and alluring. Her dark hair was up, with loops and curls hanging in an elaborate and baffling manner that only added to her beauty. He couldn't speak, but Becker had found his voice, though it was hoarse.

"Is that . . . Jenny Sweet?"

Stone looked again at the third woman and was surprised to find that it was Jenny. Her turquoise dress stood out brilliantly in the drab courtyard, and she wore a peach-colored hat with white lace. Megan's dress was a deep blue, and the epaulettes on the shoulders were trimmed with bronze-colored bows. The wide sash, too, was bronze.

Stone became aware of the absence of noise. Every man had stopped what he was doing and now stared at the beautiful newcomers.

"Isn't that a sight, now, lads?" Macleod breathed. By the sound of his voice, even he was hypnotized. "Where's an army I can defeat for them?"

Del intruded on their thoughts by asking, "Where'd that dandy get the carriage and that nice team of sorrels?"

"Who cares about the carriage, Dekko?" Macleod growled.

"Don't you have eyes in your head? Can't you see those gorgeous women?"

"Oh yeah."

"They're coming over," Becker announced in awe.

It was only then that Stone saw Louis behind them. He ruined the scene like a roach at dinner. The girl that he'd thought was unfamiliar was indeed Jenny Sweet, and if Becker hadn't suggested it, Stone doubted he would have recognized her until she was right in front of him. The change was remarkable.

Every eye in the courtyard followed the group's progress toward Stone and the others. Every eye was undoubtedly filled with envy for them, too.

Reena spoke first. "Are you gentlemen all right? You look as though you're facing a firing squad."

Macleod swept his helmet off and said grandly, "If a firing squad were to take my life right now, I'd die a happy man after seeing the loveliness you ladies have brought to us."

"Oh, my," Megan exclaimed, with a hand to her heart. "Reena, shall we send them on a quest?"

"Stop it, Megan." Her eyes came to Stone, who felt a thrill when he saw her smile.

Megan turned to Jenny. "Jenny, do you have a quest for one of these gallant knights?"

Jenny looked at Megan strangely. "What are you talking about?" The group laughed, and Jenny blushed, thinking they were laughing at her.

Stone noticed a few beads of moisture on her forehead, and she appeared ready to bolt at any moment.

Becker stepped forward and offered her his arm. Then, strangely, he withdrew it as if he were offending her. "May I show you around, Miss Sweet?"

Jenny looked at Reena, who gave a small nod. Not meeting Becker's eyes, she muttered, "All right."

Louis stepped up to Macleod. "Colonel, my name is Louis Goldsen. I'm very happy to finally meet you."

Stone felt his lip curling in pure disgust, and he moved around the colonel to Reena and Megan. "That was quite an entrance, ladies. And the late timing is so stylish."

"Are we late?" Megan asked innocently.

"Really, Hunter, we're late because of something else," Reena told him. "A surprise."

"For who?"

"For everyone."

Megan turned to look behind them and said, "Here it comes."

Through the gate rolled a horseless wagon being pulled by five Mounties. There was much commotion in the bed of the wagon, with men gathering around excitedly.

"What is it?" Stone asked.

Reena took his arm. "Come and see. And it's not a 'what,' it's a 'who.' "

Stone was more conscious of the feel of her bare shoulder against his sleeve than of anything else. At the moment, he couldn't care less who was in the wagon. The soft skin so close to him held all of his attention.

" . . . tonight," Megan was saying to him.

"I'm sorry. What?"

"I was saying that you fellows are so handsome tonight, I just want to bundle all of you up and take you back to Chicago."

The Mounties swung the wagon around so that the rear was toward the yard. In the back, propped up against the side on many pillows, was Jaye Eliot Vickersham. He looked better to Stone, but he was still obviously weak.

"Vic!"

"Hunter! And on the arms of the two prettiest women here! Why does this not surprise me?"

Stone shook his hand and placed his other over Vic's. "It's good to see you, friend."

"I wasn't planning to come, but the women simply wouldn't let me be. They had some hairy, burly men force me into this glorious transportation."

"I'm glad they did." Stone saw Vic's face brighten from a reflection, and they all turned to see the bonfire burst into flame. Thankfully, Stone noticed that it had been relieved of half of the logs he'd seen earlier. Now he wouldn't have to worry about them all cooking to death. Guests were lining up by the cook fire to be served dinner. He thought of something and turned to Reena and Megan. "I was wondering how you managed to create Cinderella over there." He nodded to Jenny and Becker in line for food.

"It wasn't easy," Reena said. "She's stubborn and didn't think she belonged here."

"Becker seems glad she came."

"I think he's sweet on her."

Stone looked at Reena. "And Jenny?"

"Jenny's not in any condition to have a man in her life right now. She's very distrustful of everyone, especially men."

"Like me," Megan said, then seemed sorry she'd spoken. Suddenly she smiled. "I'm going to drag Louis out of the colonel's face. He can be such a bore sometimes."

When she'd gone, Vickersham asked Reena, "What was that all about?"

Reena shook her head uncertainly. "I don't think everything's right in the Goldsen household."

"Oh, really?" Vic saw them look at him, and he amended quickly, "I mean . . . that's very troubling."

"Hey, Vic!" Del Dekko strode up to them. Stone was glad to see that he'd found some suitable trousers with no holes and a shirt with no visible stains.

"Hello, Del, how are you?" Vic greeted.

"Aw, better than I deserve. I knew you'd show up here somehow. You gonna dance all the ladies into the ground?"

"Look at me, Del. What do you think?"

Del cackled with a dry throat and slapped Vic on the shoulder without thinking. Vic grunted and his face twisted. "I tell ya, Reena—"

"Del, you hurt him!"

"Oh, he ain't hurt. Like I was sayin', you better keep the women away from him anyways, or he might *talk* 'em into the ground!" Del laughed some more, took out a handkerchief that to Stone's relief looked clean, and honked into it. "Tell you what, Vic ol' buddy, I'll go over there and get you some chow. You look like you need to eat."

"Thanks, Del, but I just had something a little while—"

Del was already walking away. "Back before you know it!"

Vic rolled his eyes to the sky. "Some things never change."

———

"Crown me," Sweet told Huson.

Huson placed a checker on the one Sweet had managed to get to Huson's side. "I swear, Sweet, I don't know how you get them over here so fast." Huson was in a terrible mood. He could hear the violins and harmonicas and people laughing outside.

"You're just distracted tonight, Huson."

"You can say that again."

Sweet glanced at the door for what seemed like the thousandth time in the last thirty minutes. The celebration had been going on for almost two hours now, and Fuller was due to bring Huson something to eat anytime. That is, if he followed through on his word and didn't get too distracted by some farm girl.

Huson jumped one of Sweet's checkers and said, "This is ridiculous! I mean, it's not like you're just going to escape and waltz right outside with two hundred people around!"

Sweet had heard him say this at least three times, and he was sick of it. But he had to smile and nod sympathetically for now.

"That Macleod's still mad at me for finding that little tiny bottle of whiskey under my cot. It's not like I'm the only one who has a drink now and then! In fact, I don't know a man out there who doesn't! I just got caught." Huson watched Sweet double jump and suddenly laughed. "I suppose you know exactly what I'm talking about, don't you, Sweet? Getting caught when everyone else is doing the same thing?"

Sweet wanted to reach through the bars and slap the silly smile off his face. Instead he grinned and agreed. "Yep. We're two birds of a feather, all right."

Huson moved a piece and said, "Crown me." He stood, and Sweet heard the satisfying, lovely sound of keys jangling in the Mountie's pocket. Stretching and yawning, Huson looked to the door wistfully. "I just might have to go see about Fuller. Fool probably forgot about me."

"Let's finish this game first. Crown me."

"Again?" Huson sat down again at the small table and chair he'd moved to Sweet's cell. He crowned the piece and surveyed the board. "You've got three kings, and I don't have any. I think I see the writing on the wall."

Oh no, you don't, Sweet thought with glee. *If you did, you'd bolt right out of here.* He glanced at the door again and lost his fleeting good mood. What Huson said next made his heart leap in his chest.

"I'm tired of being here, and I'm tired of losing to you, Sweet. Think this'll be my last game."

"Aw, come on, Huson. You *love* this game. Tell you what, let's make it more interesting. Double or nothing next game."

At that moment Fuller burst through the door with one arm loaded down with plates of food. Sweet mentally breathed a sigh of relief.

"Thought you'd never get here, Fuller," Huson growled. "I was getting ready to come out there and crown *you*."

"Cheer up, Huson," Fuller said with delight, "you've only got two more hours, then you can join the party. And some party it is, too."

"I don't want to hear about it." Huson moved the checkerboard to the side and Fuller placed Sweet's plate on the table.

"Yeah, let me tell you about this little farmer girl I've been dancing with." The two Mounties moved to the front of the jail so Huson could eat at his desk.

Sweet called, "Don't forget about me, Huson. Double or nothing." Huson didn't answer, and Sweet yelled, "Huson!"

"I hear you, Sweet. I'll be glad to take your money when I've got some food in my belly."

Sweet pulled the plate through the slot in the bars and munched hungrily. It was the most delicious meal he'd had since he'd been in the custody of the Mounted Police.

He smiled when he realized that it was also the last.

————

"Well, my dear, are you having a good time?" Louis asked Megan. He slipped his arm around her waist as they watched the people dancing.

Megan cringed and tried to step away from his touch, but he held her tighter.

"Now, now. Appearances must be kept."

She looked at him with loathing. "You've been drinking. I can smell it."

Louis patted his coat, grinned, and said, "Just a little preventive medicine for the dangerous snakes in the area."

"You've lost your mind, Louis."

"On the contrary, I think I've found it."

Megan turned her face to the side when he leaned over to kiss her. As she felt his kiss on her cheek, her eyes fell on Vic, who was watching them from his comfortable place in the wagon. His face showed a peculiar mixture of sympathy and anger as he smiled and waved to her. Megan realized that her attempt to hide her disgust for her husband was fooling no one. "Excuse me, Louis," she said, managing to squirm from his grasp. "I have to see about Sub-Inspector Vickersham. He looks tired, and I must arrange for someone to take him back to the boardinghouse."

"You seem to be spending more time with him than with me," Louis said indignantly.

Megan ignored him and made her way to the wagon. She wondered where Vic's ever present companion, Del, had gotten off to, and then she spotted him dancing with an older lady over by the musicians.

"He's having the time of his life," Vic commented when she reached him.

"So it seems. And how about you?"

"Actually I've had better, but not in the last couple of weeks."

Megan leaned against the side of the wagon, suddenly very tired. The stress of being around Louis was overwhelming sometimes.

"Are you all right?" Vic asked with concern.

"Yes, just a little tired."

"Why don't you go back to the house and get some rest?"

Megan shook her head. "The night's still young. Would you like to go?"

"Pretty soon. I'm tired, too."

"I'll go find some men to take you back."

Vickersham put a hand on her arm. "Not just yet. Would you mind talking with me awhile?"

Megan smiled and said, "Not at all."

Across the yard, Becker carried a hot cup of tea for Jenny. He was feeling sort of giddy; he'd been able to draw Jenny out a little bit and discover more about her. She'd been standoffish at first, but he'd attributed that to her evident nervousness. He'd patiently kept an eye on her and followed her around like a puppy, offering to get her food or drink, until she'd finally smiled at him and seemed glad he'd been persistent. As he talked with her, it had been difficult to mentally separate the battered girl he'd found in the hills from the elegant young lady that was before him. But when she opened her mouth, she was all Jenny. She said what she thought in her quaint country accent, and she meant what she said.

Jenny had declined offers to dance, and Becker understood. She was terrified enough just standing there without the added pressure to perform.

"What do you call that?" Jenny asked, motioning to the crowd of dancers. The couples took a few steps forward and back, dropped hands and faced one another, then stepped to the lively music.

"That's the Red River Jig. Look, there's Sub-Inspector Stone teaching it to Reena." They watched as Reena clumsily attempted the dance, then both of them laughed and laughed. Becker had never seen Stone so happy. He'd started to wonder if Stone ever stepped out of his hard and brooding nature. Now Becker saw that he was human after all.

When the dance was over, Becker thought it was as good a time as any to ask the question he'd been avoiding. "Jenny, do you plan on seeing your father while you're here tonight? He's the only one in the jail since Macleod sent those deserters to Ottawa right away."

Jenny avoided his eyes as she said, "No. I don't wanna see him—ever again."

"Now, Jenny—"

"I said no!"

Becker unthinkingly reached out a hand to calm her, but she flinched noticeably. "I'm sorry I asked. I was just going to offer to take you, if you wanted."

Jenny nodded but said nothing.

"How about some more tea?"

"All right."

Becker went to get her another hot cup of tea, and on his way back across the yard he spotted a man in civilian clothes talking to Jenny. He was weaving a little, obviously from drinking something stronger than tea. Jenny edged away from his persistent attempts to get her to dance. Suddenly, he grabbed her arm and began pulling her to the dance area.

Becker dropped the teacup and sprinted full speed toward them, dodging people who looked at him with fear and wide-eyed surprise. Becker heard Jenny screaming, "No! Stop it!" and then he was there. He went behind the man and wrapped his arm around the man's neck, lifting him off the ground. The man's grip on Jenny was broken as he brought his hands to Becker's arm with a strangling noise.

"We don't need that sort of behavior at this fine ball," Becker said into the man's ear.

"Becker! Put him down!" Stone ordered from Becker's right.

"What's going on here?" the voice of Macleod roared from behind him. "Unhand that man, Becker!"

Becker released his hold and pushed the man away from himself and Jenny. The man held his neck and sucked in air harshly through a bruised throat.

"Kindly explain yourself, Becker!" Macleod ordered. "This is a ball, not a knife fight!"

"Sir, I—"

"It wasn't Becker's fault, sir," Stone told the colonel. "That man was behaving rudely to Miss Sweet. He should be thrown out of here, in my opinion, sir."

"You there!" Macleod shouted, stepping up to the man. "Is this true? Do you dare cause a commotion at a *Police Ball*?"

The man looked at the sea of faces around him, still rubbing his throat and staggering a bit. "I . . . I don't know what they're talkin' about! I was just askin' the lady to dance, and this . . . this . . . *freak* with the cut-up face tried to kill me!"

Macleod turned to Jenny, who was still trembling. Reena was beside her with both arms around her. "Miss Sweet, I'll take Sub-Inspector Stone's word and have this imbecile thrown out, but before I do that, do you wish to file any charges against him?"

Tears brimming in her eyes, Jenny shook her head.

"Very well. Sergeant Stride!" Macleod shouted.

"Here, sir."

Macleod motioned to the man. "Take this . . . this person out of here."

"Right away, sir."

"And, Stride?"

"Yes, sir."

Trying his best to stay calm and regarding the man as he would a bug, Macleod said, "I would consider it a serious mistake on your part should I see this ruffian again tonight."

"You won't see him again, sir," Stride promised, with an ugly grin at the man. He took the man's arm and none too gently marched him to the gate.

"All's well, ladies and gentlemen," Macleod called to the crowd that had gathered. "The trouble is on his way out the gate. Please resume having a splendid time!"

Becker immediately went to Jenny. "Are you all right? I'm sorry I left you, I—"

"Don't touch me!" Jenny cried when he placed a hand on her shoulder. "How many times do I have to tell you not to touch me?" She broke from Reena's embrace and ran to the ladies' station that had been set up in one of the barracks' rooms.

Reena made as if to follow, then turned back. When she looked at Becker, she said softly, "It's not your fault, Dirk. She's just upset and fragile right now."

Becker nodded and his hand absently went to the scar on his face as he watched Jenny disappear inside the barracks.

———————

"I tell you, *this* is the last game," Huson announced as they set up the checkers once again.

Armand Sweet knew it was now or never. Three checkers dropped from his hand to the floor near the bars. "Blast! Could you get those, Huson?"

"Clumsy ape," Huson muttered as he stood and bent down to pick up the pieces. In his anger and frustration, he made the move without thinking. Too late, he realized how vulnerable he was.

Sweet reached through the bars, grabbed a handful of his hair, and brought his head against the iron bars with a metallic clang. Huson dropped like a felled ox.

Sweet began sweating as he pulled the still form toward the cell and searched for the pocket that held the keys. "Slow down," he whispered to himself. "Take your time or you'll mess up." His own admonishment went unheeded. If someone walked in the jail right now, it would all be over.

———————

Jenny splashed water over her face, unmindful of the carefully placed makeup that Megan had applied earlier. Her hands were shaking, and she felt her knees knocking together. She looked into the small shaving mirror over the sink. The beautiful girl from before was gone. Her hair was in disarray under her straw puff-bonnet, and haunted eyes stared back from a land of wounds.

Her trembling stopped, and she stared at the girl for a full five minutes without moving. When she came out of the trance, she thought she remembered someone opening the door, but there was no one with her. The face in the mirror reflected determination now.

"I don't belong here," Jenny told herself with cold conviction. "I wanna go home. I'm *going* home, and no one can stop me. I can take care of myself."

With a final nod, she left the ladies' station and did her best to avoid the crowd on her way out of the fort. The bright dress was her enemy now as she tried to blend into the scenery. She heard her name called from somewhere behind, but she quickened her step and didn't turn around. At the gate she lowered her head and avoided all eye contact with the few Mounties gathered there. *Almost there . . .*

"Jenny!"

She whirled to find Becker approaching. His scarred face was filled with concern, but she didn't care at the moment. She just wanted to be left *alone*.

"Jenny, where are you going?"

She pointed back the way he'd come. "Go back and leave me alone, please."

"You can't walk home by yourself!"

"Leave me alone, Dirk!" She spun on her heel, picked up her skirts, and began running off into the darkness. Chancing a look around, she saw with relief that he'd stayed by the gate and hadn't pursued her. His form was silhouetted by the bonfire and lanterns inside, and she suddenly recalled that she'd forgotten to thank him for fighting off the drunk man. She called a quick "Thanks" over her shoulder, but she didn't think it was loud enough for him to hear over the revelry inside. Maybe she would see him again in the future and could thank him then.

With no moon, the night was extremely dark. She slowed down to a brisk walk. The dress, as she'd noticed when she'd finally gotten the whole thing on, was remarkably heavy and hot. Sweat beaded on her upper lip and brow.

The boardinghouse was close, she knew, but in the blackness she couldn't make it out yet. Suddenly, arms encircled her from behind in a strong grip. A hand closed over her mouth, and she heard in a blast of whiskey breath, "You come out here to meet me, little lady?"

It was the man who'd attacked her in the fort! *How did he—?*

"We can have us our own little party now, can't we? With no big, bad Mounties around to interrupt us!"

His mouth was right by her ear, and Jenny felt his kiss with a flood of disgust. Her feet were completely off the ground, but she kicked back at his shins with her boots. The heavy material of the dress softened the impact so much, however, that he seemed not to even notice. The hand over her mouth turned her face toward him. More wet kisses, this time on her cheek. *When he tries to kiss my mouth, he'll have to move his hand. Then I'll scream like never before!*

Jenny heard a dull thud. The man's head whipped awkwardly away from her to the side. He grunted painfully, and his grip loosened enough for her to scramble out of his grasp before he slumped to the ground. She found a Mountie in the gloom behind her. Once again, the light from the fort was behind him. His white helmet hung low over his face, and in his hand loomed a pistol, which Jenny knew he'd just planted against the drunk's head.

"Dirk?" Jenny asked uncertainly. The light behind him cast the front of his face and body in a shadow that was impenetrable. Something about him told her that it wasn't Dirk, though. Dirk was a little bigger and broader.

"Hello, Jenny."

"Pa! What are you . . . how did you. . . ?"

Armand Sweet laughed low in his throat and stepped toward her. Jenny shrank back. "What's the matter, girl? Aren't you glad to see your father?"

Jenny didn't answer—couldn't answer. The shock of seeing him out of jail was enough, but in a Mountie uniform? What did it mean? Had he killed a Mountie to escape?

Sweet shook his head and holstered the pistol. "Not much at showin' affection, are you? I guess that's all right. You probably learned it from me." He glanced around to the fort and sighed heavily. "Gotta be going, Jenny. They might find that fool Huson any second. Besides, I've got a big appointment tomorrow. An appointment that will make me a rich man. You want to come with me?"

Jenny shook her head and took another step back.

"I don't think I need to tell you that you didn't see me tonight, do I?"

She shook her head again.

"I'd hate to hear that my own daughter gave me up. That would be bad for me *and* you. You understand?" Sweet didn't wait for a nod. Like a crimson ghost, he crossed the street and vanished into the shadows behind Baker's livery.

Jenny found herself trembling for the second time that night.

PART FOUR

TILL JUDGMENT BREAK

Ample make this bed.
Make this bed with awe;
In it wait till judgment break
Excellent and fair.

Emily Dickinson
A Country Burial

CHAPTER SEVENTEEN

A Limited Partnership

The Mounted Police Ball continued in full swing.

Megan found some men to take the exhausted Vic back to the boardinghouse. Louis, who'd taken up with some civilian men in drink and song by the bonfire, didn't even notice when she left.

Hunter placed some chairs for Reena and himself just to the outside of the throng that was milling about the fire, dancing, and talking. Reena inquired about the arrest of the three deserters, and after he'd told her, she asked, "So what's your next assignment?"

Stone shrugged. "Do you remember that patrol Del and Potts led north? They say they've found a site for another fort that Macleod wants built in the next year."

"Does that mean you'll be going up there to oversee the construction or something?"

"I don't know. You're aware of how it is around here. Whatever Macleod wants done—"

"Vic says Macleod picks you all the time because you're the best."

He looked at her and smiled. "He must have been delirious at the time. Macleod picks whoever's physically closest at the moment he takes a notion to do something."

"You're just being modest."

"As Vic would say: 'On the contrary, my dear.' "

They watched the celebration in silence for a while. One man who was severely overweight was still dancing—Stone had noticed him out there every time he'd looked since the beginning of the ball—but he appeared to be ready to fall from exhaustion or drop dead of a heart attack. Stone hoped it was the former. The few Indians present were keeping to themselves but seeming to have a good time watching the white man's strange jigs. Some children had run themselves out and were asleep in their parents' laps.

"Hunter," Reena said, "about that night—"

"What night?" He knew very well what night she was referring to, but she'd surprised him with the question, and he needed time to collect his thoughts.

Reena worked at adjusting the sash on her dress to keep her hands occupied. "You know . . . the night we . . . told each other about our love."

"Yes? What about it?"

"Did I make a mistake? Was it . . . too much . . . too soon?"

"Why do you think that?"

"I'll tell you after you answer the question." She smiled.

"You asked me two. Which one do you want me to—"

"Why do I get the feeling you're just talking while thinking on your feet?" Reena asked in irritation. Her face softened as she met his eyes. "Please answer truthfully."

"All right. The day after, I think we both regretted it by the way we were so on edge. But now . . ." He leaned forward and took her hand. "Now, I wouldn't trade hearing you say those words to me for *anything*. The world seems so different when you know that someone, somewhere, cares for you. I haven't had that in a long time."

Reena stared at him for a moment, then took a deep breath and expelled it slowly. "That's exactly how I feel."

Stone saw Macleod and Stride coming toward him, and Macleod didn't appear to be in a festive mood.

"I hate to interrupt your good time, Stone, Miss O'Donnell, but we have a serious situation that needs to be addressed."

"What is it, sir?" Stone asked, getting to his feet. To Macleod, a man who had no idea what an exaggeration might be, a serious situation could be anything from a hostile Indian attack to the end of the world.

"Sub-Constable Huson's dead. Sweet has escaped."

Stone looked around at the more than one hundred men in scarlet around them. "How? Where could he go?"

"Sweet took Huson's uniform and apparently marched right out of here under our collective noses." Macleod was barely controlling his temper over the daring escape, and he took it as a personal affront.

"How long?" Stone asked, already plotting what their next move should be.

"The last time anyone saw Huson was around ten." Macleod consulted a silver pocket watch. "It's now twelve-thirty. I want you to mount a troop of ten and get started at first light."

"Yes, sir."

"And, Stone? I want ten *sober* men. As much as the men try to hide it, I know they imbibe now and then. I've never caught anyone, and heaven help them if I do, but just the same . . . you understand?"

"Of course." Stone had heard the rumors too, but so far no one had been stupid enough to drink in front of him, either.

Macleod left, and Stone gave Stride a list of men that he wanted. Reena abruptly began walking away. "Reena? Where are you going?"

She said one word over her shoulder: "Jenny."

The room was empty, except for the rich turquoise dress spread neatly on the bed. Since Jenny's belongings had been few, it took Reena only seconds to determine that she was gone.

"Oh, Lord, please watch over that poor girl," Reena whispered on her way to Megan's room. The lamp was turned down low inside. Megan was on her bed, turned away from the door. "Megan? Are you awake?"

"Yes." She didn't turn over, and her voice was muffled.

"Did you see Jenny when you got back here?"

"No."

"Did you know she's gone?" Reena walked slowly toward the bed with a sudden curious fear. "Megan, are you all right?"

Megan's body shuddered, and her voice was filled with tears as she muttered, "Somebody. I've got to tell somebody. I can't be responsible for this alone."

Reena sat on the side of the bed and tried to turn her sister toward her. She'd never seen Megan out of control before, and it frightened her. With guilt, she wished that "somebody" wouldn't be her. Anything strong enough to reduce Megan to tears and incoherence would indeed be bad news. "What is it? What happened?"

Megan finally turned over, and Reena saw puffy red eyes. A soaked kerchief was clutched in her hand. "I have to tell you, Reena. But you must *promise* you won't say anything to anybody else. It's just between us two."

"All right."

"*Promise* me! He might hurt me if you tell."

"Hurt you? Yes, I promise you, dear. Now, who's going to hurt you?"

"It's . . . it's . . . Louis has gone crazy, Reena. Absolutely crazy! He's selling whiskey up here—has been for some time, apparently—and he's . . . he's turned mean. He beats me and threatens me, and he doesn't care about anything but making money! What can I do?"

Reena listened in horror as Megan poured out her pain and fear. At first she couldn't associate the ruthless, abusive man Megan described with Louis. Louis was selfish, no doubt, but a man so possessed by money and power that he would resort to running whiskey? How could that be?

Then she remembered back to when they were engaged, when Louis was learning the banking business from her father and he would sometimes speak of having to foreclose on a business or a farmer. He would try to sound apologetic and concerned, but underneath Reena had always sensed that he'd been—not *glad*, actually, but content that he'd rid the world of a man who was detrimental to the business world, a man who'd jumped into the ring and hadn't been able to outrun the lions. The weaker once again were cut out of the financial world's pack. During those foreclosings, Reena thought that Louis saw himself as the Grim Reaper for the ones who *had* made their fortunes, and the woeful business or man that went under allowed the successful to sneer down from their lofty perch.

That strange quirk of Louis's always bothered Reena, but she had no concrete proof of her intuition, and to question him about it had seemed unthinkable. He was her *fiancé*, and *couldn't* have been thinking that way!

Now, listening to Megan describe a man who cared for nothing except profit at the expense of others, she realized with a sick feeling that she'd been correct in her earlier assessment. She had almost married him! And her poor sister had!

"Oh, Reena, I can't live with a man like that! Before you know it—and it may have already happened—he'll be seeing other women. What do I do?"

Reena stroked Megan's arm. "I'm so sorry, dear. I had no idea. This must be the most horrible thing in the world to you."

"It *is* horrible, and there's no way out."

Reena thought hard. With Louis's threat of dragging Megan down with him, there didn't seem to be anything to do at all. Except one thing. "Megan, we've got to tell Hunter."

"No! Absolutely not! He'll do something about it, and—"

"Yes, he'll do something about it! He'll follow Louis and catch him with the stuff. You know Louis is up to something here, and *we* can't very well follow him around, can we?"

"No, Reena. It's too risky."

"Well, *I'll* do something, then."

Megan grasped Reena's arm painfully. "You *promised* me!"

"But, Megan!"

"You promised, Reena."

Reena saw naked fear on her sister's face and knew she had to relent, though the temptation was strong. "Yes," she whispered, "I promised. And I won't break it."

Megan heaved a sigh of relief. "Thank you. I feel so much better just having told you. I'm sorry it was you, but—"

"Oh, hush. I'm *glad* it was me. But listen. Keep your ears open and try to coax his plan out of him."

"I don't even want to *talk* to him."

"You must."

"He won't be back tonight and maybe not tomorrow night, either."

"Where's he going? Did he say?"

"No. He just said he'd be gone on business for a while."

Reena gazed at the lamp thoughtfully. "Then he's already making his move. There's nothing we can do."

"There was nothing to do, anyway, Reena. Nothing at all."

———————

The next morning Megan found that Louis hadn't come back to the boardinghouse. Panicked, she dressed quickly, had a hurried cup of hot tea, and went to the fort. A drowsy Mountie, his uniform rumpled from sleeping on the ground, met her at the gate.

"I saw him leave about a half hour ago," he informed Megan.

"Do you know where he was going?"

"No, ma'am."

"Was he alone?"

The man hesitated, apparently in fear of getting between husband and wife. "Yes, ma'am, he was alone. Pretty hung over, if you ask me, but alone."

"Thank you." On the way back to town Megan decided to check the stable. If Louis wasn't there, he might be at Tony La Chapelle's store, but she doubted it. Tony didn't hide his dislike very well, and Louis hated being around people that didn't admire him.

To her relief, she saw him talking with a one-armed man who was hitching up a wagon. Louis looked up and saw her. Something like fear crossed his face, though Megan didn't know why he should be afraid of her. The look vanished quickly, replaced by a slightly arrogant pose.

"Good morning, my dear. I was just about to stop by to see you."

"Louis, where are you going?" He did, indeed, appear hung over. His eyes were bloodshot, and he was pale.

Taking her arm and ignoring her flinch, Louis led her away from the stablemaster. "I have a very important appointment tomorrow. Unfortunately, it's a fair distance away, and I've got to leave right now."

"Appointment? With who?"

Louis gave her a knowing look but didn't answer.

"Listen to me, Louis," Megan said urgently. "It's not too late to get out of the mess you've gotten into. You know it's not right."

"I know nothing of the kind. Free enterprise, Megan. That's what made the United States what it is today, and Canada is following along nicely."

"This isn't free enterprise! It's a crime!"

"Hold your voice down, darling. I'd hate for you to give our little secret away."

"*Your* little secret! I have nothing to do with—"

"Do you remember what I said, Megan? Yes, I can see that you do. Have you told anyone?" His tone had suddenly turned dangerous, and his grip on her arm tightened considerably.

"No."

"Don't lie to me."

"I'm not lying!" Megan whispered fiercely. "Let me go!" She jerked her arm out of his grasp and took a step away from him. "Please, Louis! Please don't do this. Just do what I ask—no, beg of you—this one time, and I'll never ask another thing from you, I promise!"

The superior grin reappeared. "I've got to go now. If you send anyone after me, I'll hurt you, Megan. Don't be a fool." He turned to the wagon and called, "Are we ready, my good man?"

"Yup," came the answer. "You's all set."

Louis suddenly turned back to Megan and kissed her before she could react. "I should be back Thursday, but if I'm late, don't worry. Would you worry, Megan?"

Unable and unwilling to answer, Megan merely glared at him. Louis laughed hoarsely. "I thought so."

Megan watched him flip a coin to the one-armed stablemaster and climb up in the wagon. She felt totally helpless, as if her life were spinning off into a different universe than the one she'd left in Chicago.

"Till Thursday," Louis called jauntily as he drove by. He began to whistle and headed the wagon team down the street toward the east.

———

Armand Sweet lay sprawled on a rock outcropping of the Milk River Ridge and watched the river below. It cut through the southern edge of the ridge, winding slowly westward in a lazy fashion. This was the place he'd always picked up his shipments. If he'd known how easy it was to spy on the bend in the river from where he was, he would have checked out the spot before ever picking up the whiskey himself. Now he could see how simple it would have been to be robbed, or worse.

He'd made the trip on a horse stolen from the livery in Baker's store. He'd also helped himself to a change of clothes, some food, a new brass spyglass, and a Spencer rifle with shells. It had taken him all that night and the next day to reach the ridge.

In his anticipation to reach the ridge, he'd almost worn the horse down. He'd been forced to stop at Pothole Creek and rest the mount for three hours. After he finally reached his destination, he bedded down for the night and slept straight through until sunrise.

In the morning, after carefully searching through his spyglass to the north and west and finding nothing, he'd taken out the Spencer and practiced. He'd owned one before, and he liked the rifle. It fired smoothly and accurately and didn't jam. He fired at ground squirrels below him and once at a yellow-bellied marmot about a hundred yards to his left. Curiosity must have drawn the marmot out. He'd also died from a dead-center shot for his curiosity. Fifty-two caliber bullets left a mess, if they left anything at all. Sweet loved the Spencer.

The barge arrived about two o'clock. She looked small but loaded down as she drifted on the current. The three men on board unloaded the cargo on the riverbank, just as they'd done many times for Sweet, then sat in the sun and dozed. Sweet knew each of their names, and he hoped they followed their regular routine of leaving immediately when the pickup man arrived. They always helped Sweet load the whiskey onto his wagon, but with the surly attitude of today's pickup man, they might very well sail off after he insulted them.

It was almost five when the wagon came in sight. Sweet could see two men, and he hoped one of them was Louis Goldsen. It would make his task a lot easier.

Through the spyglass, Sweet watched the wagon's arrival and subsequent conversing among the men. The barge men did indeed help load the crates, which Sweet thought was remarkable because it was Goldsen who had come to retrieve the merchandise. The Chicago boy himself. Sweet could tell by his build, cocky swagger, and slouch hat that made him look like an idiot.

Slowly and with exaggerated grace, Sweet loaded the carbine. The Spencer was unique in that the seven cartridges slipped into the butt stock of the rifle through a tubular feed. Smooth and easy.

Such a nice piece of work, that Spencer.

The loading finished, the men waved to one another and went their separate ways. The wagon was so full it appeared in danger of tipping over at the slightest gully or gopher hole. Sweet hoped that Goldsen knew what he was doing.

Sweet took his time saddling the horse, even humming "The Little Brown Jug" as he worked. The song had been written a few years before by a man named Winner.

As he mounted the bay, Sweet suddenly laughed. The sound echoed across the ridge. "Well, Mr. Winner. I may change *my* name to Winner after today is done. All those little brown jugs down below are going to make me a winner." He almost burst out laughing again, but he didn't want to take another chance that the sound would carry all the way down to the prairie floor below. Instead, he took a deep drink of water from the canteen he'd stolen and guided the horse down the ridge pass.

The man with Goldsen, whoever he was, didn't even notice Sweet coming up behind them until Sweet was only one hundred yards away. If he was hired as a bodyguard, he was a poor one. The man reached under the wagon seat and produced a rifle, which he brandished at Sweet in a threatening manner.

Sweet shot over the man's head, then rode calmly while the man took a shot at him. The second shot from the Spencer blew the man backward over one of the wagon's horses to the prairie. Sweet was satisfied that the man had had a fair chance. He was just a poor shot.

Goldsen's shocked white face turned to Sweet. His eyes widened as he recognized him. Sweet smiled and waved. Goldsen was obviously considering whipping the horses into a run when Sweet came within earshot.

"Don't do that, Goldsen! You'll lose our load."

"*Our* load?" He was trying to flash bravado, but his face showed stark terror. "This is *my* whiskey."

Sweet rode easily beside the wagon. He was enjoying Goldsen's fear even more than he'd anticipated. "I believe you said to meet you here. Today is Wednesday, ain't it? Here I is."

"That was before you killed a Mountie. They'll hunt you down across the continent if they have to. You're too dangerous to be around." Goldsen's round eyes kept going to the Spencer held easily in Sweet's hand.

"We had a deal. You breaking it?"

Louis swallowed, started to answer, then switched the subject. "Why'd you kill Rickman? He didn't do anything to you."

"He was trying to kill me, in case you didn't notice."

"You shot at him first!"

"Look, Goldsen, I'd love to sit here and chat with you all day, but I want an answer. Am I in or not?" Sweet deliberately swung the rifle in Louis's direction a little more. It was now pointed at the horse in front of him.

Louis's face suddenly broke out in a sweat, even though the air was cool. He began coughing and put a hand to his chest.

Too late, Sweet saw the derringer aimed in his direction and exploding. He jerked the reins on the horse as the bullet whizzed by him. The last thing he'd expected was for the dandy to be carrying a weapon. He yanked hard on the reins, and the bay reared up on its hind legs, creating a shield between Goldsen and him. Another explosion rocked the air, and the bay screamed and fell. Sweet threw himself clear of the dying horse and came up firing the Spencer.

The first bullet shattered the backrest of the bench seat. The second went high. The third and fourth knocked Goldsen over the side in a shower of blood.

Sweet ran to the wagon to keep the horses from bolting. After he'd stopped the team, he turned and considered Goldsen in his awkward death-sprawl. His glasses were gone from his pale face. The ridiculous hat had sailed twenty feet away. The little derringer glinted in the sun, still clutched in his hand.

"That was real stupid, Chicago boy. Pulling that little pea-shooter on me when I'm holding the finest rifle ever invented. Dumb move." Sweet shook his head in wonder. "It was brave, though. Stupid but brave. You were just about as greedy as I am."

Sweet gathered his things from the dead horse before heading west.

CHAPTER EIGHTEEN

Becker's Detour

Three days later, Reena and Vic sat on the front porch of the boardinghouse watching Megan pace while waiting for the Mountie troop to return. Stone had sent a man ahead to arrange for more supplies since they hadn't found Sweet. Reena had heard this from Macleod, who'd paid a visit in the morning to check on Vickersham.

"Where *are* they?" Megan asked for what seemed like the tenth time. Unlike Vic and Reena, she refused to sit down.

Megan's pacing was beginning to get on Reena's nerves, but she said nothing. Since the morning after the ball there had been no word from Louis—nothing. Megan had a right to be worried. Reena hoped that Stone had seen or heard from Louis in his travels.

"I wish I had the energy you do, Megan," Vic teased. "It takes all my strength just to get up and down those stairs."

"But at least you're up," Reena reminded him.

"That's true." He adjusted the pillow behind him. "I suppose I should tell you two that I'll be going back to the fort tomorrow."

Reena looked at him in surprise, and Megan stopped her pacing.

"But you're still weak!" Reena said. "You can't go back on duty yet."

"I can go on *light* duty. Macleod hates paperwork and doesn't really have time for it, so he asked me this morning if I could help him out."

Reena shook her head. "You're not ready yet, Vic."

"I'm more than ready, I assure you. This lying around for weeks is driving me insane. I *need* to feel needed, Reena."

"Who will take care of you?" Megan asked.

Reena noticed again how pale she was. Her problems with Louis had managed to drain the life from her usually lively face, and Reena thought she'd lost weight.

Vic leaned back in his rocking chair and laced his fingers behind his head. "Now, you ladies know I can take care of myself. You've just been spoiling me."

"You just got on your feet two days ago!" Megan exclaimed.

"If I'm on my feet, I can do what it takes to care for myself."

Megan turned to Reena and asked, "Have you ever met a man who *wasn't* stubborn?"

"No."

"They must be born with it."

Vic looked at them seriously. "I can't tell you how much I appreciate what you both have done for me."

Reena smiled and said, "You're a remarkably good patient. Much easier to take care of than Hunter was."

"Oh? Do tell."

Megan said, "You two shouldn't be talking that way, even in jest. Hunter had lost his poor wife."

Reena and Vic both nodded and agreed with her.

"What a horrible death that must have been," Megan said flatly.

"Let's not think about it," Reena said. "I'm tired of thinking about death. Besides, Betsy Stone and our mother are happier now than they ever were here."

They sat in silence for a while, unable *not* to think about death now that it had been mentioned. Reena was very sorry she'd brought up the subject of Hunter and his tragedy.

The noise of squeaking equipment, horses, and men's voices reached them, and they all stood to look down the street. The Mountie troop, with Stone in the lead, slowly made its way toward them and the fort. Reena could see that the men were worn out. The horses walked with their heads low and bobbing, as if any step might be their last. Except for Buck, Reena noticed with pride. The buckskin had his head up and ears twitching alertly. His rider was another matter.

Hunter's uniform was dusty, and his boots were caked with dried mud. His white helmet hung from the saddle pommel by its chin strap. He spotted Reena and smiled, but it was a tired smile and for some reason seemed a little sad.

"They've been going nonstop," Vic commented. Then, with dread coating his voice, "One of *those* patrols."

"You mean they haven't slept in four days?" Megan asked.

"Oh, I'm sure they have—in the saddle."

"Is that possible?"

Vic looked at her, amused. "You'd be surprised."

Stone spoke a few words to Sergeant Stride and broke from the column toward them. He was no longer smiling, and Reena began to feel a curious knot of dread in her stomach. The man riding toward her wore the same look on his face that she'd seen when he'd been the lowest in his life: a grim, tight mouth below haunted eyes. Reena was suddenly very afraid and unconsciously grasped Megan's hand and squeezed.

"What's the matter, Reena?" Megan asked worriedly. "You've gone pale."

Reena didn't answer but tried to smile as Hunter reached them. "Hard ride?"

Stone nodded and dismounted. To Vic he said, "Good to see you up and around."

"Thank you. Good to see you back."

Reena thought Vic sensed something was wrong, too, by the strained expression that had appeared all at once.

Stone ran his fingers through his hair and sighed. "We didn't catch him."

"I know," Reena said. "Colonel Macleod told us."

"We picked up his trail southeast of here, heading toward the border. He stopped at the Milk River and turned west. I think he's going to the mountains. We'll have to stock up on rations and go dig him out." His gray eyes came to rest on Megan, almost as if expecting the question she asked.

"Hunter, Louis has disappeared. I haven't heard from him in days. Did you hear any news of him? For all I know, he's back in the U.S. now."

In the silence while they waited for Hunter to answer, Reena knew. Maybe it was the silence itself, or the way his face seemed to age ten years in an instant. Whatever it was, Reena gripped Megan's hand harder and reached over to grasp her arm with her other hand.

"Hunter?" Megan asked in a small voice.

"Let's sit down," Stone suggested.

"Yes, let's," Vic chimed in, taking Megan's other arm.

"Why? What's wrong?" If possible, Megan's face lost more color. "Did you see him?" Her gaze went to the column that had passed up the street. "Where is he?"

Stone looked at Reena in obvious pain. She wished she could do something, but her voice had left her.

"Talk to me!" Megan wailed.

"We found him on the prairie, Megan. He was dead—probably killed by Sweet. I'm very sorry."

Reena watched for signs of fainting, but Megan only stared at Hunter intently. Her mouth worked silently, but no tears came; only time would tell if that was a good sign or an ominous one.

Insistently, Vic whispered, "Let's sit down, Megan."

"I don't want to sit down! Why is everyone telling me to sit down?" She broke from their grips and moved to Hunter. Buck threw his head nervously at the sudden tension so close to him. "What . . . where is the . . . the . . . body, Hunter?"

Stone looked down at his hands as they twisted the reins. Bringing his eyes to hers, he told her, "We had to bury him out there. He'd been there for a couple of days. We had no choice." He looked at Reena helplessly.

He's never done this before, she reasoned all at once. *He's always let someone else break bad news to people.*

Megan turned toward Reena, her lower lip trembling. "Everyone's dying, Reena! Everyone's dying!"

Reena went to her and wrapped her arms around her. Still no tears came, but Reena could feel Megan's taut body humming with unreleased tension.

"Who's next, Reena? You? Liam? Daddy?"

"Shhhh. Don't talk that way. You're just upset. We'll get through this together." Reena patted her back gently and met Hunter's eyes over Megan's shoulder. He was frowning and shook his head in empathy.

"There's no hope anymore," Megan murmured in a voice so

low that Reena doubted Vic and Hunter could hear. "There's no hope."

The Mountie troop ate a hot meal, donned a change of clothes, and made all the preparations for moving on after Sweet. Stone offered each man the chance to be replaced and stay at the fort, but all refused.

After Stone's meeting with Macleod, he was walking to his quarters to shave and change clothes when Becker stopped him by the quartermaster's office. Becker looked freshly scrubbed and energetic, momentarily making Stone feel old and tired.

"Sir, I have to talk to you," Becker said without preamble. "It's important."

"What is it?" Stone was ready to get cleaned up, and he couldn't keep the irritation from his tone.

"It's Jenny Sweet, sir—"

"We've already discussed this, Becker, and the answer's still no."

"Yes, sir, but things have changed—"

"How?"

Becker looked around them as if ready to divulge an important secret. Finding no one within hearing distance, he stepped up to Stone and locked eyes with him. Stone had never seen Becker as serious and grim as he was now. "I've been talking to Del, and I think Sweet's heading for his cabin."

Stone shook his head and said, "That's the last place he'll go. He knows *we* know about that cabin. He'll think we've already got men up there."

"That's my point!" Becker stated emphatically, stepping even closer to Stone. He saw something in Stone's face and amended, "I mean . . . sir. We don't *have* any men up there. He may think that since it's so obvious, we won't even bother covering it. And guess what? It turns out he's right, sir."

"I don't care for your tone, Becker."

"Sorry, sir, but Jenny's up there all alone! He's a ruthless, hunted man who's already killed two men in only a few days. What chance do you think she will have with him?"

To Stone's chagrin, he realized Becker was right in everything he was saying. To allow his tired mind to absorb the facts and search for the right thing to do, he asked, "You don't really think he'll kill his own daughter, do you?"

"Neither you nor I would—we couldn't even consider the act—but we're not insane, either. What if . . . what *if* . . . something happened to her, and we're off in the mountains chasing decoy signs? It wouldn't make me feel very well, Sub-Inspector."

Stone rubbed his face with his hands and sighed deeply. "What does Del say?"

"He says it'd be very easy for Sweet to lead us into the foothills—maybe even into the mountains—then turn straight north and make his way to the cabin through passes in the Porcupine Hills."

Stone took another deep breath and let it out slowly. He should have thought of this. What was the matter with him? "All right, Becker. Take three men and—"

"Pardon me, sir, but I think I should go alone. If Sweet does come there, we'd have a better chance of surprise with one man instead of four, don't you think?"

Stone nodded and smiled tiredly. "Right again. Go on."

"Thank you, sir!" Becker sprinted for the stables.

"Becker!"

He stopped and turned back, his face mirroring the same irritation Stone had felt earlier.

"Good thinking, Becker. And be careful."

Becker grinned, nodded, and ran for Egypt.

Stone watched him for a moment before heading for his quarters. His birthday, April 19, was approaching fast; he would turn twenty-six. Observing Becker's exuberance and seeming tirelessness, his bones felt as if they were on the verge of forty-six.

After he'd cleaned up and changed uniforms, Stone found Del at the stables. The grizzled scout gave him a knowing, smug look. "What's on your mind, Del? I know that look, and I don't really care for it."

"What look?" Del asked innocently.

Stone rubbed Buck's nose and gave him part of a cookie he'd taken from the mess hall. Buck's large brown eye said thank-you as he munched. "You've got something to say," Stone said to Del with a smile. "Out with it."

"You sent the bear cub to the cabin, didn't you?"

"Yes."

"Thought so." Del spat a stream of tobacco juice behind a pile of hay. "By hisself?"

"Yes."

"Mmm. Don't know as I'da done that."

"Why not?"

"Young cub like that all alone against the scum we're chasin'? What sorta chance you think he's got?"

Stone explained his reasoning for sending Becker alone. "Besides, we don't know Sweet's heading for the cabin."

Del's face turned serious. "I do." He looked away and added, "We should be heading straight for it, Hunter."

Throwing a blanket over Buck's back, Stone said, "I have to follow the tracks, Del. You know that."

"He'll beat us to the cabin, then. And Becker's alone."

"I thought you didn't like Becker. Why are you so worried about him all of a sudden?"

"Oh, I like him all right, I guess." Del suddenly cackled. "He sure is sweet on that little gal."

"Yes, he is. I just hope he stays alert. Sweet won't give him more than one chance."

"There's one more thing, Hunter. What if they's already some men at the cabin? Sweet had some men when we arrested him. Maybe he got a message to them to join up with him there. Then what'll Becker do?"

Stone stopped smoothing the blanket and looked at his friend. That was yet another factor that he hadn't considered, and his blood chilled.

———

Becker watched the cabin through the cold rain. He'd left Egypt tied to an aspen tree and hiked to a spot behind the cabin with a view of the area. So far, through the wet twilight edging on darkness, he'd seen no one. A light burned somewhere inside, and smoke curled from the chimney. Its warm glow made him want to abandon all caution, get inside, and drink coffee with Jenny by the fire. His grin at the foolish thought stretched his scar, making it shine white in the gloom.

It had occurred to him on the ride that there could be some hired men at the cabin. He thought the possibility was remote, for no particular reason other than a gut feeling. Sweet's escape sounded as if it were on the spur of the moment, with no planning whatsoever. However, Becker didn't want to blunder into a house full of outlaws.

Jenny passed by a window. Instinctively, though he was sure she couldn't see him, Becker ducked behind the bush in front of him as he watched. The curtain was open. Jenny's hair was wet. She began brushing her hair with an amber-colored brush. She was wearing a white cotton shirt, and by the way it engulfed her, it looked like a man's shirt. He couldn't see below her waist and sincerely hoped she didn't suddenly remove the shirt. She stopped brushing and stared at the mirror before her. Leaning forward, she brought a hand to her cheek and gently stroked it, as if she were enjoying her own softness. Becker wished he could do it for her.

Shaking his head in self-reproachment, Becker looked away. This was too much; he had no right spying on her this way. Far away he heard a wolf howl, the most lonesome sound in the world. *And I'm lonesome, too,* he thought suddenly, with a jolt of surprise. *I've never felt that way before. Used to be I was happy with my surroundings. If I wasn't happy, I'd make myself happy. But since I've known Jenny . . .*

The thought of her made him look back to the window. She was gone and the brush was by the mirror. Becker wagered that the warmth from her hand was still on the handle. He wanted so badly to go inside, to make his presence known. How would she react? Glad? Cold? Overjoyed? Angry that he would think she couldn't take care of herself? But he wasn't here for her, really, he told himself. He was here to catch a very bad man who just happened to be her father. That's what he told himself.

Becker waited for what seemed like another hour. Then he carefully moved to the cabin, took a deep breath, and looked in all the windows. The bedrooms were empty as far as he could tell. Jenny was in the kitchen making herself something to eat. He wanted to watch her for a while, but he made himself scan the interior for signs of additional people.

In full darkness he made his way back to Egypt and untied the horse. As he went toward the cabin, he prayed that Jenny was alone, and that she wouldn't shoot him. If there *were* men in the house, they were hiding themselves well. And, if there *were* men in the house, he was about to give them an excellent target to shoot at, too.

The rain had stopped, and his boots made squishing sounds in the mud. His heart pounding like a galloping horse's hooves, Becker stood twenty feet from the front door and shouted, "Hello, the house! Jenny! It's Dirk Becker! Don't shoot me!" His voice echoed off the mountain behind the cabin, serving notice to anyone miles around that he was here. He wondered if the wolf he'd heard earlier had stopped what he was doing at the sound of the human. He wondered crazily if the wolf thought Becker's howl sounded as lonely as the wolf's had.

No movement. No door opening. No young girl rushing out to meet him with arms wide, tearful with gratitude that he'd come to protect her. Nothing.

"Jenny?" Becker waited, then looked at Egypt. The horse eyed him as if to say, "Are you sure you know what you're doing?" Becker reached over and wiped the moisture from Egypt's nose. "No, I'm *not* sure about this, boy. If there's any sign of trouble, you run and find Hunter Stone for me, all right?"

A tiny creak brought Becker's attention back to the cabin. A thin slit of light around the front doorframe was broken by the shape of Jenny's head as she cautiously looked out.

"Dirk?"

"Yes, Jenny. It's me. Can I come in?"

"What do you want? What are you doing here?"

He took a few tentative steps toward the door. "I'll explain if you'll share your fire. It looks very inviting." He winced inwardly. From where he stood he couldn't even *see* the fire. If she caught his mistake and questioned him . . .

Jenny, looking very small, stared out at him. Becker couldn't see her face since it was silhouetted by the lantern, but he sensed her reluctance. "There ain't nobody here, if that's what you're lookin' for. He ain't here."

The rain suddenly came down again, and Becker glanced up at the sky accusingly. "Jenny, I'm already soaked. Tell you what—I'll go stable Egypt, and by the time I'm through maybe you'll want to let me in. How's that?" He didn't wait for an answer and headed for the barn.

"I gotta get dressed and clean up a bit," Jenny called to his back.

Becker waved without turning around. He hadn't planned on being so abrupt with her, but he was tired and soggy and cold.

When Egypt was taken care of and eating contentedly in the stall beside Splash, Becker wearily walked back to the cabin. Jenny met him at the door wearing a soft blue cotton dress with white lace around the high neck and on the cuffs. Her hair was still damp, and Becker wondered if it was from a bath or if she'd been out in the rain for some reason.

"Some of Pa's clothes are in that room," she told him. "You can change if you want, and I'll make some coffee."

"Thanks." At that moment, Becker couldn't care less about wearing an outlaw's clothes. He went in Sweet's bedroom and changed into black cotton pants and a thick cotton plaid shirt. The fit was less than perfect—the sleeves and pants were a few inches too short—but at least he was dry now.

He glanced around for character clues of the man whose clothes he wore, but the room was simple, empty, and bare—severely bare. No pictures on the walls or dresser, no trinkets or hobby pieces. Shrugging off a pang of guilt, he searched through the dresser drawers and found nothing but a few clothes. Becker supposed the stark nakedness of the room was a clue in itself. Armand Sweet was neither sentimental nor materialistic, interesting or attractive. He was a shadow without form.

A hint of a smile crossed Jenny's lips when she saw the poor fit of the clothing. Becker didn't comment and sat on a worn, stained sofa by the fire.

Jenny moved behind him and said, "Lean forward." When he did, she wrapped a blanket that smelled like hay around his shoulders.

"Thank you." The coffee she brought him was extremely hot and strong, just the way he liked it. Jenny sat across from him on a wooden kitchen chair and watched him carefully sip the scalding liquid.

"So why are you here?" she asked.

222

Becker told her about the danger she could be in, leaving out the fact that it was his own idea.

"Why am I in danger? He's my father, you know."

"Forgive me, Jenny, but since when *weren't* you in danger around him?"

She dropped her gaze to the floor. Becker saw a look of such vulnerability come over her face that he instantly despised Armand Sweet more than anything in the world.

In a small voice, her lips barely moving to form the words, she asked, "Why does he always want to hurt me?"

"Because he's a very bad man. And I think he's . . . not right in the head."

"Did your daddy ever hurt you?"

Becker smiled. "I took a few lashes from an oak switch, but I deserved it. Nothing like what you've been through. My father was a good man."

"Was? Is he dead?"

"Yes. Killed in the war. Both he and my brother."

"I'm sorry."

"Me too."

"They were on the Confederate side?"

"Yes."

"I remember hoping they'd win. I don't know why."

"Maybe it's because you identify with lost causes."

Jenny didn't answer, but she brought her eyes back to his. In them he could see doubt and pain.

Becker leaned forward and put his elbows on his knees. "Listen to me, Jenny. If your father does show, or anyone else, I want you to hide in your room. Two men have already been killed, and I don't know how your father will react to finding me here. Do you understand?"

"I ain't hidin'."

"Please, Jenny. For me."

"You may need help."

"I'll be fine. I've got surprise on my side."

"No one ever surprises my pa. Never."

"Jenny—"

The front door burst open, and Armand Sweet filled it. A Spencer rifle was pointed directly at Becker's head. "Well, now, ain't this cozy?" Sweet asked with an ugly grin.

CHAPTER NINETEEN

A Light in the Darkness

The doorbell chime sounded, and Reena called to Mrs. Howe that she would get it. Vickersham, in full uniform and looking healthier than ever, stood on the doorstep.

"How is she, Reena?"

"Good evening to you, too, Vic. She's . . . about the same."

Vic stepped inside, removing his helmet. "Is she resting?"

"I don't know if she's rested since she got the news this morning. Every time I check on her, she's awake. She's not eating, either."

"What I mean is, can I . . . we . . . see her right now?"

"Come upstairs with me and I'll see." Reena glanced at him as they ascended the stairs. "Is something wrong, Vic? You seem nervous."

"I'm just . . . it's only that . . ." Vic twisted the helmet in his hands and sighed deeply. "Yes, something's wrong. I just don't know what it is. I feel . . . sort of strange tonight. That's the only way to describe it."

"I'm surprised Colonel Macleod let you come back so soon."

"When he heard the news about Louis, he was more than happy to let me try to help."

Reena nodded but said nothing. She knew that Vic was specially attracted to her sister, but she didn't know the full extent of it. Vic was such a caring person that it could very well be innocent concern. However, something was definitely bothering him.

Reena knocked softly on Megan's door and tentatively stepped inside. The curtains were drawn with no light burning. Through the light cast from the hallway, she could see Megan sitting on the bed, facing the wall. She was still wearing the dress she'd put on that morning. "Megan? I thought you were asleep."

Megan didn't reply.

"Vic's here. May we come in?"

In a whisper that Reena barely heard, Megan answered, "Yes."

Reena nodded to Vic, waiting outside the door, and went to light a lamp. "You need to try to get some sleep, dear. I know you don't feel like it, but you're probably more tired than you feel."

"Hello, Megan," Vic said quietly, coming into the room. "I hope you don't mind me intruding so late."

"It's all right." Megan stood and faced them. When Reena had lit the lamp, the soft glow revealed her pale drawn face. "Sit down."

Megan and Vic sat on either side of a mahogany writing table, while Reena sat on an open armchair by the window. No one said anything for a few moments. Vic kept his helmet in his lap, still fidgeting with it. Megan stared at one of the candlesticks that stood on each end of the writing table. Reena noticed that the stems of the candlesticks were lightly channeled with a slight spiral swirl.

Obviously uncomfortable with the extended silence, Vic crossed one leg over the other and told Megan, "I've been thinking about what you said today—that there was no hope left. Do you still believe that?"

Megan shrugged, not meeting his eyes.

"What are you thinking?"

After hesitating, Megan said, "That it's all my fault Louis is dead."

"What?" Reena blurted. "*Your* fault!"

"Megan, you don't believe that. . . ?" Vic asked, too stunned to finish.

"If I'd reported what he was doing, he'd be in jail right now instead of dead." Megan's voice was wooden, but it held a terrible certainty about the words. "Because of my fear of him, he's dead."

"That's just it, Megan," Reena told her firmly. "He threatened you if you told anyone. You *couldn't* tell."

"Threatened you?" Vic asked. "How?"

Megan shook her head.

Reena sat up straighter in her chair and told Megan, "Well, if you won't tell him, I will." She turned to Vic. "Louis had gotten to the point where he felt it was all right to knock Megan around a bit with his fists."

The instant shock on Vickersham's face quickly turned to a blushing anger. Megan was finally looking at him, interest in his reaction showing on her face. When he saw her watching, his features softened with sympathy. "I'm so sorry, Megan. I didn't know. I'm . . . very sorry."

"Thank you."

"Did he . . . hurt you badly?"

"Just a few bruises. He'd only recently started being violent."

"I apologize if this hurts you, but my respect for the dead has just vanished completely. He had no right. No man has that right."

Megan smiled just a bit, but it was gone so quickly Reena wasn't sure if she'd seen it or not.

"Now, about this guilt you feel," Vic went on, "pardon me for saying that it's ridiculous. If he physically threatened you, you had no choice. You did the right thing by keeping silent to protect yourself. Do you understand?"

Megan's lips tightened.

"You told me it was his idea to come here originally, not yours. Is that right?"

"Yes. What does that have to do—"

"It was *his* choice to come here, Megan. He *chose* to get in the whiskey business. He *chose* to place himself in danger. He *chose* a profession that could have fatal consequences. You had nothing to do with all that."

"He's right, Megan," Reena insisted.

Megan began to cry. Reena recognized it as the sort of cleansing weeping that had come over her after hearing of her mother's death. Megan, however, wasn't as demonstrative as Reena had been that day. The tears, seemingly an endless amount, spilled from her eyes, but she made no sound.

"There, there," Vic said softly, placing a handkerchief in her hand. Before he could pull away, Megan's other hand closed over his.

In a choked voice Megan asked him, "So there *is* hope?"

"Oh yes, there's hope. There's hope for all of us." Vic turned in his chair to face her fully. Both of his hands closed over hers, but he looked at Reena instead. "You sensed that something was wrong with me tonight. You were right. I already told you that, but I wasn't as honest as I should have been." He faced Megan again. "Megan, I'd planned on talking with Reena alone after our visit, but I've changed my mind. I want you to hear what I have to say, and I hope—there's that word again—that you'll be a part of something wonderful with me."

Megan nodded as she wiped her eyes. Reena had no idea where Vic was going with this.

"I've been thinking about this a lot lately, and . . ."

Reena desperately wanted to say, "What, what?" But she knew that wouldn't be proper. She watched Vic's mouth work as he struggled to finish.

"And I've come to realize that as human beings—by ourselves, I mean—we have no hope. None at all."

Reena unconsciously put a hand to her mouth. *Could this be. . . ?*

"Our only hope is God and His Son Jesus," Vic finished, looking slightly embarrassed and very uncomfortable with the alien words he was speaking. "I know that now. After watching Reena deal with her pain and finding help from God, after seeing that death is waiting for *any* of us at any time . . . I want to be prepared. And I want to have a relationship with our Creator."

Reena took the wet handkerchief from her sister and dabbed at her own eyes. "Vic, that's wonderful. I'm so happy."

"Megan," Vic went on, "will you pray with Reena and me? I think deep down you know what I'm saying is true and want the same thing that I do. Peace . . . a new life . . ."

Megan began shaking her head, lost for words.

"Don't say no. It's time, I think . . . for both of us."

"No. You don't understand. I wasn't saying no," Megan said. She took a deep breath as if she'd been holding it all the while Vic had spoken. "It sounds . . . wonderful!"

"Really?"

Reena could keep her seat no longer. With a joyous cry, she leaped at Megan and threw her arms around her neck. Then she did the same with Vic and gave him an exuberant kiss on the cheek.

"You two have no idea how happy and . . . and *surprised* I am! But what a tremendous surprise! Praise the Lord!"

"Will you tell us what to pray, Reena?" Vickersham asked.

"May I . . . say it?" Megan asked them. Now it was her turn to color with embarrassment. "I think I remember, Reena. You know . . . from when we were growing up and going to church."

"Of course you remember, Megan."

"I hope I can do it right."

Reena smiled. "There is no right or wrong way, dear."

Megan nodded and glanced at Vic, who said, "You start, Megan."

Bowing her head and clasping her trembling hands together, Megan began, "Dear Father . . ."

The pause was so long that Reena thought she was going to have to ask Megan if she wanted her to take over. Glancing up briefly, Reena saw that Megan had her eyes tightly shut, and tears were leaking through and rolling down her cheeks. Vic waited patiently with his head bowed. Reena couldn't see his face.

"Dear Father," Megan began again in an unsteady voice, "please forgive me for my sins against You. I've been so . . . so . . . *lost* without You, and I ask You to come into my heart and dwell there . . . forever."

Vic repeated Megan's words with a strong voice.

Reena looked up, her own tears tickling her face as they ran down, but Megan wasn't finished yet.

"Please make me into what You would have me to be. I don't know what to do without . . . my husband." Her voice broke pitifully, and she began crying in earnest. "I need You now, Lord. Please help me and guide me."

Reena and Vic both placed their hands on Megan's shoulders as her body shook with sobs. Over Megan's head, Reena saw that Vic had a pained look on his face, as if he were experiencing Megan's pain right along with her. Despite the expression, he managed to smile at Reena.

Megan's crying continued for a long time, interspersed with cries for help from God. As she held her sister, Reena's heart was torn between empathy and an incredible, soaring joy.

———

"I know you're tired," Stone told his men, walking their horses through the dark. "But we may have a man in trouble at that cabin. We've got to move fast."

The troop had been pushing the horses unmercifully for two hours. Now, as they walked along in front of their tired mounts, a few of them shook their heads in exhaustion and self-pity.

"I *knew* we shoulda just headed straight for that cabin," Del grumbled. "The bear cub was right all along."

"We've been over this, Del," Stone told him tiredly. "Our orders were to follow the tracks." The temperature was around freezing, with a strong wind that had somehow made its way through the mountains. Stone buttoned the top button of his coat. He was alternating between being hot and sweating to shivering with cold, and the changes in his own body temperature were making him even more testy than he already was.

"That rat Sweet was prob'ly laughing all the way down to his boot heels when he turned north. Prob'ly thinkin' how us poor, stupid Mounties was eatin' up his every trick with a spoon—"

"Del," Stone said with a dangerous edge to his voice, "shut up."

"Yes, sir."

"How much farther, do you think?"

"I'd say about ten miles."

Stone glanced at the men behind him. The normally good-natured banter had vanished with Sweet's turn to the north and Stone's order for quiet as they'd picked up their pace. One young sub-constable was limping noticeably. Another sneezed wetly. Stone recognized the sound since he'd heard it a few times before and knew the man was coming down with something.

"Bad luck. That's what it is," Del growled. "We ain't had a smidge o' good luck since that rat escaped."

"Luck's got nothing to do with it, Del."

"Humph. Gotta be *somethin'*." Del turned to Stone with a cautious look. "What you think Sweet'll do to that kid?"

"Who? His daughter or Becker?"

"Both of 'em, now that you mention it."

Stone paused and shook his head before answering. "He'll probably take Jenny with him, wherever he's going."

"What makes you think he's going anywhere?"

"He knows we'll turn up eventually. A five-year-old could follow his tracks."

Del squinted as he asked, "And Becker?"

"I don't think he'll take Becker with him."

"What'll he do with him, then?"

Stone looked at him, expressionless.

"Oh no," Del breathed. His strange eyes took on a haunted, faraway look.

"What does he have to lose? He's already killed one Mountie and two civilians—that we know of."

They walked in silence for a few steps, both of them struggling to exorcise grisly thoughts from their minds. Stone heard another sneeze.

"Let's mount up," Del suggested suddenly.

"Too soon. The horses need—"

"Hunter! That boy ain't got a chance against Sweet, and you know it!"

Stone turned on his friend savagely. "Yes, I know it! I don't need you to remind me of it, either!"

Del turned away, his lips tight.

Stone sensed a sudden tension behind him, and he knew the men were growing uncertain about the whole excursion. Exhaustion topped with doubt was a dangerous thing in a troop. Stone forced himself to apologize loud enough for most of the men to hear him. "Del, I'm sorry. What I'm trying to say is that it wouldn't do us any good to kill all these horses by driving them too hard. They need rest."

"I know. I'm sorry, too. My mouth gets ahead of my brain sometimes."

"It happens to us all." Stone spent the rest of the walking time moving among the men, trying to reassure them that everything was all right by showing confidence that he didn't feel.

He began sweating again.

———

"Pa, what are you doing here?" Jenny asked, leaping to her feet from the kitchen chair. Her heart was pounding in her chest so hard she was afraid it would overwork itself and stop. First Dirk Becker appeared, a not unwelcome event, and now her father, which was another matter entirely. She glanced at Dirk, who was staring at the Spencer as if hypnotized.

"What am I doing here?" Sweet grinned. "I *live* here. I *built* this place, remember?" He turned to Becker, casually waving the barrel of the Spencer at him. "What are *you* doing here, scar boy?"

"Don't call him that!" Jenny exclaimed. She couldn't help taking a step back when the impossibly dark eyes swung her way again. Her father's eyes launched an almost physical jolt at whoever was on the receiving end of his glare. Now she saw dawning comprehension in them that produced a gnaw of dread in her belly.

Without warning, and so quick that neither Jenny nor Becker comprehended the move until it had been made, Sweet stepped to Becker and thrust the barrel of the Spencer under his jaw. Grinning, Sweet crooned, "Has a wolf been playing in the hen house while I've been away?"

Jenny saw Becker swallow involuntarily, and she moved toward the men.

"Stop right there, girl!" Sweet told her as he jammed the rifle into Becker's neck even harder. "Or your boyfriend may lose his head."

"He's not my boyfriend, Pa! It's nothing like that—"

"Ah, then you tell me just how it is."

"He's . . . he's . . . a *Mountie*, Pa! He just came up here to—"

"To what, Jenny?" Sweet's tone was deceptively gentle and overly curious. He cocked his head to the side, and Jenny saw a few raindrops glistening in his goatee.

"Pa, did you kill a Mountie? And some others?" Jenny saw the playfulness suddenly vanish from his face.

"That what he told you?"

Jenny hesitated.

Becker said, "Yes, I told her that—"

"Shut up! Nobody talking to you, boy!"

"—because it's the truth."

Sweet pushed Becker back on the worn sofa with the Spencer until Becker's head was against the arm. "I told you to shut it!" He reached down and savagely tore the Adams pistol from Becker's holster and threw it behind him.

Jenny felt the urge to leap on her father's back and scratch and claw until he dropped the rifle. Good sense told her it would be a foolish and dangerous move. Sweet stood over Dirk, finger on the trigger, white teeth flashing through his beard.

"I didn't kill old Huson, boy! He was alive when I left him."

Becker didn't respond. Jenny wondered if it was because of caution, or because his face was pressed against the arm of the sofa so hard.

"What about the others, Pa?" she asked.

"That was a business deal gone bad, Jenny. I didn't have a choice. Two men holding guns on me—*shooting* at me! What do you *think* I should have done?" When Jenny didn't respond, Sweet suddenly shouted, "Boggs!" over his shoulder in the direction of the partially open door.

In walked Boggs, all six foot four of him, smelling like he hadn't bathed in weeks. "We got company?" he asked, grinning at Becker.

"Yeah. His name is insurance. Do you like it?"

"Huh?"

"Never mind. Jenny, find something to tie up our insurance with."

Jenny didn't move.

Sweet roared, "Go on, girl, do what I say!"

Jenny went in the kitchen. Passing by the butcher knives and cleavers, she hesitated. The blades were a cold flame in the dimmer lighting of the area. The fingers of her right hand flexed and flexed, over and over. Behind her, not daring to turn around, she heard her father tell Boggs, "Move all this furniture against that wall and start bringing it in."

"In the rain?" Boggs asked. "Can't it wait till—"

Sweet gave an exaggerated sigh. "*Now*, Boggs."

Flex and flex. Over and over. Her fingers were starting to ache, but she didn't really notice. A gray wall was forming in her mind. She dimly heard Boggs.

"What about him?"

"You let me worry about him."

"But if *he's* here, there may be more on the way!"

"Then let me worry about more on the way. Move!"

Boggs' heavy boots thudded across the floor, and Jenny heard the rasp of chair legs on the wooden floor.

Then she heard nothing but the blood rushing through her veins.

If he pushes one fraction of an inch more, Becker thought miserably, *my head's going to explode.* Lightning bolts crashed on the side where his ear met the bare wood of the sofa arm. He'd managed to place his head exactly where the fabric and padded cotton had worn away. He couldn't take much more of this without making a move. His left hand was six inches from his boot knife, shielded from Sweet by his legs. *Call it desperation from agony. Call it suicide. But I'm going for it on three. One . . . two . . .*

The Spencer eased away. "Sit up, boy."

"My name's—"

"I don't care what your name is. Sit up. Jenny!"

No answer.

"Jenny, what are you—? Oh, great, she's having one of her spells."

"Spells?" Becker asked as he carefully sat up. He desperately wanted to rub his head, but he kept his hands on his thighs. The Spencer was still inches from his head.

"I thought I told you to shut up. Boggs! Get in there and find me some rope."

"What's wrong with *her*?"

"She's having a spell."

"Spell?"

"Just go! I'm tired of questions!"

"All right, all right, I'm going!"

Becker watched Boggs go to the kitchen, give Jenny a wide-eyed berth, and begin rummaging through drawers and cabinets. Jenny made no move, and even though Becker couldn't see her face, he knew it was blank, the muscles slack. He tensed for retaliation for what he was about to say. "You know, Sweet, you probably caused those spells." The barrel once again came against him.

"What are you talking about?"

"I'm talking about the beatings you've given her. Probably caused some sort of brain damage, and her head just . . . shuts down sometimes. Especially in times of stress, which I'm sure is a lot of the time. Living with you, I mean." Becker tensed, but Sweet made no move with the rifle—yet. He moved his hand down to his boot a half inch. Boggs would be back any second, and if Sweet would just make one careless mistake . . .

"What are you, some kind of head doctor?"

"No."

"And who says I beat that girl?"

"Do you deny it?"

"Yeah, I deny it!"

"You caused it, and you know it." Lightly and gently, the end of the barrel began tracing Becker's scar.

"How'd you get that scar?" Sweet asked softly.

Up and down, from Becker's jawline to below his eye, moved the cold iron. Becker knew the path well; sometimes he would find himself absently investigating the exact same line with his finger.

"That's a dandy scar. Do the women like it, or does it disgust them?"

"I haven't really noticed." Up and down, up and down. His hand moved another inch toward his boot. Almost there. "How does it feel to know that you've damaged your own daughter? Your own flesh and blood?"

The barrel stopped in the hollow below Becker's cheek and indented slightly.

"Found it!" Boggs called triumphantly.

The cold barrel left his face.

Now! Becker thought. A curious, blinding light exploded into his vision and dissolved into specks against a black background. A fraction of an instant later, a pain ten times more excruciating than any sofa arm could cause bit into the back of his head with relentless force. The pretty lights winked out, and all was ebony, inky darkness.

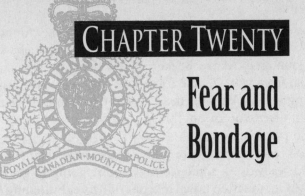

CHAPTER TWENTY

Fear and Bondage

When Becker woke, he found much activity around him. He was sitting in a corner between the sofa and a storage bin, with his head protesting at every move. The bonds around his hands and feet were incredibly tight and prevented him from checking the back of his head for a lump or broken skin.

Both boot knives were gone, as was the knife he carried in the small of his back. The belt buckle that doubled as a small blade was intact but impossible to reach. His hands and feet felt numb.

Becker watched as Sweet, Boggs, and Jenny hauled crate after crate of whiskey into the cabin. By the looks of it, they'd already stacked twenty or thirty on the wall opposite the fire. Becker was at a loss as to why they were bringing the contraband inside instead of putting it in the barn where Becker had found Sweet's earlier stash. The rain must have stopped, because all three of them were dry.

Jenny had obviously controlled her strange spell, but her movements were wooden and seemingly automatic, with no animation or expression on her face. The word *defeated* crossed Becker's mind. She had probably been hoping that her father would be out of her life forever, and now here she was back under his thumb. Becker tested the ropes again, but the only thing he accomplished was increasing the pain in his bound wrists and drawing Boggs' attention.

"He's awake, Armand."

Sweet looked at Becker, then said to Boggs, "Get everything ready. Jenny, fix us something to eat. We haven't eaten since this morning."

Without a word, Jenny went to the kitchen. Becker found himself disappointed that she didn't even look at him as she passed by.

Sweet sauntered over to Becker. "Now then, am I gonna have any more lip from you? 'Cause I can sure crack your head again."

Knowing that shaking his head would only bring more agony, Becker didn't move or say anything.

"Not so talkative now, huh?"

"Do you really think you're going to get away again?"

"Yeah, I really do. I don't see how you're going to get up and stop me." Sweet squatted down in front of Becker, watching Boggs come in with a huge wooden vat. "Boggs and me got a little thing to take care of, then we'll be gone before dawn. You and Jenny will be coming along, too."

"Where are we going?"

Sweet waved his arm expansively. "Away."

"I know you have to take me, but why don't you just leave Jenny here?"

Surprise covered his dark features. " 'Cause she's the only family I got."

"Lucky her."

"You want your head broke again?"

"Not particularly."

"Then shut your mouth and leave it shut." Sweet stormed outside and returned with a large plain box. "You ready, Boggs?"

"Ready."

"Then start pouring."

Boggs opened one of the whiskey crates and took out a bottle. Becker heard the light sloshing sound of the liquid and was reminded of water. He found that he was very thirsty.

Boggs poured the contents of the bottle into the vat, then picked up another one. One by one he emptied ten bottles. Becker looked over at Jenny in the kitchen, but she was ignoring the activity as if it were the most common thing in the world to pour out ten bottles of whiskey. Becker could smell it from where he sat.

When he turned back to the vat, he found Sweet grinning at him. With exaggerated showmanship, he reached into the box he'd brought in, produced a large bag of chewing tobacco, and untied the string at the top. Then he turned the bag upside down and the moist, dark tobacco leaves fell into the vat with a *plop*.

"Bet you think I'm crazy, huh?" Sweet asked him, still grinning. "You think I'm ruining my own whiskey, don't you? Well, watch this." He reached in the box again and drew out another bag. Becker couldn't read the writing on it. Sweet told him, "Red pepper, in case you can't see that far." He withdrew a handful of the pepper and dumped it in the vat, then repeated with another.

Becker was stunned to silence.

Sweet's hand dipped into the box again. Next came a dark bottle that produced a buff-colored liquid when Sweet poured it into the vat. "Jamaica ginger," Sweet informed him.

Becker recognized the next item, but Sweet told him anyway in a grand fashion. "Molasses. Kind of counteracts the kick from the pepper."

Swallowing, Becker pushed back the nausea that rose to his throat. He looked over at Jenny again. She was facing him and gave him a sympathetic look. No doubt she'd seen this process many times before.

"Now, here's the secret ingredient," Sweet remarked, and he emptied a few ounces of a red liquid into the concoction. "Red ink. For a robust color, you understand. Or maybe it's tasty. Never tried this stuff myself."

"Why are you doing this?" Becker asked in a hoarse voice.

"Adds to the flavor, and the Injuns love it. Whoop-up bug juice is what they call it. Oh, and it adds to the quantity, too."

Boggs took a large ladle from the box and began stirring the mixture.

"But," Becker said slowly, "wouldn't that be *dangerous*? Even toxic?"

Sweet shrugged and replied, "Nobody's died from it yet that I know of."

"And you've never tasted it?"

"What? Are you crazy?"

The refreshing smell of frying meat came to Becker, and he was immensely grateful. The horrid mixture's odor had been starting to make him sick. *To think that a human being could actually drink that and like it!* he reflected. *God help them.*

"How's that meal coming, Jenny?" Sweet called.

"Nearly ready."

Sweet and Boggs began using ladles to scoop the adulterated whiskey back into the bottles. The color of the mixture was a dark reddish brown. When the vat was empty they began the whole process again. It seemed to Becker that the crates would be too numerous to finish before dawn. However, he had a feeling that Sweet knew what he was doing.

Becker turned his attention to Jenny. His situation seemed hopeless with the close confines of the cabin and no object in sight to saw through the ropes. If Sweet had told the truth about taking him along, Becker had no doubt that once a comfortable distance had been covered between Sweet and those pursuing him, he would kill Becker. At least, he had to believe that way; Sweet didn't seem too interested in leaving witnesses.

He watched Jenny intensely, willing her to look his way and give him some idea of her intentions. Would she meekly go along with whatever her father told her, or did she have a plan for getting them both out of this? Becker shook his head grimly. She was blatantly ignoring him as she set food down on the small dining table.

Helplessly, Becker felt the scar on his cheek beginning to itch.

"Looks like they're havin' a party," Del whispered to Stone.

The moon peeked out from behind the heavy thunderclouds, washing the brightly lit cabin in a pale glow. The woods around the Mounties allowed some moonlight to flicker among them, and then it was gone. Stone stared at the cabin, surprised to find the lights still on. It had to be two or three in the morning.

"You think that's Sweet's wagon there at the front door?" Del asked.

"Yes. Becker took the only wagon that was here when he arrested that Frenchman. The wagon's still at the fort, and Jenny took her horse when she left, not a wagon. It's got to be Sweet's."

"What about the bear cub? Think he's all right?"

Stone looked at him and shook his head. "We have no way of knowing, Del."

"Well, I do," Del stated as he moved toward the cabin. "I'll just go peek through—" Stone's iron grip on his skinny arm stopped him.

"You'll do nothing of the kind, pal. We sit here and watch for a while."

"But, Hunter—!"

"That order's not debatable, Del. If you or anyone else went down there and got caught, then they'd have *three* hostages. For all we know, Sweet could have a lookout anywhere around here. We may have already been spotted."

"So we just *sit* here?" Del asked indignantly.

"That's right." Stone was quickly losing his patience with Del. The man *always* questioned everything.

"Well, that makes us about as useful as an umbrella to a buffalo," Del grumbled.

"That's enough, Del. I mean it." Stone motioned Sergeant Stride to him and told him his intentions. Stride nodded and moved to pass the word quietly among the men. Stone said to Del, "That's why you'd never make an officer. Did you see what Stride did when I gave him the order? He nodded without a word. That's an officer."

"Humph. Man prob'ly never had an original idea in his life."

"Del, make yourself more useful than a buffalo's umbrella and go get my field glasses."

"Yes, *sir*." Del made a point of showing Stone an enthusiastic nod.

Stone nodded to the men, some of whom looked at him uncertainly. They knew Becker was inside. Stone was sure that the idea of charging the place full force was on their minds. In Stone's opinion, that was just asking for casualties. If the lights were out it would be another matter.

Taking the field glasses from Del, who gave them with a small, sarcastic flourish that only Stone could see, he trained them on the windows.

"See anything?" Del asked anxiously.

Stone lowered the glasses and gave him a slow, burning look. Del just grinned.

"Why don't you get your glasses and make your way around to the back of the cabin?"

"You got it!"

"Del, wait! Listen to me very carefully. Go *slowly* and *quietly*. Do you understand?"

"'Course I do. I ain't stupid."

"In fact, why don't you stay completely out of sight of the cabin until you get behind it?"

"Sure, Hunter."

"Del, if you get killed, Vic will never speak to me again."

His smile broadening in the dim light, Del asked, "And that would be a *bad* thing? I try to get him not to speak to me all the time, but it never works."

Stone watched him go before studying the cabin again. The curtains were drawn on both front windows, and no shadows crossed them. "Why would they be up in the middle of the night?" he whispered to himself.

"What was that, sir?" Stride asked. Stone hadn't heard him move so near.

"I said, why would all the lights be on this time of night? What are they doing?"

"Mixin' whiskey," said a voice behind them.

Stone turned to find one of the newer recruits. For the life of him, Stone couldn't remember his name. "What did you say?"

"They're probably mixin' whiskey in there. I've seen it done before, and if this Sweet fella's as good as everyone says he is, he'll be mixin' his up, too. Makes for more to sell."

"You mean they dilute it?" Stride asked.

"No, Sergeant. They add stuff so it'll pack a punch to curl your hair, then rebottle it."

Stone said, "I'm not going to ask how you know all that . . . um . . . what was your name again?"

"Deakins."

"Right, Deakins."

"Sir," Stride interjected, "Dekko said that by the depth of Sweet's wagon tracks, he was really weighted down. If the wagon had that much whiskey in it, and now it's all inside—"

"That place could blow sky high, I know. I can't believe Sweet's not mixing it in the barn."

They stared at the cabin for a while before Deakins whispered, "That'd be quite a fireworks show, wouldn't it?"

The anticipation in Deakins' voice made Stone want to tell him to shut up. The only trouble was, he was right.

The itching grew steadily worse.

Becker was never unaware of the fault line on his face. The eyes of the people he met unfailingly flew to it like magnets to steel. It was there every time he looked in the mirror. If he smiled, he would feel the tissue stretching unnaturally, as if it protested the very act of being happy. It was a pale brand that marked him as damaged.

He remembered the searing, burning pain at the moment of that branding, and he grimaced involuntarily. At only fourteen years old, he thought the amount of blood staggering. It was a knife fight. A ridiculous knife fight.

The man's name had been Lucas. A drifter, he'd seen Becker practicing throws and parries and had challenged him to a friendly duel and wager. Becker, brash and confident in his skill at his relatively new hobby, had accepted. "First one to draw blood wins," Lucas had said. "Go easy on me."

Less than ten seconds later, Becker was on his knees, watching an alarming amount of blood spill through his fingers to the dirt of the street. He'd never even seen the slash of Lucas's knife, but he'd sure felt the pain of it. Without a word, Lucas had reached in Becker's pocket and extracted the agreed upon two dollars. Then he'd walked away, and Becker had never seen him since.

For the chance of winning two dollars, the young Dirk Becker had paid an awful price that had come up for renewal every day since; each day forward he would wake up to the same payment.

"You can give him something to eat, I guess," Sweet told Jenny at the dining table, with a nod to Becker.

"Untie him," Jenny suggested with no conviction.

"Forget it. You can feed him. It'll be *romantic*," Sweet finished sarcastically.

Jenny ignored him and prepared a plate for Becker.

"I'm gonna get some sleep, Boggs. You keep mixing, then you can take a nap."

"All right."

Jenny brought Becker the food and a cup of coffee. She didn't meet his eyes as she knelt beside him.

While Sweet and Boggs talked about fixing something on the

wagon, Becker whispered, "Jenny, we've got to do something."

She held out a forkful of boiled corn, her eyes on his mouth.

"Something to drink first, please," he asked. She brought the steaming cup to his lips. His parched mouth resented the hot, strong coffee at first, then soaked it up like a sponge. "Are you listening to me, Jenny?" he asked, louder than he'd intended.

"No talking over there," Sweet ordered at once.

"I was just asking her to scratch my scar. It itches." The admission was embarrassing, but it was the first thing that came to his mind. Jenny looked at him as if to say, "Are you serious?"

Sweet laughed and told Jenny, "Well, scratch the little boy's itch, daughter."

Jenny produced a dish towel from the waistband of her apron. Bringing it to his face, she hesitated with a questioning look.

"Go ahead, I'm serious," he whispered.

"I said that's enough talking!" Sweet roared.

Jenny jerked at the sound of her father's anger. After closing her eyes tightly for a brief moment, she brought the towel to his cheek and gently ran it up and down the scar. Becker sighed contentedly.

Jenny fed him, though he wasn't really hungry. He knew he might need the strength later, so he ate as much as he could before shaking his head. Through it all, Jenny's blank expression never changed, and she didn't try to communicate with him at all. Becker was extremely frustrated.

"I'm going to lie down," Sweet announced, rising from the table. "Jenny, you help Boggs." He took a step toward her. "You aren't planning anything stupid, are you?"

Jenny cringed back from him the tiniest bit, even though he was ten feet away. Eyes wide, she shook her head.

"It'll go bad for you if you do. Real bad."

Jenny nodded slowly. As Sweet turned toward his room, Jenny gave a quick glance at Boggs and reached for the towel she'd placed beside Becker. Her small hand disappeared inside the folds, and Becker saw a metallic flash as she quickly reached behind him and left something.

A knife. A small kitchen paring knife, but still, a knife.

Becker closed his eyes in relief and gratitude, then looked at her. The tiniest of smiles crossed her lips as she got to her feet.

Once again the moon was concealed by clouds, and Stone could barely see his men in the forest. All had removed their white helmets. He could, however, see enough to notice Stride glance anxiously at him. "I know, Sergeant. It's been long enough."

"I didn't say anything, sir."

"You don't have to."

"They must be staying up all night and leaving at dawn."

"Yes, but we're not waiting until dawn." Stone shook his head. He'd seen a shadow cross the left front window a few minutes earlier, but nothing else. They still didn't know how many people were inside. "If they had a lookout posted, we would have seen him go inside by now."

"Maybe Dekko's seen something."

"How long has it been since he left?"

Stride consulted a gold watch that managed to gleam dully in the dim light. After bringing the watch within inches of his eyes, Stride said, "Forty-five minutes."

"All right, here's what we do. I'm going to make my way around to Del, and in exactly thirty minutes . . . no, make that forty-five minutes, we rush the cabin. That'll give me enough time to make it back and warn you off in case we find that Sweet has five men with him."

"Understood, sir. But don't you want someone to go with you?"

Stone shook his head. "More chance of being spotted." Stone checked his Adams pistol for what seemed like the tenth time, picked up his Henry rifle, and told Stride, "The signal will be one shot. I'll give you time to make it to the front door, then Del and I go through the back windows. Don't be late."

"In about forty minutes, I'll move the men closer to the cabin."

"Good." Stone took a deep breath and vanished into the inky night.

———

"Go outside and bring me another box of tobacco and stuff, Jenny," Boggs told her.

Jenny got a lantern and glanced at Becker on the way out, no-

ticing his shoulders bunched with strain as he worked the knife behind him. His eyes never left Boggs as he worked. Boggs, who'd
tied Becker's bonds, apparently had no worries that they would be
broken, since he'd barely so much as glanced at Becker for the last
half hour.

Just before she opened the door, Becker gave her a quick nod
and mouthed, "Almost." Instead of being relieved, Jenny felt fear
gather in her belly. Too much could go wrong here.

Light from the open cabin door bathed the wagon enough for
her to find the box. As she lifted it, her eyes went to the woods, and
she thought she saw movement. She froze, staring intently at the
spot, but she saw nothing else.

Telling herself that she'd seen a bear or wolf, Jenny turned back
to the cabin with the box. She had no idea how to pray or call on
God, so she merely whispered, "Please send help," as she went back
through the door. The idea that God was listening when anyone on
the planet talked to Him was a bit ludicrous to her, but she was
feeling desperate. She was feeling so desperate, in fact, that she
asked Becker when she came through the door, "If everyone in the
world started talking to God all at once, would He hear us all?"

Becker was so stunned, he was caught speechless. Boggs looked
at Jenny as if she'd lost her mind and had suddenly become dangerously unstable.

"Would He?" she persisted.

"Um . . . why, yes, He would, Jenny."

"Every one of us?" she asked skeptically.

"Yes, every one." Becker smiled and added, "He's God, Jenny.
He's not confined to understanding only one conversation at a
time. We can't even imagine what it's like to be God. He's total
perfection. Total knowledge."

Jenny nodded and turned away as if no one had said a word.
"Where do you want this box?" she asked Boggs.

Boggs regarded her warily. "Set it down right here in this other
one. What made you think of that God stuff?"

"Nothin'. Just wonderin'."

"Whooee. You're a wild card sometimes, girl."

Jenny began helping him, careful to keep herself between Boggs
and Becker so that Boggs was blind to what the Mountie was doing.
Any minute Pa's gonna be getting up. Do something, Dirk!

Stone had no problems at all until he spotted Del down the mountainside gazing at the cabin. When he took another step, he stumbled over a rock outcropping that he never even saw and began rolling down the steep incline directly toward Del. As he desperately avoided trees and boulders through the dizzying fall, he saw Del's white face turned to him in horror. In the quiet night, Stone imagined the noise he was making would alert anyone within miles.

Del moved up the mountain with arms stretched wide, ready to stop Stone's momentum. At the last minute, Stone managed to turn his body parallel with the incline enough to stop himself. Gingerly moving his arms and legs, he was relieved to find nothing broken.

Del was over him in an instant, whispering harshly, "Why didn't you fire your gun over and over while you were rollin' and make the most noise possible?"

"Help me up."

"You all right?"

"Yes, except for my ego." They became immobile as they watched the cabin for signs of alarm. Stone noticed that one of the window curtains glowed with light, while the other was dark. "Hey, is that curtain open?"

"Yep. I already watched Sweet lie down to take a nap."

"He's in that room?"

"Yep."

"Did you see anything else?"

"Yep. I snuck down there after I thought Sweet was asleep and peeked in. Saw Becker in the living room on the floor, tied up tight as you please, but alive. Jenny's in there, along with that Boggs feller."

"That's all?"

Del shrugged. "All I saw. Ain't that enough?"

"Plenty for me. What time do you have?"

"Four ten."

Stone told him the plan while he stared in Sweet's window. It would be so easy to—

"Hunter, we ain't got to wait on Stride! We can hop through

that winder there and give Mr. Armand Sweet a nightmare he'll never forget!"

"And have Boggs shoot Becker and maybe Jenny, too?"

"Then we go in separate winders and—"

"*No*, Del! Stop arguing with me! I'm not going to tell you again."

"You got it." Del checked his watch again. Unlike Stride's immaculate gold pocket watch, Del's was battered silver. "We got twenty minutes."

"I saw Jenny, too," Stone said quietly.

"What? Where?"

"She came outside to get something from the wagon. She looked right at me."

"What'd you do?"

"Nothing. She couldn't really see me, and now I regret that I didn't show myself to her."

"What good would that have done?"

Stone's lips tightened. "She was scared. I could tell from fifty yards away . . . by her movements or . . . something. Maybe she wouldn't be scared if she knew we were out here."

"Ah, don't beat yourself up, Hunter. Too late now to change it."

"That little girl's been scared her whole life." Stone's eyes came around to Del, who for some reason took a step back. "After tonight, she's not going to be scared anymore. I'll see to it."

CHAPTER TWENTY-ONE

An Absence of Darkness

Becker desperately flexed his hands, trying to bring back some feeling. They were slick with his own blood since he'd stabbed himself more than once while awkwardly cutting the rope. His shoulders ached terribly from the extended amount of time his arms had been pulled behind him and from the bunching of muscles in order to work the knife.

But he was free—almost. When the feeling fully returned in his hands, he would have to move quickly and accurately to release his feet. That would be the crucial moment. But if Boggs were to glance his way while he moved . . .

Jenny's question about God had taken him completely by surprise. They were the first words she'd spoken to him since her father's arrival, and the subject matter had confused him. Was she really wondering about God, or was it part of some sort of diversion, the likes of which he was beyond understanding?

Jenny Sweet was strange and disturbed, but in an intriguing way that made him long to get to know her better and help her face a past full of violence. She had seemed like a mute schoolgirl, watching instead of participating in the world around her.

At the moment, she was chatting in an animated fashion with Boggs about Fort Benton, Montana.

"Did you like it?"

"Mmmm. It was all right, I guess. Just a cattle town mostly."

"I've never been there. Are the Americans anything like us?"

"The ones I met were."

"Ain't there a river there?"

Becker had never heard Jenny talk so much. He imagined that Boggs would become irritated with the small talk before long. Becker couldn't see him, but—*I can't see him, and he can't see me. Jenny's spoken more words in the past five minutes than I've heard since we met.* He shook his head in irritation at his mental lapse as he groped for the knife. Bringing his arms nearly to his sides, with his shoulders protesting at the unfamiliar movement, he wiggled his toes to make sure he'd be able to stand when he *did* cut them loose. The feeling was strange, but he thought his feet were serviceable. *Only one thing left to do . . .*

With one last look at the hidden Boggs, Becker brought his arms forward, and the knife bit into the cords of the rope.

"How much longer?" Stone asked Del.

"You just *asked* me that, Hunter—"

"I'm asking again."

A pause. "Fifteen minutes."

"Should've told Stride thirty minutes instead of forty-five," Stone muttered. He took a deep breath and said, "I can't wait any longer. I'm going in that window."

"What! You said we wait no matter what—"

"I know, and you *are* going to wait. I said *I'm* going in that window."

"Uh-uh. No, sir, it ain't gonna be like that. We go *together.*"

"What did I tell you about arguing, Del? When the time's here, fire a round in the air and come charging. But wait until the agreed upon time, Del, do you hear?"

"Yeah," Del agreed glumly.

"I just have a feeling. . . ." Without finishing his sentence, Stone began moving toward the cabin through the sighing aspens.

Jenny was ready to kill Boggs herself. She wasn't accustomed to carrying on a conversation, and Boggs was absolutely no help in that department. Her nerves were frayed and crackling at the edges.

If Becker didn't make a move soon, she would. Boggs began filling bottles with ladles of the horrible concoction in the vat, his head bowed and vulnerable in front of her. She could snatch up a bottle, bring it down on his head, and run. That's what she could do.

Deciding to give Becker some sort of warning of her intention, she turned to him, and her heart skipped a beat.

Becker was on his feet, but he had a strange look on his face. Taking two lurching, stiff steps, he began to list to the side. Now his face was puzzled and a bit helpless.

Understanding that his legs were numb, Jenny immediately reached down and grabbed the nearest thing—a half-filled quart of molasses. Boggs must have sensed the quick movement, for his head began to come up toward her. Jenny held the bottle high and came down with all her strength. The jar glanced off the top of Boggs' head, not even breaking until it hit the floor.

"What the—!" Boggs roared. His eyes grew wide as he saw Becker.

Jenny looked over at Becker just in time to see his legs give out as he staggered toward them. Reaching out to steady himself, he grabbed the walnut worktable that she'd placed the lantern on, and all came crashing down. The lantern flew directly at a crate of unopened whiskey bottles, the glass oil reservoir shattering and spraying flaming oil over the contents.

With a growl, Boggs grabbed Jenny by the arms and hurled her across the room. She landed against the partition between the living room and the kitchen, stunned.

Boggs pulled out his pistol, but Becker managed to get to his knees and grab Boggs' gun hand. With a huge effort, Becker pulled the big man down on top of him.

"What's going on here?" Armand Sweet yelled from his bedroom doorway. His eyes were wild as he took in the two fighting men and the fire licking at more liquor crates. Then he turned to Jenny with a look so vicious she had to cower against the wall. "*You* let him loose, didn't you?" He started toward her, one hand gripping a pistol. "You're a traitor just like your mother."

"Dirk!" she cried in a choked voice. She'd never seen her father so murderous looking. "Dirk, help me!" The sounds of grunts and blows came from the floor by the fire, behind stacked crates.

"Get up!" Sweet cried, grabbing her hair and using to lift her up. "I got something special planned for you!" He lifted the gun and fired in the direction of the struggling men he couldn't even see.

"No!" Jenny screamed.

His hand still locked in her hair, Sweet spun her toward the back door and sneered, "They're dead anyway! That whiskey will blow any second!"

Jenny saw the heavy wooden door coming toward her at blinding speed. Her feet didn't even seem to be touching the ground. With a cracking jolt, she hit the door and was propelled right into someone else's arms, who somehow managed to roll her to the ground and out of the way painlessly.

Sweet stood in the doorway in complete shock. "Stone! How did you—?" With an unearthly howl, he raised the pistol and started firing blindly.

Stone grabbed Jenny and dragged her behind a thick cottonwood tree. With a sickening feeling, he saw Del fall in the woods behind him while the wild shots rang out. When the hammer of the pistol fell on a spent chamber, he charged out from behind the tree, ducked his head, and slammed into Sweet with a teeth-jarring thud.

They tumbled back into the cabin, and Stone understood the situation at once. Becker and Boggs were struggling right beside the fire that had spread to three crates. Boggs knocked Becker's legs out from under him, and the two men fell over more crates to land only a few feet away from Stone and Sweet.

Straddled over Sweet, Stone felt a jerk at his belt and found himself staring down the barrel of his own pistol. Jerking his head to the side, he grabbed Sweet's hands just as the pistol roared. A white-hot pain flashed on his face as the bullet streaked by. He slammed Sweet's hand down to the floor, and Sweet fired again. Becker, underneath Boggs, twitched and cried out.

Sweet glared up at Stone with murderous eyes and gritted teeth. "I'll kill you!"

Boggs raised to his knees over the writhing Becker, grinning triumphantly. Taking a crate of whiskey beside him, he lifted it over Becker to bring it down on him.

Stone let his hand up a few inches and rammed his finger over Sweet's in the trigger guard. Turning Sweet's wrist upward, he applied pressure on Sweet's finger and shot Boggs in the chest. The big man was thrown backward, shattering a full crate. Stone saw liquid seep toward the flames. They were out of time.

Feeling Sweet trying to bring the pistol back to him, Stone suddenly let him. Sweet gave a victorious cry. When the barrel was nearly pointed at him, Stone used Sweet's momentum to twist the gun inward to Sweet's chest. Surprise crossed Sweet's face just before the gun popped, muffled by Sweet's clothing.

The leaking whiskey reached the flame, burned a trail back to the broken crate under Boggs' body, and began burning the wood. Stone leaped off Sweet, who groaned and muttered, "Help me!" Ignoring him, Stone grabbed Becker's lapels and with all his strength lifted him off the floor. Becker appeared to be only shot in the arm, but he was obviously groggy.

"Come on, Becker!" Stone shouted in his face, "Run!" He spun Becker around toward the door. Flames crackled and spat behind them.

"Help me!" Sweet yelled, his face suffused with blood. Both hands covered his bleeding chest. "Help me, *please!*"

Stone glared at him as he whisked Becker toward the back door. He could only carry one man, and there was no question who it would be. At the door, over his shoulder, he shouted, "I'll be ba—"

An ear-splitting, booming roar drowned his words. Stone closed his eyes against blinding light and felt both himself and Becker being *lifted* by a forceful hot wind that carried them into the yard behind the cabin. Opening his eyes as he flew, marveling over the incredible feeling, he saw Jenny crouching beside Del in the woods. Both had their arms over their heads.

In midair, Stone lost contact with Becker. They finally came down twenty feet away and tumbled along the ground another ten. The air left Stone's lungs somewhere along the way. Over the painful ringing in his ears, he heard Becker cry out and Jenny screaming. He caught his breath sharply, breathing in heat and smoke that nearly choked him.

Fiery debris began raining down around them. Stone gained his feet and pulled Becker deeper into the woods toward Del and Jenny. Del came out to help him, hunkered down against the burning rain, and together they raced under the shelter of the forest. The three men fell to the ground.

"I ain't ever seen *nothin'* like that!" Del bellowed hoarsely. "Nothin'!"

Stone looked over at the scout. "I thought you were shot."

"Shot?"

"When Sweet was shooting out here, I thought I saw you go down."

"That's called *ducking*, Hunter! You oughta try it sometime."

They all sat up and, with Becker painfully holding his arm, looked at the cabin, or what was left of it. The explosion had blown down three walls but left the far wall with the chimney standing. Burning pieces of wood surrounded the flaming foundation. The area was lit up as bright as day, and Stride and the other men were easily spotted as they took a wide berth around the structure and came toward them.

Holding his arm, Becker scooted over to Jenny and touched her shoulder. "Are you all right?"

With her eyes locked on the cabin, and her mouth turned down in a fierce frown, Jenny didn't even notice that Becker was wounded. "He was in there, wasn't he?" she asked. Her voice was barely audible over the noise of flames.

"Yes, he was. I'm sorry."

Shaking her head slowly, Jenny began leaning toward him. Becker moved closer to her until her head came to rest on his shoulder. Through the thick smoke that hung in the air, he could smell the clean scent of her hair. It seemed like days ago since he'd seen her drying her hair through the window.

His gaze fixed on the massive destruction, Becker told her in a low voice, "He can't hurt you anymore, Jenny. You don't have to be afraid."

She mumbled a sentence he couldn't hear.

"What did you say?"

After a long hesitation, Jenny said, "Always something. There's always something to be afraid of."

Becker wiped the blood from his hand on his trousers before tentatively taking her own. "It'll get better, Jenny. I promise."

At Becker's touch, Jenny didn't flinch or pull away from him.

A week later, with the weather so fine that Tony La Chappelle had wedged the door of his shop open, Megan and Reena sat at a table that Tony had placed out on the sidewalk. On the edge of the sidewalk at their feet sat Jenny and Lydia. The three women, for the most part, kept their eyes on the little girl as she played with her new and very cherished possession.

"How are you feeling, Jenny?" Megan asked suddenly. Their talk had been sparse and brief as they'd simply enjoyed the beautiful day and the serenity of one another's closeness.

"I'm good," Jenny said, without turning around. "I'm doin' real good."

Reena could tell from her tone that she was telling the truth rather than putting the question off with the answer they wanted. Jenny had stayed with them at the boardinghouse since the death of her father. She'd helped Mrs. Howe around the house every day, played with the children, and basically done anything to keep active. Reena was so proud that Jenny hadn't retreated to her room to grieve and isolate. Now, she actually looked better than she ever had. Color was in her cheeks, she wasn't nearly as aloof in conversation, and since the long talk she'd had with Megan the day before, she'd been positively cheerful.

"So much death," Megan said softly, bringing Reena back to the moment. "The West is hard, isn't it? For everyone."

"It's just a way of life, I think," Reena replied. "We choose it, trust God to live in it, and go on."

After a moment Megan said simply, "Yes . . . yes." She took a sip of her creamy coffee and asked in a lighter tone, "Lydia, do you know that you'll be going to school in the fall?"

"Ain't no school around here."

"There will be. I'm going to teach Jenny how to read and write, then we're going to *start* a school. Won't that be fun?"

For the first time since receiving her gift from the three women, Lydia looked up. To Jenny she asked, "Izat true?"

"Yes." Jenny clenched her fists in front of her and looked to the heavens. "I'm gonna learn to *read*, Lydia, and so are you. Ain't it exciting?"

"Both of you stop saying 'ain't,' " Megan admonished playfully.

"I guess it's all right," Lydia mumbled, then went back to her playing.

"Overjoyed, isn't she?" Megan asked Reena, and the women laughed.

"And you, Reena?" Jenny asked. "What are you going to do?"

Reena smiled. "You know where my place is. I'll be going back to the Blackfoot this summer."

Jenny looked sad for a moment, then she nodded. "I hope it goes better for you this time."

"I'm sure it will, Jenny. Thank you."

"Here comes the cavalry," Megan announced, and Reena saw Stone, Vickersham, and Becker riding toward them from the direction of the fort. They were all dressed as civilians in plain, comfortable working clothes.

"Now where are they going?" Reena wondered aloud.

"They look strange in clothes," Jenny commented.

Megan snickered and asked, "As opposed to. . . ?"

Jenny turned with a confused look. "Huh?"

"Never mind, darling, I'll explain later."

The men pulled their horses up in front of them. All three were grinning broadly.

"Morning, ladies!" Vic crowed. "And what a peach of a morning it is, eh?"

Reena said, "You three are in too fine of a mood to be up to any good. What's wrong?"

Stone sputtered and exclaimed, "Nothing's wrong!"

"Just three gents out for a ride," Vic said innocently.

"I'm sure," Megan said in disbelief.

Jenny pointed to Becker's side. "How's your arm?"

Becker lifted his arm and suddenly whirled it in an alarming fashion. "Never better."

"That's quite a recovery!" Reena said.

Jenny said wryly, "Now tell us about your *bad* arm."

"Oh, that one." Becker lifted the other one more gingerly. "Better every day!"

Laughing, Reena asked Stone, "Would you please tell us what you're up to?"

"All right. We heard about a man who needed a new barn." He leaned forward in the saddle toward Lydia. "Lydia's father, actually. Good morning, Lydia!" he sang in a tune.

Lydia barely glanced up from her playing.

"So we're going to introduce him to something Becker calls a 'barn raising.' "

Becker gave the other men a dark look and said, "It can't really

be called a barn raising because *some* men, who will go unnamed"—
he winked and pointed at Stone and Vic in a showy way—"wanted
to get their beauty rest until almost noon. A *real* barn raising starts
before dawn."

"It's our day off, Dirk!" Vic told him, feigning a sulk.

Stone said, "Besides, that's mighty big talk for a one-armed
man who'll probably just watch us do all the work."

Becker shrugged, grinning. "Someone has to supervise." He
began backing Egypt. "Let's go!"

Vic tipped his hat to the ladies and said, "Now I know why Del
calls him the bear cub. Good day, ladies!"

Stone turned Buck, smiled at Reena, and said, "Think about us
under the blazing hot sun, our skin peeling off, while you sit in the
shade and drink your lemonade. We *may* be back, unless we die of
exposure out there."

Reena waved him off, laughing. "It's sixty degrees! What blazing sun?"

The women watched the men ride down the street, whooping and
waving their hats and generally making a spectacle of themselves.

"What a bunch of show-offs!" Jenny observed.

"They're such . . . *boys!*" Reena sputtered, and she laughed
harder than she had in weeks.

Megan asked, "They *don't* ever grow up, do they?"

"Ain't it wonderful?" Reena asked, and when she saw the shocked
looks from Megan and Jenny, they all began giggling even harder.

When their laughter subsided, they could still make out the riders beyond the edge of town. All three men wore white shirts that
bobbed up and down in the distance.

As all three women watched the men fade from sight, Reena said
in a wistful, hushed voice, "Ain't it wonderful."

They watched in silence until the white shirts blended together
into one dot, then disappeared.

"You're tired, aren't you?" Lydia asked her one-armed doll. "It's
time for night-night." Clutching it to her chest tightly, she gave the
doll a kiss and gently placed it in her brand-new cherrywood cradle.

Reena, Megan, and Jenny watched her as she carefully swung
the heart-decorated base back and forth and hummed a lullaby.